Mistaken Destiny

A Brenner Falls Romance

Book 4

Kyle Hunter

Copyright 2025 by Kyle Hunter. All rights reserved.
Published in the United States by Monceau Publishing.
P. O. Box 40152
Raleigh, NC 27629
www.Kyle-Hunter.com

No portion of this publication may be copied, retransmitted, reposted, duplicated, or otherwise used without the express written approval of the author. Any unauthorized use of any part of this material without permission by the author is prohibited and against the law. The only exception is brief quotations in printed reviews.

This is a work of fiction. Names, characters, and situations are products of the author's imagination and are used fictitiously. Any resemblance to persons living or dead is entirely coincidental.

Cover design by Erika Alyana Sañga Duran.

ISBN 979-8-9895265-7-4

More novels by Kyle Hunter

Circle Back Around
One December
Postcard from Nice

The Provence Series

Prodigals in Provence
A Promise in Provence

The Second Chance Series

Marissa Rewritten (A Novella)
Julia Redesigned
Sydney Rewound
Eden Redefined

The Brenner Falls Series

Good Gifts
Custom Made
Embracing the Broken
Mistaken Destiny

Yet I still belong to you; you hold my right hand. You guide me with your counsel, leading me to a glorious destiny.

Psalm 73:23-24

Prologue

The September breeze swirled with balmy temperatures, yet whispered the approach of fall in Flagstaff, Arizona. Stephen took the hand of his wife, Annika, as they followed their favorite walking circuit along the pine shaded sidewalk on the edge of town. The streets were quiet that Sunday afternoon, save the occasional jogger or dog-walker.

"What a perfect day." Stephen drew a full breath into his lungs. "Especially after such a busy and rainy summer."

"*Really* busy," agreed Annika, knowing they weren't just talking about the unusually warm season that had just bade them farewell. It was their second month of an empty nest. The preparations, shopping, and packing right beforehand had occupied her mind for a while, staving off the emptiness to come. But once they took Derek to campus, waved goodbye, and drove away without him in the car, reality shook her to the core.

It had been easier when Bryan had left in July to start a campus job. He'd already been gone from the house for two years, so Annika considered herself broken in for his departures. But Derek's absence left the house too quiet.

"I think it's already easier now without both boys." She voiced thoughts that were never far from her mind, as if to convince herself. "I'm bouncing back." She was trying, in any case.

"Yes, you are." Stephen smiled and squeezed her hand. "And it'll keep getting easier." He cocked his head and met her gaze. "I sort of like having you to myself."

She grinned back at him. "I'm sure I'll enjoy the rhythm too. No more early mornings. And less laundry. And quiet while we're reading and having coffee after breakfast."

"We'll have to plan a trip soon. It'll be different with just us. I'm looking forward to it."

"That sounds nice." Annika let out a sudden chuckle. "Call me crazy, but I just thought about the mess I left in the kitchen. I *never* do that. Maybe I'm already adjusting to the freewheeling empty nest lifestyle." After church, they'd had a hurried lunch of leftovers and rushed outside, impatient to enjoy the afternoon, calm and clear after a series of thunderstorms the previous week.

"They'll wait. Now, how about we talk about the trip we want to take next spring? Any ideas? Maybe Europe, or even a cruise."

"Hmm. You can give me some options, since you've been thinking about it already. We can talk about it later tonight."

They fell silent as they kept a steady pace. Once both boys were away at college, they began the habit of walking together daily. It helped soften the transition between a full house of noisy teenagers with assorted friends and...just the two of them.

The full foliage of cottonwoods blended with the darker shades of evergreens, so numerous at that elevation. Soon it would transform to an orange and red painting, splashing the pine-dotted mountains and fields with color.

On the return toward the house, they approached a stone bridge which had been there forever. The rain had filled the stream beneath to a higher level and the gurgle of tumbling water added natural music to the peaceful day.

Something beneath the bridge caught Annika's eye. "Stephen, what's that under the bridge?"

"Huh? I didn't see anything." His graying brows furrowed.

Annika slowed her steps. Maybe her eyes had played a trick on her. "I thought I saw someone down there who might be hurt."

"Sometimes homeless guys hang around down there. We should keep our distance." Caution laced his voice.

Annika had already crossed the bridge and was scooting around the embankment. Stephen jogged to catch up with her.

"I know what you're saying, Stephen, but my gut is telling me this is different." When she felt that nudge, she needed to follow it. Maybe God was telling her something.

"Okay, but let's go slowly. Could be an ambush."

Stephen and Annika edged toward the shadow under the bridge, taking in the scene. A lone man lay on his back, unconscious. Near the curve of the bridge's underside sat a knapsack, a rolled-up sleeping bag, and a couple of empty food cans.

The man groaned and his head turned to one side and the other, as though thrashing in pain. His eyes remained closed. Through his dark beard, Annika saw him gasping for breath. "He's not sleeping, Stephen. I think...I think he's sick."

"Keep an eye out and I'll see if he's awake." Stephen crept closer to the man. "Sir, are you okay? Are you alright?"

The man didn't respond, though another groan spiraled from his throat. Stephen reached out to touch his forehead. His grim gaze found Annika's. "He's burning up. He's sick, just like you said."

"Can we...can we take him home?" Annika crossed her arms, a rumble of concern filling her chest and weighing inside. The man looked to be in his late twenties. Her stomach squeezed. This was someone's *son*. Someone who likely didn't know where he was.

"Or to the hospital." Stephen felt for a pulse. "His heart rate seems fast. The hospital is safer for him, since we don't know what's going on. He may have pneumonia, especially if he's been sleeping here outdoors."

Annika swallowed the lump in her throat. "Okay. Let's take him to the Medical Center. We can check on him tomorrow. Maybe they'll find ID on him and can notify his family, if he has one."

"First thing is to get him safe. I can stay here with him. Can you bring the car?"

"Yes, good idea." Annika rose. "I'll be back as soon as I can."

They exchanged a worried gaze. "I hope it's not too late."

Stephen's ominous tone caused a chill. Dread for this youthful stranger gripped Annika's chest. "Me too."

She took off jogging toward the house, praying all the way home.

Chapter One

Rick Russo pushed the lukewarm mug of coffee away from him as he sat at his mom's kitchen table. He opened the Brenner Falls Times to the Help Wanted section and folded back the front page, creasing it carefully with two fingers. Funny, they still had help-wanted ads in a physical newspaper. Suited him, since he didn't have a computer. As he shifted his chair closer to the tabletop, he grunted. Though he was only thirty-one, the print seemed too small to read.

"You're up early." The voice of his mother, Debbie Russo, reached his ears before he saw her. He wasn't used to her voice anymore, not after nearly fourteen years away. Nor was he used to living in her house, but he'd only arrived in early May. Less than a week ago. He'd give himself time to adjust. He hoped he could.

"Hey, Mom." He turned his head and smiled at her. She laid a hand on his shoulder. She'd been doing that a lot since he'd come home. Though he liked the physical connection, it stirred guilt inside. He'd been gone so long, he had the impression she wanted to hold on to him to assure herself he was truly there and not some kind of mirage.

It was Friday, but she'd taken the morning off for a dental appointment, so she still wore her bathrobe. She went to the counter and poured a cup of coffee then sat across the table from him. "Are you finding anything interesting?"

Rick shrugged. "*Interesting* isn't really my criteria at this point. I need a job and about anything will do." He scanned the column again. "But I may draw the line at garbage collector. I know it's honest work, but imagine the smell."

His mom chuckled. "I'd have to agree. Anything else?"

He held up a finger and scoped the bold print. "Yeah. Door to door surveys."

"No." They both said at the same time, then laughed.

"Here's one. A restaurant called The Grateful Fork needs a dishwasher and busboy. Pay seems pretty good."

His mother took a sip of her coffee. "That's a good option. It's a popular place in town. Kind of a gathering spot for locals. And you've got to start somewhere." She took another sip. "You have restaurant experience, right?"

"Loads. Too much to count." It was true. He'd bussed tables, he'd waited tables, he'd cooked, he'd washed dishes. For over a decade living mostly on the streets of Arizona he'd held many short-term restaurant jobs. They were easy to get and easy to leave, whenever the money ran short, which was all the time. Get and leave the jobs, over and over for more than a decade. He let out a deep sigh. A *wasted* decade.

"That sounds like it has potential. Not forever, just to get you on your feet."

Rick met his mother's gaze. "Yeah. Need to do that. Thanks for letting me crash here, Mom."

She touched his hand. "You're not crashing, Rick. This is your home, don't forget. Just because you haven't lived here in a while, you still have a room, and you always will. Please stay as long as you want." She swallowed. When her eyes filled, she looked away. "I'm sorry. I...I've missed you so much. And I worried about you all those years."

She returned her gaze to him and forced a smile, swiping a rogue tear from her cheek. "I know I'm pressuring you. I don't mean to. I'm just thrilled to have you back, so please don't hurry off yet." Wordless pleading poured from her eyes.

Rick's chest clutched. He covered her hand with his other one. To lighten the moment, he made a gruff sound in his throat. "No way. Not hurrying anywhere, Mom. I was gone too long and I'm...I'm sorry about that."

She pushed her chair back and withdrew her hands from his. "Well, you're home now." She forced a cheery smile then added, "I'm not trying to mother you. I respect the fact that you're an adult."

"Of course." Rick grew uneasy with the exchange but pushed the feeling down.

"So, how about some breakfast?" Her voice became brisk. She rose and went to the fridge.

"You don't have to cook breakfast every day either, Mom. How about I cook for you?"

"Okay. It'll give you that much more experience to get the restaurant job." They laughed.

While he stirred up scrambled eggs and laid out the bacon on the griddle, his mind flitted around. It still felt weird being home again, after no more than a handful of visits, financed by his brother, Ben, over the last fourteen years.

Mom had renovated some of the rooms, freshened them up, so the house didn't look exactly like the one he'd grown up in. Again, courtesy Ben, renovator extraordinaire. The first example of that was the kitchen. Soft yellow painted walls glowed in friendly welcome, along with updated artwork, a new counter and cupboards, and new fixtures. At the windows over the sink and by the table hung matching curtains. Mom had replaced most of the rugs throughout the house and had the bathroom redone.

But aside from cosmetic changes, the real reason it felt foreign to him was that so *many* years had passed since he'd lived there. Even his memories of childhood fought through filmy webs of time to regain conscious access.

Rick often had to remind himself of the moment he'd had a conviction that he should return home to Brenner Falls. He'd just finished dinner with Stephen and Annika, helped with dishes, and returned upstairs. The minute he entered the bedroom he'd occupied for nearly two years, he *knew*. Otherwise, he'd never have returned home. He would have eventually found his own place and a different job in Flagstaff, which he'd grown to like, and had felt like home.

Not that he didn't like Brenner Falls. He had good memories up to a point. That point was about the age of seven. Then everything went down the toilet. His mom had started drinking. Before long, she was a full-blown alcoholic. Several years later, when Rick was fifteen, his dad died of lung cancer. He and Ben had raised themselves, more or less. And the stuff they'd gotten into back then… He grimaced. Such stupid stuff…

With time, he and Ben took completely different paths. Ben got into church and eventually convinced their mom to go. Ben went on to college, and now was a respected engineer for the city of Brenner Falls. He was also newly married. Meanwhile, Rick left home to seek adventure out west.

He snorted with regret. Some adventure *that* was. He thought living with his adopted family, his band of fellow druggies, would fill in the gaps of what he'd left behind. All he'd lost. For a while, it seemed to.

That was then. If he'd had any idea back then how God would get ahold of him, he'd have doubled over laughing in disbelief. Or shock. Despite his momentary regret and despair, a smile pulled his lips. God must be crazy to run after a foul-up like him.

"Eggs are ready, Mom," he called toward the table, giving the fluffy yellow pile a final flip with the spatula.

"Already?" She grinned and put her hands on her hips. "You're quick. *Quick Rick*, they're going to call you over at The Fork."

"Yeah, that's it." He smiled and held out his palms. "But what can I say? I'm a pro."

☙ ☙ ☙

Kelsey Brewster logged out of her computer and gazed through the kitchen window at the dainty green maple blossoms making their spring appearance. Her office consisted of a corner kitchen nook at her parents' house. From her chair, she could simply shift her focus to the outdoors and escape her screen for a few moments. She'd worked all morning at her online job, but it was time to stop. She'd get back to it later that evening.

She stood, stretched, and crossed the entry hall to the den, a long, comfortable room with an expanse of windows on the back overlooking several acres under pine trees. "Molly, are you ready to go?" Her sister sat cross-legged on the floor, coloring at the square coffee table surrounded by a sectional sofa. "We have to leave in a few minutes."

"I did a picture for you." Molly's grin stretched out, making her round face look wider and happier. "You have to come here if you want to see it."

"You're stalling, Molly." Kelsey smiled in spite of herself as her chest swelled with affection for her sister, who was two years older, but much younger in mental capacity.

Kelsey rounded the coffee table and squatted to look at Molly's picture, a unicorn and a princess. "That's beautiful, Molly. Is that princess me? Or maybe it's you."

Molly giggled. "It's for you, but I don't know who she is. She's just a pretty princess."

"Very pretty. "You're going to love Treasure House today. Miss Joanne said it's a surprise, but I think it has something to do with *painting*..." She finished her phrase in a sing-song voice. Painting was one of Molly's favorite things.

Molly let out a loud squeal and pulled herself up from the floor. "I like painting." Then she frowned. "I don't work today?"

"Not today. You'll go on Monday and work with Miss Aggie on napkins and things."

"I like Miss Aggie."

"Me too." Aggie had owned The Grateful Fork Restaurant for forty years. And grateful was what Kelsey felt each time she went there to help. Her regular job consisted of remote online work for a medical records company, which registered below zero on her excitement scale. But a few times a week she took shifts at The Fork to help Aggie out. Well, filling in when they were short-staffed in the kitchen or with waitstaff was only *one* of her motivations. Another one was simply getting away from the house and computer, being around the upbeat energy of The Fork. *And* around food preparation and service, her happy place.

Along with that, she got a change from keeping an ever-watchful eye on Molly, who had been born with Downs Syndrome. Molly could be fairly independent, but Kelsey still took her responsibility seriously, her promise to take care of her older sister while their parents were away for a nine-month mission trip in Uganda.

After dropping Molly off at Treasure House, an innovative adult daycare, she drove to The Grateful Fork. That day, she'd wait tables. She preferred kitchen work, or overseeing the shift, but enjoyed the atmosphere either way—the people contact, the laughter, and the good smells flowing from the kitchen. One day, if she stayed on target with her heart, she'd have her own restaurant and she'd probably end up modeling it after The Grateful Fork. The thought brought a smile to her lips.

Kelsey pushed open the glass front door and greeted the hostess. The restaurant extended a homey welcome to those who entered under its turquoise awnings on Restaurant Row, as the locals called Charleston Alley, since a few more eateries lined the narrow street. Folk art and antique implements hung on the warm golden-yellow walls. In one corner was a stage for music groups who performed on Friday or Saturday evenings.

Stenciled over the pine-paneled bar near the ceiling were the words, *Give us this day our daily bread.* Aggie and Charles hadn't had children, but they'd had a dream to own a restaurant. Aggie had grown up hearing stories of food shortages in England during the Second World War from her mother, who had been a British war bride. This inspired the restaurant's name and, as Aggie said, reminded anyone who came in the door why they should be grateful.

The kitchen already buzzed with white-clad cooks moving briskly under bright lights. "Hi Aggie. Hi everyone." Kelsey reached into a bin and laced a clean server's apron around her waist.

The woman paced through the kitchen, surveying large bubbling pots on the stove and making suggestions to the chefs. She turned to Kelsey. "Hello, Kelsey. Come over and try this sauce Vince just created. It's good." Her dark hair streaked with silver framed a bird-like face webbed with wrinkles. Despite her seventy-two years, she always seemed to abound in energy and creativity. She and her late husband, Charles, had made The Fork a Brenner Falls institution.

"I'd love to." Kelsey took the spoon of the creamy liquid.

"Guess what's in it, Kelss." Burly Vince, head chef for the last twelve years, prompted her with an inviting smile. He frequently quizzed the savvy of her taste buds and cooking knowledge.

"I taste..." Kelsey moved her tongue around the creamy sauce. "It's not anise...Is it tarragon? And butter and lemon. And is that nutmeg too?"

"Yes, a pinch. I tried fennel, but the flavor competed too much with the tarragon. We'll use this over fish."

"Rather fancy for The Fork." Kelsey smiled. "Is it becoming haute cuisine around here?"

"Depends on the day," Aggie said as she sat on a nearby stool. She waved Kelsey over. "Come here, dear. I want to tell you something."

Kelsey went to Aggie's side and waited.

"I've decided I'm going to retire soon. I've been thinking about it for the last year, and it's time to pass the baton."

Kelsey's smile fell. "Oh, Aggie. I don't know what to say." Sudden sadness quivered inside, but she forced a supportive tone. "But of course, you deserve the fun and rest of retirement. What...what will you do with The Fork? Sell it?" She held her breath. She had to admit, The Grateful Fork was a little like family to her.

Aggie shook her head. "I may do that eventually, but I'm not planning to right now." The woman took a long pause as her gaze laser-focused on Kelsey's. "I'd like you to think about something, Kelsey. I don't necessarily want you to give me an answer yet, but I thought about *you* taking over as manager."

Kelsey gasped and one hand went to her chest. "Me? Oh, Aggie." A surge of hope peaked then fell with a thud. "That's such an honor, and I'd absolutely love to. But...but I can't, not until my parents get home in November." Six more months. She couldn't ask Aggie to wait until Kelsey was ready for her dream job.

"Because of Molly?"

"Yes. Otherwise, I'd come in a heartbeat. You know I would." Kelsey wouldn't allow her mind to imagine managing the restaurant. The mental picture would only torture her, since it wouldn't happen.

Aggie offered a restrained smile and a nod. "Yes, I know, dear. I'd forgotten about the commitment you made to your parents. The job would be too demanding, I think, to give adequate care to Molly." She shrugged and let out a sigh. "Maybe it's best to keep it in our family, then. I also thought of asking Danielle to step in as manager. You know Danielle, my great-niece."

"Yes, we were in high school together."

"Well, she's been out of work for a couple months, since that IT job laid her off."

Kelsey swallowed. "Has she ever done this kind of work before? Being a restaurant manager is rather involved, isn't it?"

Aggie shrugged. "She's been around here and there. She's waitressed, she's been a hostess. I'll stay on for a bit to train her."

Danielle lived in a small apartment on the edge of town and Kelsey didn't see her often anymore. And she likely had *no* experience running a successful restaurant.

"It might be risky, Aggie, since she doesn't have experience," Kelsey said. It would be a shame to put The Fork into the hands of an unproven if well-meaning manager. "Hostess is one thing. Manager is quite another, but I don't need to tell you that."

Aggie waved the air. "After a month with me training her, she'll be fine. I mean *intensive* training. Danielle's smart. She'll catch on. And she'll have Vincent and Claire to rely on. They've been here forever."

Kelsey held down a sigh. She doubted Vince and Claire would be able to bring Danielle up to speed. They were chefs, not restaurant managers. They wouldn't have time to tutor Danielle in restaurant management.

With a sad smile, Kelsey laid her hand on the older woman's arm. "I'll miss you, Aggie."

"I'm not gone yet." Aggie chuckled. "But I'll still drop in from time to time. Are you working only lunch today?"

"Yes. I have to pick up Molly after my shift."

Aggie nodded. "How are your parents doing over in Africa?"

Though the topic had shifted, a lead ball of regret still lay in Kelsey's stomach. "They're enjoying it, even though it's hard sometimes. It's quite primitive where they are, in a remote village. We talk on the phone every month. They have to travel to a larger town to call us."

"I'm glad they're able to stay in touch. They probably need it as much as you do."

"That's for sure. Well, I better get out there."

The restaurant wasn't too busy yet, so Kelsey could get her bearings. She forcibly pushed aside her disappointment at not being able to accept Aggie's offer, as well as her misgivings about Danielle's lack of experience. It was out of her hands. Instead, she took note of her section then went behind the bar to capture a moment of calm before the front door swung open and the lunch rush began.

Along the wall, a man sat at one of the empty tables filling out a job application, probably for dishwasher/bus boy. The job had been posted for over two weeks. He seemed old for that kind of job, maybe around thirty. Though she'd been in Brenner Falls all her life, she didn't recognize him. Dark wavy hair curled below his ears around an olive complexion. Maybe he was passing through or had just moved to town.

Just then, he lifted his head, and his gaze found hers, as if he'd known she had noticed him. Her face grew warm. She offered a slight smile, then busied herself at the bar.

The man's dark, serious expression stayed imprinted in her mind. Who was he? Why would a guy his age want a job washing dishes?

"Party of four at table six, Kelsey." The words of the hostess caused Kelsey to spring into action.

Time went by quickly, since Kelsey didn't stop moving for two hours. She didn't think about the stranger again or notice when he left. The lunch shift started to wane until only a few customers remained. Time to finish up then scoot off to get Molly.

These days, she didn't have much time for herself, unless Molly was occupied at the house with one of her hobbies. Kelsey had happily offered to take care of Molly while her parents were in Africa. They'd taken care of her all the preceding years. But it was tiring whether she was busy doing things for or with her sister or merely *thinking* about what Molly might need or an activity Kelsey could do with her. She could easily imagine how a working parent felt.

She'd pick up Molly and get her settled with her books. Then maybe Kelsey would have time to fiddle with one of her recipe inventions. She'd serve it for dinner, since Molly was usually a willing guinea pig for Kelsey's culinary experiments. They could eat outside at the picnic table under the pine trees.

That mental picture of a peaceful Friday evening caused a layer of acceptance and calm to seep down inside, diluting her disappointment after Aggie's news and the mismatch in timing for the manager role. It was clear that as perfect as the job seemed to her, it wasn't meant to be. She had to accept that painful reality and keep going.

Chapter Two

Congealed grease and smears of mayo covered the plates Rick sprayed with hot water and placed into the industrial sized dishwasher. This didn't faze Rick after all the contact he'd had with dirty plates over the years. He could stack eight plates on one arm and grab four condiments in the other. It might be nice to have a different set of skills, but at least he had that. And he wasn't in a position to be choosy. He could always wait tables and earn more money, but didn't feel sociable enough. Without drugs, he was back to being an introvert. Small price to pay to be clean.

Three days after completing his application at The Grateful Fork, he'd been called back for a perfunctory interview, which consisted of two questions. He'd been hired on the spot and asked to work the dinner shift the same day, so there he was. Michelle...Danielle...Rachelle? He couldn't remember the name of the chubby blonde who'd interviewed him. He later learned it was only her third day on the job, but she was the great-niece of the owner. Of course, they'd done a background check on him, so thankfully, he'd stayed relatively legal during those lost years in Arizona. The only crimes he'd committed were against himself.

That last crazy night almost killed him. Literally. His so-called adopted family left him for dead under the bridge. When he awoke from a bad trip paired with pneumonia, he was in the hospital. A couple he'd never seen in his life hovered in his hospital room. The concern on their faces made him want to weep with a strange mixture of longing and loss. That's when the fog of his last decade began to clear. Clarity was painful, especially in the beginning. But sobriety eventually felt good, hopeful. Hope was something he'd lost somewhere between the ages of ten and sixteen. He didn't think he'd ever find it again, but he did. And hope was followed by faith. After that, everything changed quickly.

"You the new guy?" Rick heard a gruff voice behind him as he rinsed the dishes. He turned and faced a tall man who might have been in a boxing ring at one time. A graying crew cut topped a long, pocked face, and tattoos graced his upper arms.

"Yeah. Name's Rick. Rick Russo." The new grunt laborer, yet thankful for a job.

"Any relation to Ben Russo?"

"He's my older brother. I just got back into town after a long time away."

The man nodded. "Nice dude, your brother. I'm Vince, head chef. *Also* Italian." He grinned and bushy eyebrows danced. "Welcome to the team. And welcome back to the Falls." The kindness in the man's eyes belied his imposing physique.

"Thanks. Nice to meet you, Vince." *The team.* He'd never been called part of a team in other restaurants where he'd worked. Vince then introduced Rick to the other cooks. That too had never happened before. He'd always been a nobody, a fill-in dishwasher. Nameless, short-term.

Might be a nice place to begin his new life.

His new life would consist of working full-time, or as many hours as he could get. And church. Brenner Falls Community Church. He'd attended once so far with his mom. Ben had already set him up for *follow-up* with the pastor, a friendly middle-aged guy named Frank. Rick could sense Ben's compulsion to ensure Rick would get plugged in and avoid backsliding. Not a chance. Not after tasting death.

So, he'd met with Pastor Frank once and would continue every week or two for Bible study and discussion. Frank was a nice enough guy, but it was already getting stuffy under his wing.

Frank had also recruited Rick to help the youth pastor with youth group on Thursday nights. As soon as Rick mentioned that last year he'd volunteered with the youth at the church in Flagstaff, the pastor had signed him up. That made Rick nervous, since his backstory was anything but inspiring. What could he offer to a bunch of church teenagers? They'd probably never even heard of some of the drugs he'd taken back in the day.

"We're always in need of volunteers," Pastor Frank had told him. "And you're the right age to connect with them. Especially the boys. We have fewer boys, but some of them need an older guy in their lives."

Rick had stifled laughter. "And you want *me* to be a role model? What've you been smoking, Pastor?"

Frank had merely laughed, unoffended. He knew Rick's story—all of it—and hadn't backed away one bit. "Not a role model, just a friend. They need an older male friend. Some of them don't have dads."

"Huh. Not sure I'm better than nothing." Yet, he knew what it was to lose his dad. Maybe he could offer something to these kids. Might as well let God recycle some of his pain for the good of these fatherless teenage guys.

Rick gave in to a slight smile at the thought, then drew his mind back to the basic but filthy plate, transforming back to white under a spray of hot water. He rinsed the next ten in record speed and returned to the dining room.

The people he'd met at The Fork were likeable, especially the kitchen staff. Friendly. Accepting. They didn't ask a lot of questions, which he liked. He'd met nearly everyone who worked there, except a few of the servers. That included the pretty redhead who'd smiled at him the day he filled out his application. Her eyes, a dark blue—he couldn't quite tell from the distance—were striking. Along with an eye-catching heart-shaped face. Her smile had been his first greeting, his first glimmer of warmth he'd seen in his future place of employment. Her smile had remained in his mind like an angel sitting on his shoulder.

☙ ☙ ☙

    Kelsey measured the oatmeal into a bowl, added brown sugar, milk, and salt, and microwaved it. She'd rather have made a puff pancake with Boursin cheese, sauteed shallots, a hint of Dijon mustard, and topped with a brown-butter glaze. But Molly wanted oatmeal. That was fine. Kelsey would make the special concoction for herself the next day and, if it tasted good, make a note in her folder. Inside the folder were the food experiments she'd been conducting for two years. She had almost enough recipes to publish a book, but not quite. She'd even taken photos of the finished product for most of them. She could put the puff pancake on her blog too, *Kelsey's Kitchen*. Maintaining it was a challenge, but she posted weekly and her list of followers grew slowly but steadily. For now, it was a deferred dream, since there never seemed to be enough time. Little by little, she'd achieve something with her food passion, even without managing The Grateful Fork. She refused to dwell on that loss.

    It was Tuesday, and she needed to work all day at her online job. She'd promised Molly she'd take her to The Fork for dinner that night instead of working a shift. A local band was scheduled to play. Aggie hoped to draw more people on a weeknight, though she always seemed to have a good crowd, regardless of the day.

    Kelsey's computer job was dull but less pressured than the online analyst job for a pharmaceutical company she'd held for six years prior. The money had been good, but often she'd had to travel as well as attend a multitude of meetings. When her parents announced they wanted to leave for a nine-month mission trip in Uganda, she knew she'd need a job that would be simpler for her to maintain while caring for Molly. She'd lived at home for the last three years and had helped with her sister during that time, but now she was Molly's sole caretaker.

A home-based job allowed her the flexibility to work at The Fork or do her own kitchen experiments. She ought to be more consistent with *Kelsey's Kitchen* and other goals, but she was already juggling a lot between work, Molly, and The Fork.

Of course, she didn't *have* to work at The Grateful Fork. She just *wanted* to.

"Am I folding napkins tonight?" Molly asked once they were driving across Brenner Falls.

"No, we're both off today. We're having supper at The Fork. *Not* working. There's music tonight. Doesn't that sound fun?"

"Yeah. Funner than working."

"*Much* funner. I like working there too. Don't you?" Kelsey glanced over at Molly in the passenger seat.

"Yeah. I like folding napkins. I like helping Miss Aggie."

"Me too." Kelsey smiled. Aggie was like a grandma or aunt to her. Or at least a good friend. They had the same heart for food and hospitality and were on the same page in many ways. That might be why Aggie envisioned her in the manager role. A wave of sadness sailed through her at the thought of Aggie leaving, of no longer seeing her regularly. Danielle had begun her new role last week, so Kelsey saw her often when she worked lunch shift. Uneasiness pooled in Kelsey's stomach. Hopefully, Danielle would learn quickly and be able to maintain Aggie's success.

Kelsey and Molly settled at a table near the stage. The dining room was already half-filled, though the band wouldn't start for another hour. Sounds of conversation, laughter, and clattering silverware hovered in the air. There were always a few familiar faces, those of regulars or friends, making the place feel even more homey to her. She could already smell the fried chicken breasts Vince was likely preparing for the evening special.

"Hi, Kelsey. Hi, Molly." Annette, the waitress, grinned and handed them menus.

While Kelsey and Molly pored over them and discussed what they wanted, Danielle arrived and stood beside the table. Her blond hair hung in a bob to her chin. "Hey, girls."

"Hi, Danielle. How's the new job going?"

"So far, so good. There's a lot to learn. Aggie's like a firehose. But I'm getting the hang of it. She has me doing hostess this week, then I'll move on to ordering inventory, stuff like that."

"I hope it goes well, and you'll like it." Maybe Danielle would surprise Kelsey and find her niche in restaurant work. Behind Danielle, Kelsey glimpsed the guy who'd filled out the application the previous Saturday. He was clearing a nearby table. She lowered her voice. "Is that the new busboy?"

Danielle shot a glance over her shoulder. "Yeah. That's Ben Russo's little brother, Rick. He's back in town, saved and sober, I hear."

"Oh? That's good. I know Ben pretty well. His wife, Amber, is a good friend of mine." So *that* was the famous Rick Russo. She knew a little too much about Ben's little brother. But saved and sober...that was great news. "I saw him the other day when he filled out the application. I didn't recognize him, but I must have known him or known about him in high school. I think we're about the same age."

"*Surely* you guys ran in different circles." Danielle gave her a knowing look.

No doubt about that. Danielle returned to the bar. Kelsey's gaze followed Rick's movements around the dining room for a few seconds. He had a certain focus and militant determination about him. She returned her eyes to the menu in case he saw her watching him yet a second time. He was cute. But if he was fresh off the streets, he likely had nothing in common with her.

Guilt pinched her inside. *Lord, forgive me for that thought, for feeling superior, maybe even judgmental. That's the last thing I should feel. There but for your grace...* The same grace that had pulled Rick in had pulled her in too.

Kelsey ordered a chef salad with fried chicken tenders on top. A compromise between healthy and not, she told Molly. Her sister had no such limits, and fully enjoyed her smothered fried chicken and southern green beans loaded with bacon. The dining room filled little by little while they ate, and the noise kept pace. Soon, a full crowd stretched to each corner of the room as they anticipated the concert.

A few minutes after Kelsey and Molly finished, the musicians began testing microphones and tuning their instruments. Kelsey felt a presence beside her.

"Are you finished? I'll get these out of your way." Dark eyes met her gaze, startling her. Rick Russo stood by her table, awaiting her response.

"Oh, oh yes, sure. Thanks." She offered a little smile, and darned if her heart wasn't pounding. He'd surprised her was all.

Rick nodded and stacked the plates along one arm, clearing the entire table at once. Impressive.

"Um, I'm Kelsey," she told him as he turned to leave. "I work here sometimes. Just wanted to say hello, and welcome."

Without smiling, he nodded. "Thanks. Nice to meet you, Kelsey." He shifted his gaze to Molly. "And who is *this* young lady?" A tiny smile tugged the corners of his mouth.

"I'm Molly." Molly awarded him with a wide grin. Her chin still sported a splash of gravy.

"My sister," Kelsey said.

"Nice to meet you too, Molly." After that, he disappeared into the kitchen, not wavering under his load of dishes. Kelsey didn't watch him leave, but felt touched by the way he'd reached out to Molly.

The musicians began their first song, a rousing country tune, and the volume hampered discussion. Kelsey glanced across the room just as Cooper Dawson and his wife, Blair, scooted in the front door. She waved at them in case they wanted to sit with her and Molly. Cooper was Amber's older brother and had recently married Blair, a former neighbor and single mom to Jake.

Cooper and Blair settled across from them with smiles and greetings. "Did you already eat?" Cooper shouted over the din.

"It's good to see you both," Kelsey shouted back. "Yes, we just finished. There's Annette, if you want to order something." She pointed to their server at the next table over.

They caught up on their news and lives for a few minutes—the new subdivision Cooper was working on, how they loved married life, Blair's business, and her son Jake's life as a growing ten-year-old.

Blair leaned toward Kelsey. "How is your food blog going?"

Kelsey gave a wan smile. "It's coming along, but it's tough finding time to post consistently. Since it's a food blog, I like to post recipes I've tested, but I need time to do that too before posting. Once it's more established, I can sell my cookbook there."

Blair pushed a lock of blond hair behind one ear. "Oh, right, I hadn't thought of that. It's more involved in your case than simply writing up a blog post." She gave Kelsey a sympathetic smile. "I started mine with a few posts and tips, and it gradually gained momentum. Consistency is important, if you can pull it off. Along with lots of patience."

"Yeah, I know." Suddenly Kelsey felt glum. Blair was a good example of a motivated entrepreneur who'd done the hard groundwork before launching her own clothing label. It hadn't been easy for her, while she'd juggled a factory job and single parenthood. But she'd taken baby steps, and it had paid off. She now had an online store with her designs and a collection of faithful customers.

The same would be true for Kelsey, if she was more consistent... at everything. And maybe give up sleeping, which would supply a few more hours in the day. She forced out a smile. "You're a great example for me, Blair. Even though clothing and food are different, the mechanics of steady focus and consistency are the same. There are no shortcuts."

"True. But don't forget constant learning. Experimentation."

That, Kelsey could do. She loved experimenting with food, just as Blair must love trying and creating new clothing designs. But Blair had graduated from fashion design school. Kelsey was self-taught, thanks to her favorite cooking shows and many books, but primarily experimentation and a few classes here and there. Otherwise, it was *The Kelsey Brewster Cooking School.*

"Hey, what about a video channel?" Blair brightened. "That would be perfect for you. You could show a recipe and different techniques, then the finished product. That would drive interest to the blog too."

"That's a great idea." She'd certainly seen plenty of cooking videos. But that would have to wait for the next phase.

Blair touched Kelsey's shoulder. "You'll get there, Kelsey. You're a natural."

"Thanks, Blair." Though she didn't always feel like one, Blair's comment spread warmth into her doubt, nudging some of it aside.

"Here's the server," Cooper told them. "Are you ready, Blair? No talking shop tonight, okay?" He grinned playfully and squeezed his wife's hand.

Cooper and Blair ordered sandwiches and conversation died down while everyone listened to the band. Blair's encouragement was helpful, yet reminded Kelsey of how much she *hadn't* done in her own fledgling business. Though time was her primary challenge, she also had to admit to being gun-shy, lacking confidence, so she dragged her feet.

Taking shifts at The Fork wasn't helping her find time to work on *Kelsey's Kitchen*. But she *enjoyed* The Fork. If she gave it up, not only would she leave Aggie short-handed, but she'd snuff out the highlight of her week. There was no easy answer.

After the band had played a few songs, Kelsey's gaze panned the dining room. There were a lot of unfamiliar faces, people who'd recently moved into Brenner Falls, mixed with other faces of regulars she knew. The town was small, but grew steadily, changing month by month.

Her gaze strayed to one familiar face, Pete McGowan, sitting with a group of friends. Her heart did a tiny flip. He was back in town. She'd had a crush on him while they were in high school and church youth group together years earlier, but he was never more than a friend back then, despite her hopes. They'd gone to different colleges. A few years later, she returned to The Falls while Pete had moved to another town. According to the grapevine, namely Amber, who had the scoop on former Brenner Falls residents, he'd married someone from college, a woman who later left the marriage. And now, he was back in his hometown.

He looked even better than he had the last time she'd seen him. More mature, more seasoned, less cocky...though his short sandy hair and blue eyes were the same.

Was she grabbing at straws? Feeling desperate? Kelsey shucked off the thought. She refused to think there was *no* hope for her to find love like her friends had. But when they all got married, and she didn't even have a date, it made a girl wonder what was wrong with her. Maybe nothing. It wasn't God's timing. But she'd been saying that to herself for years.

At her age, it was easy to assess whether a man she met had potential for a romance or not, according to age, faith, interests, background, and a few other things. There were two categories, *Potential* and *Not*. It was simply practical to think that way. It avoided wasting time, and having those things in common generally led to more stable relationships.

Was Pete back for good? While she pondered the question, his gaze found hers across the room, startling her. He too looked surprised to see her, then grinned and gave her a little wave. She responded with a wave of her own just as the band began their next song.

After the concert, Kelsey and Molly prepared to leave. They said goodbye to Cooper and Blair. She turned and almost bumped into Pete, who stood close to the table.

"Kelsey Brewster! How long has it been?"

She broke out into a wide grin. "Hi, Pete. I don't know, a few years at least. Are you visiting for the weekend?"

"Nope, I'm here to stay. I lived in Harrisburg for a while, but I missed my small town. Feels great to be back."

"I'm sure you've noticed it's not as small as it was before."

"Yes, I've observed that during a few visits over the years. That's a good thing. Progress and more amenities. I got my real estate license while I was away, so all the growth is great for me."

"Oh, that's good." Kelsey nodded. "I think you'll have plenty of clients. You remember my sister, Molly, don't you?" She turned to Molly, who stood beside her, fidgeting with her purse.

"Sure do. How are you, Molly? I'm Pete. You might not remember me."

Molly gave him a blank look. Apparently not.

"Well, it's good to see you again, Kelsey," he said. "I'm sure I'll see you around town."

No guarantees, but she hoped so. Maybe *he'd* have potential. She might ask him more questions, strike up a longer conversation if it weren't for Molly. She responded with a smile, hoping he'd make a more concrete statement.

"In fact," he added. "We should get together one of these days."

"Sure, I'd love to." For a split second, she wondered if he'd ask her for her number, but he'd turned away with another wave.

"See you around!"

Kelsey forced another cheery smile while her hope seeped out like a leaky balloon. "See you around."

Story of her life.

Chapter Three

Rick parked in front of the Brenner Falls Community Church at six-thirty Thursday evening. He came a few minutes early to breathe, be alone, to find his bearings. In thirty minutes, he'd become a volunteer youth leader.

What were they thinking?

So, he sat still in the second-hand car his mom had bought for him. As soon as she knew he was heading home, she started looking, she'd told him. He ran a hand along the clean vinyl dashboard. It was a decent car, so probably Ben had helped her pick it out. She wouldn't have known what to buy. It had a good engine, relatively low miles. A brief mental image of his mother scanning the aisles of used car lots brought a smile to his lips, despite the flutters in his stomach.

"Lord, what do you have in mind with all this youth stuff?" he asked aloud. Yet, he'd worked with the youth in Flagstaff and had liked it. He didn't mention the fact of liking it to Pastor Frank, who would've planned out his entire future career. The kids had gravitated toward him for some reason. He hoped he'd somehow helped them. The Brenner Falls kids might be different. But maybe he could help them too. The very thought made him shake his head. *Help* them? He was barely out of the gutter himself.

"I shouldn't think that way, Lord." He admonished himself. "You saved me two years ago and put me on another path. It isn't a small thing, so I shouldn't think like I'm still in that gutter. Or under the bridge." Yet, it was hard not to feel like he'd never change his identity. Like he was permanently tattooed with labels like *druggie. Homeless.*

He prayed silently for strength to walk through the doors. For God's will, whatever that was. And to grasp his new place as a surrendered and redeemed son. He got out of the car and walked toward the large double doors of the church.

"I'm looking for Jesse Holmes, the youth pastor," he told the first person he saw, a maintenance man mopping the hall to a glossy glow.

"He'd be down in the gym by now." The man pointed. "Go down the stairs at the end of the hall."

"Thanks." He was supposed to meet Jesse at six forty-five.

Rick had been in the church building a few times by now, but hadn't been to the gym. He knew it was a floor below the sanctuary. When he entered the cavernous room, he saw Jesse right away, along with a few teenagers who'd arrived early. Some were shooting baskets at one end of the court, while others fidgeted awkwardly in a cluster as they waited for the program to begin.

Pastor Frank had introduced him to Jesse at church the previous week. Rick had a good first impression of the man, who was about Rick's age. Rick explained he wanted to observe the group the first few times. Over the years, he'd developed a habit of easing into things slowly as he learned the lay of the land. In this setting, it was crucial.

"Hey, Rick. Glad you're here." Jesse's warm tone echoed from the high ceiling as he gave Rick a firm welcome slap on the shoulder. He stood at least five inches taller than Rick, who was already five ten. A mop of frizzy brown hair and kind gray eyes topped Jesse's towering but skinny stature. "We usually average about twenty kids, more or less. About half to two thirds are church kids, and the rest come either from around town or other churches. Some aren't in any church. We often start out with a game, which we'll do tonight. That gets the kids active and having fun. Then we pull them into that room there." He pointed to an open carpeted area to one side of the gym. "We sing a few songs, and I do a short devotional. Sometimes we have discussion, sometimes not. Other times, I show a movie. It varies. Then we break and have snacks over in that area."

He gestured toward a long table against the wall where a couple of kids arranged bags of chips and cookies. "I have another leader, Rhonda, but she couldn't come tonight."

Rick nodded several times during Jesse's description of the evening's events. Sounded similar to the program in Arizona. That calmed his butterflies somewhat until the kids started filing into the gym. Maybe it hadn't been a good idea to agree to work with the youth this soon after his arrival.

A few minutes after seven, Jesse called the kids together in a circle in the middle of the gym. Rick counted eighteen kids, about ten girls and the rest, guys. They looked like the teens he'd met in the past, a continuum of expressions on their faces. Eager, bored, friendly, surly. He recognized himself in some of them...guarded. Hurting. Hopeless. His tension loosened. Maybe he *did* have a role here.

"Listen up, everyone," Jesse called, his voice reverberating. "Welcome to youth group. Maybe this year we can come up with a cooler name for ourselves." That brought titters and grins from the small crowd. "So, this here is Rick." He fanned a palm in Rick's direction. "He'll be helping out with the group. He just moved to town." Rick was grateful for a sketchy introduction, but hoped it didn't elicit tons of questions.

Introductions completed, Jesse corralled the kids, divided them into two teams, and explained the game, which involved a flag, a ball, and Rick forgot what else. Before long, he was running around with the teens and forgot he wasn't one of them. Felt great, since he hadn't really *been* a kid himself.

Back in Flagstaff, he'd enjoyed his time with the youth, but had never fully let go of his reserve. He always feared they'd discover his story and back away from him in disillusionment. Feared he'd be the ultimate bad example, though he was a believer by then. So, he'd been an adult friend, a *good guy*, but a surface guy. A guy with secrets.

Following two different games, the group headed into the room with chairs and a screen. Rick slipped into the last seat in the last row, but a couple of the guys seemed eager to pile into the folding chairs next to him. He smiled at them, then shifted his attention to the front where a couple of kids tuned guitars.

Rick scrutinized everything that happened, everything Jesse said and did, as well as the kids. Observing, taking mental notes. It was another skill he'd learned over the years, changing places so frequently. That is, while he was sober. Get the overview, notice the details. He liked the fact that the kids were the ones playing guitars, preparing snacks, and running the slides.

After singing two or three songs Rick didn't know, Jesse quieted the group and sat on a stool. He propped an electronic tablet onto a simple wooden stand, then opened with a story that introduced the devotional before launching into his topic. Rick scanned the faces of the kids around the room. Some paid attention, others drifted or fidgeted. But Jesse's message was decent. Likely, it would hit some of the kids' hearts.

All in all, it wasn't a bad two weeks back in Brenner Falls. He had a home, a car, a job, a mentor, and a ministry. *And* he had a family again. The thought brought a clutch of both gladness and agony to his gut. Of course, Ben and his mother had been ecstatic when he told them he'd given his life to Christ and was living with a Christian couple, working a real job doing lawn and other maintenance at the church. It was the most stable he'd been in over a decade. Then two years later, when he told them he was moving back home, it was as though he'd given them winning lottery tickets. Some lottery. But their joy broadcasted their love, and that touched him deeply. *And* filled him with tons of guilt.

How could he ever erase what he'd done to them? The way he'd treated Ben over the years, like nothing more than a cash machine? And his mom, worrying about him for twelve long years, praying for her prodigal to return home? Maybe that's why God nudged him that night and told him it was time. Maybe it was for their sakes.

ଔ ଔ ଔ

On Friday in the late morning, Kelsey parked in front of Treasure House. "I hope you enjoy your day, Molly." She touched her sister's shoulder. "I'll pick you up at four-thirty, okay?"

"Okay. Bye." Molly slipped from the car and disappeared into the brick building.

Next stop, The Fork, this time, to help in the kitchen with prep for a couple of hours. Then she'd return home to her regular job until time to pick up Molly.

She didn't totally dislike the rhythm. Going to The Fork made her computer job bearable. She could complete her work projects on her own time, even in the evening, if she needed to. How many evenings had she spent on the couch with her laptop in use while Molly watched a show or colored pictures?

She walked down the narrow, European-looking alley and spotted the familiar blue awnings of The Grateful Fork, its metal sign swinging from a horizontal pole. She recalled the day years ago when she was talking to Aggie, who'd just lost a couple of employees during the busy season. Kelsey jumped at the opportunity to help her friend, but also to slip behind the scenes at The Fork, preparing or serving meals occasionally. She'd been there ever since, a few hours here, a few hours there.

"Hi, Claire," Kelsey called to the sous-chef as she reached into the linen closet to snag an apron. "I'm ready to cut veggies or whatever you need. Your wish is my command." She folded her hands and gave a bow.

"Hiya, Kelsey." Claire grinned over one shoulder as she stirred a steaming stockpot on the stove. Her motion made her dark blond ponytail swing back and forth. "I've set everything out for you there on that counter. You know what to do." She hitched her head toward a stainless-steel surface covered with piles of vegetables and a few sizes of knives.

Kelsey laughed. "Yes, I do." She'd prepped too many times to count. Salads, vegetables for the salads or the meals people ordered at lunchtime, beverage prep. She spent the next hour chatting with the kitchen staff, who seemed a bit like family, while slicing vegetables and tearing lettuce.

The kitchen door swung open. In walked Rick Russo. He greeted everyone in his reserved way, nodded at Kelsey, and pulled an apron from the closet. She tensed, unsure of why. Because she didn't really know him yet. Or, she had to admit, because she found him attractive, mysterious. And off limits.

Just as quickly, without indulging in any news or small talk, he disappeared into the dining room, likely to make sure the tables were clean, and condiment bottles filled before the lunch crowd arrived at eleven-thirty.

A few minutes before noon, Kelsey finished her prepping duties. She put her knives into the huge dishwasher and tossed her apron into a bin, then said goodbye to the lunch crew. She wasn't sure what day she'd be back, since Aggie usually called her in advance on an as-needed basis. Maybe Danielle was now in charge of scheduling.

The kitchen door opened into the bar area on one end of the dining room. When Kelsey entered the area, Rick was behind the bar arranging washed glasses and other items. He glanced her way and continued working. She went toward him.

"Hey, Rick. How are you settling in here?" Hopefully, he'd find her welcoming since he was new.

"Hi." He stopped what he was doing and his dark eyes found hers. "Your name's Kelsey?"

She nodded and offered a friendly smile.

"It's going pretty well. I've done restaurant work in the past, so it's easy to get up to speed."

"I heard you'd just moved back into town. Were you gone a long time?" She thought she saw him stiffen slightly. He didn't need to fear she'd learn his story. She knew it already.

"Yeah. Almost fourteen years. The town has changed a lot." He shrugged. "I think I'll like it here."

"I hope so. Where did you live before coming back here?"

"Arizona. I left after high school. I wanted a warmer climate."

"I guess you found one in Arizona." She grinned. "I hear the summers there can be brutally hot, though I've never been there."

"It depends on what part of the state you're in." His face relaxed a little. "I spent a lot of time in Flagstaff, which is in the mountains. Summers were good there. Phoenix is a couple hours away, and that's where it's hot in summer. But the winters are milder."

"Best of both worlds, I guess."

The chill returned to his eyes. "I guess that's one way to think of it." He paused. "How long have you worked here?" He snagged a towel and dried a few drops of water from a glass before setting it into a rack.

"I don't actually work here. And I'm not a mirage, either." She grinned, hoping to draw a smile. "I know that sounds confusing. I have a full-time job I do at home online so I can keep an eye on my sister, Molly. But I come here to fill in when Aggie needs me, and because I enjoy being around people and food."

A half-smile quirked his lips. "I could ask why you don't work here full time since you like it, but I guess that's because of your sister?" He crossed his arms and leaned against the counter.

Kelsey ignored the stab inside at his words, reminded of her lost opportunity. "Yes, primarily. My parents are out of the country for nine months on a mission trip, so I'm Molly's primary caretaker. Coming here allows me to be around people and I like that. Otherwise, I'd be in front of a computer screen."

Rick nodded. "Yeah, I can see why you'd want a break. It's good for some people. My brother Ben, for example. He's an engineer and spends a lot of time on the computer. But he goes out to worksites too."

"I know your brother and his wife." She wouldn't tell him Amber was one of her closest friends. "I bet Ben's happy you came back to town." Hopefully, she wasn't opening Pandora's box during her first conversation with Rick Russo. Knowing his background already caused her to walk carefully.

Instead, he smiled, the first smile she'd seen on him, and it made him, unfortunately, more handsome than he already was, white teeth against an Italian complexion. "Yeah, he is. We were close as kids, then I was gone a long time. We're working on getting that back."

"That's wonderful," she said sincerely. An eager welcome from family would help him in his transition.

Kelsey shot a glance at the dining room, which was filling up with lunch customers. "Well, looks like you're about to get busy here, so I'll let you get to it."

"See you around." He turned his attention back to the sink.

Kelsey walked to her car, but her brief conversation with Rick stayed in her mind. She was glad they'd broken the ice. She felt so curious about him. What had driven him to the streets? How had he become a Christian? What was it like now for him to adapt to a completely different life?

Those questions would remain unanswered, since he wouldn't likely want to discuss his past with a coworker he'd just met. She'd seen him once at church, sitting next to his mother, while Ben and Amber sat on the other side. She had the impression he was making a valiant effort to succeed in his new life.

Her afternoon sped by and soon it was time to pick up Molly. After preparing a hurried supper for her sister, Kelsey changed into jeans and a colorful top, pulled her thick auburn hair into a ponytail, and added a bit of makeup and earrings. It had been ages since she'd gone to a church singles event. Or any group social. Just the other day, she realized she lacked a social life. It had been too easy to get caught up in work, Molly's needs, The Fork, and creating recipes for her cookbook project. Putting her own priorities on the back burner was a longstanding habit. So, she called her friend, Sophie, and convinced her they should go together to *socialize*.

That evening, the event would be games and pizza around tables in a reserved room at the church. The group did a variety of activities, like restaurants or parties, potlucks or day trips. Occasionally, Kelsey took part, but found it challenging to juggle what she already did without adding more.

Since moving back home, Kelsey often helped her parents with her sister, so hadn't expected the extra time and attention it took to be Molly's sole caretaker. Despite that, she still needed balance, which included socializing with others her age. Seeing old friends and maybe even meeting a new guy—hopefully one with Potential—though she wouldn't count on *that*. Newcomers were rare, and usually female. Maybe Pete would show up. Although games weren't her favorite activity, she decided to go anyway. Molly would be fine on her own for a few hours. The landline was set up to speed-dial Kelsey, just in case.

Kelsey parked in front of the church among several other cars and approached the front door, where her friend Sophie stood waiting for her. Sophie's business, Sophie's Coffee Shop, was another Brenner Falls hub that always seemed crowded with fans of her sweet specialties, both French and American. Aggie often ordered desserts from Sophie for the restaurant at Kelsey's suggestion. And of course, she and Sophie often talked about cooking and baking, swapping recipes, and learning from one another's cultural traditions.

"Hi, Sophie." Kelsey gave her friend a hug. "Haven't seen you in a while, so I'm glad you were willing to come."

"Only because you're here," Sophie said. "I don't know a lot about American games." She spoke softly and an intriguing French accent laced her words.

"I can't say I know them any better than you do," Kelsey admitted. "The point is to socialize. I'm lacking that lately."

"Yes, socialize. We both work too hard."

Sophie spoke the truth. But she was living her dream, making pastry from scratch as she'd been trained back in Brittany, France. Kelsey wasn't living her dream *yet,* even though she enjoyed being at The Fork a few times per week.

As the women approached the room reserved for the evening, the sound of conversation and laughter grew louder. Kelsey knew at least half the people in the room, including Danielle, who greeted them warmly.

Kelsey was glad to see Pete McGowan across the room. Seated at a round table, he was engaged in a conversation with a pretty brunette. He looked up and waved at Kelsey, who waved back. Maybe it was a start, but it reminded her of the last time she saw him at The Fork. Casual, disinterested. The wave simply didn't cut it. But hey, the night was still young.

People played a variety of card or board games at different tables. Kelsey and Sophie chose a table with a card game that looked easy to learn. At the end of one round, they changed tables to try something else. Soon, the pizza arrived and the men and women around the room swarmed to a long table enveloped by enticing cheesy aromas.

"Are you enjoying yourself, Sophie?" Kelsey murmured as she slid a piece of hot cheesy pizza onto her paper plate.

"It's okay. Once I learned the games, it was more fun." Sophie shrugged. "But it's not really my thing."

Kelsey smiled. "Me either. But we're being *social,* aren't we?"

Sophie grinned back "If you say so."

"We meet again, Kelsey." A male voice spoke over her shoulder.

She turned. "Hi, Pete. I didn't expect you here tonight," she said. "Maybe because you just got back into town." Her hope ticked up, since he'd made the effort to cross the room. Would he pursue his earlier suggestion of getting together after all?

"I saw the event posted on the church website, so I thought, why not? I need to get integrated again after being gone so long." He turned a glance at Sophie. "Hi, I'm Pete McGowan."

"Oh, I'm sorry," Kelsey said. "I forgot you two probably didn't know each other. This is my friend Sophie, as in Sophie's Coffee Shop."

Pete's eyebrows lifted. "Really? That's impressive. I'll have to try it. Is it downtown?"

"Yes, it's in the center of town on Warren Street," Sophie told him.

"Is that an accent I detect?"

"Yes, I'm from France."

"I love it!" Pete chortled. "Bet you get that all the time."

Kelsey suddenly felt invisible as her previous hope dripped away.

Sophie gave him a gracious but subdued smile. "I am used to it now. I've been in America for many years."

"Well, I'll have to stop by your shop sometime. Do you make French pastries?"

"Yes. I have both French and American desserts and breads."

"Can't wait to try one. Well, it's good to see you both. Good to meet you, Sophie."

When he left them to return to his table, Kelsey and Sophie exchanged a glance. "Don't be surprised if he comes to your shop tomorrow," Kelsey murmured with a wink.

"*Ah, non! Je ne veux pas* !" Sophie put a theatrical hand to her brow, and they both giggled.

"I guess that means he didn't win your heart. Believe it or not, I had a crush on him when I was in high school."

Sophie looked perplexed. "What is this *crush*? What does it mean?"

"It means I liked him. Then he left for many years."

Sophie looked dubious. "Do you still have a crush now that he's back?"

Across the room, Pete approached a different woman at another table, this time, a redhead. Kelsey's previous enthusiasm sagged, and she heaved a sigh. "Nope."

Chapter Four

The Monday lunch rush was a tornado of activity, more than any weekday Rick had seen in the two weeks he'd begun working at The Fork. He must have covered forty miles, going from the dining room to bus tables, then to the kitchen to rinse and stack them in the dishwasher. Back and forth. The increased crowd was due to the specials of the day Aggie posted to stir up more business for a weekday. As far as he could tell, business was always brisk, though Monday lunch was the slowest. That was natural, since it followed the weekend.

On a chalkboard by the front door was a list of meals Aggie called *Monday Motivation Specials*. It was a great idea, and not the only indication he'd seen of Aggie's creativity. For seventy-something, she seemed to have double his energy and a clear mind as well.

That day, Kelsey waited tables and looked just as busy as he was. He caught her eye once, giving her a reserved smile and a nod of greeting. Just trying to be as friendly as she'd been to him. Who was he kidding? His spirits lifted when he saw her in the room, zipping from table to table, her wavy auburn ponytail swinging with her swift and nonstop motion. Each time he overheard her speaking to customers, her gentle tone and kindness struck him, as if she weren't juggling sixty tasks at one time.

Gradually, the dining room emptied, looking like a mild war zone. Every table needed to be bussed. Rick dispatched the task with focused precision. Aggie often told him with an elderly trill to her voice, "Rick Russo, you're like a one-man army. I wish I had five of you."

To that, he'd usually grin and say, "You'd regret that, Miss Aggie." That drew laughter and a playful swat from the older woman. Often, she insisted he go home for a couple of hours if he was also working the dinner shift. Hopefully, that would be the case that day, since his shoulders ached with fatigue from hours of carrying dishes on his arms.

He slipped behind the bar and poured a glass of cold water, gulping it down without stopping.

"Bet you're tired." A soft female voice beside him. Kelsey.

Warmth surged inside. "You'd win that bet." He offered a smile and grabbed a glass. After filling it with water, he handed it to her.

"Thanks." She took it and drank as greedily as he had.

"Aren't you? Tired, I mean."

"Exhausted." She let out a sigh. "But that's the price we pay for Aggie's marketing genius."

"No wonder this place is a goldmine. I assume it is, at any rate."

"*And* a hub for all of Brenner Falls," she supplied with a smile before she finished her water.

"The town has definitely changed since I lived here," he said. "Of course, that was a long time ago. I hope the new eateries that are bound to come don't overtake Aggie's customers one day."

Kelsey shrugged. "There are plenty of new places, and people like them. But Falls natives are faithful to their landmarks too. Like Seasons, for example."

Rick cocked his head. "Seasons?"

"It's a Brenner Falls institution, like The Fork. Seasons is a dinner theater and restaurant in that big Victorian house across from City Hall."

"Oh, *that's* what it is. I wondered." He'd seen the stately mansion and wasn't sure what kind of business was inside. "What about Seasons?"

"Seasons is around eighty years old, and the building was getting kind of run-down. The owner was sick and couldn't keep up with it. He died and left it to his nephew, Nathan Chisholm. At first, Nathan wanted to sell it, but the people in town didn't want him to.

They didn't want a developer coming in and tearing down their dinner theater, even though a lot of them never even went."

Rick grinned. "Figures. They want their landmark, but don't take part in keeping it alive."

"Well, they did eventually. That's a story I'll let Nathan tell you one day." Her full pink lips held a tantalizing smile.

"I don't know if I've met Nathan, but I'm sure over time, I'll meet everyone in Brenner Falls."

The kitchen door swung open, and Aggie marched out. "Good work, everyone," she called to the employees assembled there to catch their breath. She passed through the bar and into the empty dining room. "It was a busy shift, and everyone pulled their weight. Thanks for making my experiment a success. *Monday Motivation*. We'll keep that going for a while and track the results."

She sat at a nearby table. Her strength and energy seemed to escape from her body all at once, leaving her looking wrung-out and owning all of her seventy-some-odd years. She motioned to all the wait staff with one arm. "Please come, everyone. I have a short meeting for the staff to give you some news." The chefs and cooks' assistants emerged from the kitchen and clustered around the bar.

"This won't take long, but it's very important. First, I've owned The Grateful Fork for forty years. I've seen all its ups and downs and loved every moment. But I'm almost seventy-three years old and I'm getting tired. My relatives and friends have urged me to retire. I've thought about it for over a year because, quite honestly, I didn't want to. This is my family, now that my Charles is gone. You are all family. I hope you feel like family to each other to some degree. But it's time for me to pass the baton. At this point I'm not planning to sell it. As a first step, I'm going to keep The Fork in the family and pass the manager role to Danielle Locklear, my great-niece." She extended her hand with a flourish in Danielle's direction. No one applauded. Maybe they were in shock?

Instead, Rick heard Kelsey let out a sound, as if a whimper had tried to escape, but she'd muzzled it down. He shot a glance at her, seeing a stricken expression, probably at the loss of regular contact with Aggie. He'd observed their rapport and guessed they were close. But maybe Danielle wasn't Kelsey's first choice for the manager either. Or maybe she and Kelsey didn't get along. Whatever the reason, Kelsey seemed unhappy about the news.

Aggie continued. "I'll leave officially in two weeks, but I'll phase out between now and then. I've done some training with Danielle and will continue until I leave. I'll stay in touch, of course, especially for her first few weeks. But I want you all to help her learn the ropes and help each other through the transition. I already know you're a good team, but just wanted to remind you of that. I'm staying in town after I retire, but I'm planning to travel once in a while. That's something I've always wanted to do more, but couldn't get away. Now's my chance."

Only two weeks to train a new manager? Rick stifled a sarcastic laugh, but it wasn't at all funny.

"We'll miss you, Aggie," said Janet, one of the servers.

"Yeah, wish you all the best, Aggie," Bruce, one of the cooks added, and several people echoed his sentiment.

As other employees added their good wishes, Rick noticed Kelsey remained in place, not speaking. Another surreptitious glance led to surprise as he saw her blue eyes glassy with tears. He understood, having known Aggie for only two weeks, yet sensed there was something else going on.

A few minutes later, he took a load of plates into the kitchen and saw her with two of the line cooks discussing Aggie's announcement. He got the gist as he headed to the square metal sink. They all seemed astonished that the woman would retire only two weeks after making her announcement. It seemed quick to him too, but maybe Aggie had kept the news under her hat to keep people from quitting or morale from tumbling. Judging by the looks on their faces, morale had already slid out of control, beginning with Kelsey.

The next few days passed like the ones before, except for one difference. Danielle was now the manager of The Grateful Fork under Aggie's watchful eye. Aggie took a proactive approach with her great-niece, explaining the important routines of the restaurant. She'd made a notebook for Danielle to follow, and he often spotted one of them carrying it around while Aggie explained things, like ordering inventory, keeping the accounts straight, payroll, and confirming music artists. Her protégé nodded mutely, looking shell-shocked most of the time.

There seemed to be a lot involved in managing a restaurant. Danielle might be capable of following everything in Aggie's notebook, but would she be able to dream up something like *Monday Motivation*? Maybe Danielle would fall into step and own it once she'd learned everything. He'd only been at The Fork a short while, but he already felt a sense of belonging that made him care what happened to it. That had never happened in any of the countless restaurants where he'd worked in the past.

Alongside caring about The Fork, he realized something he'd forgotten. He *liked* restaurant work and had a knack for it. Some of his managers back in Arizona had told him that, and back then, he'd blown it off. He'd considered it a short-term gig that had no future, not that he even desired one back then.

But now, things were different. He'd arrived in Brenner Falls a new man with the capacity to think of the future, to want something for his life. Maybe his many hours of restaurant work weren't a waste after all, as he'd once considered them. He'd felt comfortable there and had occasionally made suggestions for improvement. Then while he lived in Flagstaff, one of the courses he'd taken and enjoyed at the community college was in the hospitality field.

"Rick, Aggie wants to talk to you for a minute." The voice of Trina, one of the servers, broke into his thoughts. He looked toward the bar and saw Aggie and Kelsey engaged in discussion. Aggie looked toward him and motioned with one hand.

He wiped his grubby palms on his apron and slipped behind the counter.

"Rick," the older woman said. "I wanted to ask you and Kelsey for a special favor. I realize Danielle is getting broken in and though she's learning quickly, she'll need some extra help once I'm gone. Now, the two of you have good insight about restaurants. Kelsey, you know *this* restaurant quite well, even if it's not your regular job. Rick, you spend a lot of hours here and have good experience elsewhere. So, I thought the two of you could be two extra pairs of eyes and hands. Hopefully, that will add a layer of assurance for Danielle. You can keep an eye on things she might miss, remind her of things if needed, and so on."

Kelsey nodded. "Sure, Aggie. I would have done that anyway. I'd like to be of help when I'm here."

"Same for me." With Aggie's authorization, he could do more. But the obvious bonus for him, collaborating with Kelsey. Though he kept a poker face, a warm flush surged through him.

"Thank you both. I knew I could count on you to be my extra set of eyes. Protective eyes, I mean, to support her. You'll be helping Danielle succeed in her new role."

Kelsey and Rick both nodded in agreement and Aggie slipped back into the kitchen.

"You heard the boss." Rick offered a restrained smile.

Kelsey's gaze met his. "So, we'll become Danielle's safety net. I...I'm relieved and glad. I think she'll need one."

Was she glad for the chance to help Danielle or glad to be working with him on it? He hoped it was both, although whether they could help Danielle succeed or not remained to be seen.

Later that evening, Rick entered the church gym for his second youth group meeting. Right away, he noticed some new faces. Like the last time, a few kids were shooting baskets at one end of the room. Rather than shift his weight until the program started, Rick joined them. He'd played often during a random pickup game while on his sojourn out west, and could hold his own. Before long, there was a rousing competition underway and good-natured banter.

When Jesse arrived just after seven, he called everyone in. "Sorry I'm late. I had to pick up my car at the shop and they weren't ready on time. Looks like we have some new folks tonight." He looked around the group with a smile. "I'm Jesse, this is Rick, and that's Rhonda. What are your names?"

One guy was lanky and pale, with dark blond curly hair and a blank expression. "I'm Chris," he said. "Rod invited me, so I thought I'd check it out."

"And I'm Sal," piped up another guy, shorter and rounder. He offered a wide grin and panned the group with dark, eager eyes. "Rod invited me too."

"Way to go, Rod." Jessie grinned and pumped one fist. "A great reminder to everyone. Invite your friends." He turned back to Chris and Sal. "Welcome to both of you. I hope you'll enjoy yourselves and make some new friends."

Rod was a tall kid with wavy reddish hair, a muscular build, and a confident air. Rick took a mental note. *Might be an influencer.* He'd talk to the guy later and feel out his spiritual commitment level.

Everyone played the game, then headed to the carpeted room for the devotional.

"Are you from Brenner Falls, Chris?" Rick asked the new guy who walked beside him toward the room.

"No. I've been here since the beginning of high school when my parents split up, so about five years. I was in Arizona before that."

Rick's heart pounded against his ribs for a few seconds. *Settle down. There's no danger whatsoever that Chris would have ever seen you in the past.* "I used to live there too."

Chris looked startled. "Get out, really? Where'd you live?"

"Flagstaff, mostly. Sometimes I'd go down to Phoenix in winter, since it was warmer there." Especially on those nights when his little band didn't have housing.

"I lived in Scottsdale till my dad left," Chris said. "Then my mom and I came here with my little sister. My mom has a sister here, so we moved in with her until my mom got a place for us."

"Do you work? Go to school?"

"I work. Autobody. It's okay."

Rick nodded in response. They sat in the last row as the guitarists tuned.

After Jesse's devotional, the group rose and ambled toward the snack table. Jesse pulled Rick aside. "Hold up just a minute, Rick," he said. "I was thinking you could take on some more leadership, maybe start by choosing and leading the game from time to time, or even every week if you want. What do you think?"

Rick laughed. "I don't know diddly about games."

Jesse frowned. "You didn't play games growing up?"

Not really. Games like how to stay away from home as long as possible. He knew that one pretty well, but doubted that would count. "Not that I remember. Dodge ball, stuff like that?"

"Dodge ball is okay, but there are others. I have a booklet I'll loan you. You can pick one and lead next time, okay?"

"Sure, I'll try." Up to then, Jesse hadn't asked Rick to do more than gather the kids after the game, connect with them, and keep an eye out for newcomers. He'd been relieved, but had observed or thought of small ways to improve the program. Maybe invite someone from the outside who could talk about a topic of interest. Initiate better follow-up for new kids… Maybe during the weekdays when he wasn't working, he could meet some of the guys for a game of basketball, either there in the gym or at a local court outside. He already sensed some acceptance and trust building. That encouraged him, since it might be the hardest hurdle for them.

Teaching a game? He guessed he could do that. If only he could project his mind back to his teen years and rewrite his history, what would he have enjoyed back then as a normal teen, instead of packing up for the vagabond life on an unknown road?

He frowned. A normal teen? Nothing about his life had been normal, so he'd have to use a lot of imagination.

ಌ ಌ ಌ

Kelsey peeked into Molly's bedroom. Her sister, who'd stayed up late the previous night watching movies, was fast asleep. Hopefully, she'd stay that way for a couple of hours.

With a sigh of satisfaction, Kelsey padded into the kitchen, savoring the silence and her aloneness. It was rare to be alone on a Saturday morning with no responsibilities, no work to do, save a bit of housework. Nothing else but her own projects, which included food experiments.

The first one would serve as breakfast for her and Molly, acorn squash pancakes. She'd never eaten acorn squash, but one day at the grocery store had been drawn by its sculptured beauty and deep green skin. A quick online scan confirmed its health benefits. After roasting it, she dug out the softened flesh, pureed it with maple syrup and cinnamon, then folded it into her pancake batter. A few pecans, a dollop of Greek yogurt, and she'd made a healthy breakfast and a new entry for her cookbook, and maybe the blog too.

She had some of it left, so what could she do with it? Fritters came to mind. Less sweet this time, with a touch of curry powder or garam masala...

Three weeks had passed since the announcement of Aggie's retirement. For the two weeks following that even, as promised, Aggie continued to mentor her great-niece, providing checklists and working through the ever-present notebook day by day. When the moment of Aggie's official departure arrived, the staff hosted a retirement party for her. The restaurant was packed that evening with Brenner Falls residents, Aggie's friends and family, and faithful, long-term customers. A rich blend of nostalgia and festivity animated the evening, which Kelsey found bittersweet.

Since that time, Danielle had been on her own managing The Fork, but Aggie had dropped by several times a week to check on her and get an overview. Danielle also sent weekly summaries of the accounts and copies of her completed checklists to Aggie by email. The other employees gently explained or reminded her of routine tasks, and Danielle seemed grateful. Kelsey and Rick stayed watchful, but didn't have to intervene much yet, especially during Aggie's training. So far so good, but Danielle had been flying solo, with Aggie's remote support, for only one week.

Rick had been at The Fork almost every time Kelsey took a shift. She had the impression he worked more than full-time. Whenever she spoke to him, he seemed less reserved than the previous time. She imagined tightly furled leaves gradually unfolding in spring. At times, one of them quipped or shared a grimace, depending on the situation.

Though she warmed at the thought that he was increasingly relaxed around her, agitation simmered below the surface for one reason. As their working acquaintance developed and touched on friendship, this countered her efforts to suppress her growing attraction to him. Of all the people to make her insides flutter when her gaze connected to his dark eyes, or she happened to observe his arm muscles flex under a load of dishes...

More than his manly physical appeal was her impression of him as being on a mission to reinvent his life and make good decisions.

Despite his past, she respected him for that, especially when she looked across the sanctuary at church and saw him surrounded by teenagers, some of them tough-looking, as he once must have been.

Even if Rick *were* a suitable match for her, he wouldn't likely be attracted to her. She didn't have the zing that men went for, men like Pete, but she couldn't help it. Kelsey was who she was. Unruly hair, pale skin, and average build, though she did her best with what she had, like sometimes accenting her blue eyes with makeup. That's why, when new male faces entered her world, they made a beeline for women like Amber and Sophie with their undisputed beauty. At least she had other gifts and qualities that made her unique, and she wouldn't minimize those. She sighed and pushed the thoughts aside, falling back on God's timing once again.

Following Aggie's official departure, Kelsey became vigilant for opportunities to do as Aggie had requested, be an extra set of eyes for Danielle. One Wednesday she came in to work the lunch shift, and began with a quick scan around the dining room. She saw only two servers, and neither Danielle nor Rick.

The pre-rush tranquility of the dining room contrasted with the buzz in the kitchen. She greeted everyone, her voice lost in the melee of shouts and clanging cookware, and slipped on her apron. Rick came in then and did the same, then returned to the dining room, not wasting words on anyone, including her. She frowned. Had he forgotten they were a team now? Did that mean each one to his own duties with no communication, no complicity?

Kelsey shoved her hurt feelings aside. She was reading too much too soon into anything with Rick Russo. To him, it was likely a directive from the boss and nothing more. *Fine.*

She found Rick behind the bar prepping the drink counter. "Hi, Rick. Is Danielle here? I don't see her."

He greeted her with a smile. "She'll be here tonight."

"Who's covering until then?"

"I don't know. Aggie must have a plan for times she couldn't be here. You could ask Vince."

Kelsey took a breath, and her gaze roved the dining room again. A lot could fall into the cracks if neither Danielle nor Aggie were there. That's why Aggie had wanted her help, along with Rick's. "I'll do that. And check inventory too."

Rick frowned. "You don't have to do that unless you really want to. Danielle might have already done it. You could ask her when she comes in."

"But don't you think it would be wise to keep an eye out anyway? Even before something goes wrong? I can catch it before it happens."

Rick placed the wadded towel on the counter and crossed his arms. A grin teased his lips. "Kelsey, my advice is don't worry until there's something to worry about. Check inventory if it makes you feel better." He glanced at the door and hitched his head in that direction. "But you probably have some lunch customers first."

Kelsey huffed and returned to the kitchen. Was he patronizing her? Whether he was or not, he was pretty blasé about doing as Aggie had asked. Wasn't it their role to be watchful? A second set of eyes? Why wait for something to fall apart when they could prevent it?

Her conscience pricked at her. She fully expected Danielle *not* to succeed, and wasn't giving her a fair chance. Still, she wanted to fulfill Aggie's request.

She took a glance inside the walk-in refrigerator, but realized she didn't know what to look for. Why did she feel it was suddenly her responsibility as if she were the manager? Rick had a point. They were there to prevent or put out fires if they occurred. Not to predict them.

"Kelsey," Trina called from the kitchen doorway. "Party of two at table three."

Oh, right. Back to work.

For the following two hours, the immediate task of waiting tables rerouted her thoughts. Finally, she took a cold bottle of water from the fridge and slipped out to a small fenced-in area behind the restaurant. In the small patio sat a round picnic table. A few more chairs lined up against the fence and a gate led to a set of dumpsters. Kelsey closed her eyes for a moment and coaxed the quiet and summer warmth to soak into her bones.

A moment later, the sound of the back door swinging open jarred her from her sleepy state. Rick slid into the chair across from her and popped the lid from a cold drink.

"Sorry to wake you up." He grinned and took a sip.

Kelsey couldn't help but smile back. "Hey. I'm sorry I was…um, touchy a while ago. I want to be conscientious, but I don't need to obsess."

"Conscientious is good. And watchful, as if it were yours."

"That helps. I'll pretend it's mine." If only. Rick met her gaze, and a flutter rustled deep inside her.

"We can be helpful, but it might not lead to a successful outcome."

"Yeah," Kelsey said glumly. "I want to be more optimistic. I can't explain why The Fork means so much to me, when I'm not the owner or even a regular employee. It's sort of like my family." She shrugged. "I'd hate to see it…change." Even if Danielle succeeded, The Fork might shift according to *her* vision.

"What's your family like?"

Her head lifted at his question, which seemed unrelated, but wasn't. "It's great, really. My parents are supportive. They're strong believers." But? "Honestly, I can't explain why The Fork is like family. Maybe restaurant work is my thing, where I can be around what I love, whereas in my family, I try to be helpful because of Molly. My focus there is being a team player."

"You're a team player here," he pointed out. "But at home you have to sort of lay low about your own wants." He took another sip of his drink, but his eyes didn't leave hers.

"I guess so. I never thought of it that way. I always feel responsible for a lot when I'm there. At The Fork, I still feel responsibility, but I've chosen it." She gave him a crooked grin. "Don't get me wrong. I love helping Molly." Would he think she was selfish because she sought a corner of her life that fed her passion?

"Makes perfect sense to me. At home, you're part of a family and don't get to fully do the thing you love. Here, you can get a little closer to it."

She fell silent. He'd given her a pretty good description, summarizing in a way she hadn't.

"So, did you check the inventory?"

Kelsey smirked. "I tried, but realized I didn't really know what to look for. I'm sure there's a system and I haven't learned yet." She would have, though, if she'd been able to take the manager role. She'd be on top of everything by now.

Her eyes lifted to his. "Before Aggie announced her retirement, she asked me if I wanted the manager role."

Rick's eyes widened. "She did?"

"I *really* did want it, but had to say no because of Molly."

His lips tightened and his eyes showed sympathy. "What a shame for The Fork and also for you."

"It would've been perfect, but not perfect timing."

"Maybe it *was* perfect timing, but you won't see it until later."

Kelsey weighed his words. Did everything happen for a reason? Was that the same as everything working together for good? "Yeah. That's undoubtedly true." She leaned forward on her elbows. "The other day Aggie said you had good experience elsewhere. I guess that means you worked in a restaurant before here?"

"Many restaurants," he answered. "Too many to count."

"Why restaurants? Do you like this kind of work?"

Rick seemed to consider her question. "I do. But they're also easy jobs to get if you don't mind what role you play. I did a lot of what I'm doing now, since there was always a need for busboys and no skills were required. I did dishes, and a little cooking. I waited tables when they needed someone."

Her brows rose in surprise. "A lot of things, then. What did you like best?"

"I don't even know. I didn't like waiting tables that much, but the money was better. I like being behind the scenes. Short-order stuff, maybe. Nothing gourmet."

"So, you have some varied experience. It's a shame you're bussing tables, then."

"Not really. I'm new in town so I have to start somewhere. It was a natural place for me to land."

"What does the future hold?" She grinned, intrigued by what he might say.

"Ah, that is a mystery, isn't it? For you and me both." He chuckled then glanced at his watch. "Time to go."

He rose and returned inside without another word.

Chapter Five

Rick enjoyed being busy, especially following all the lost years. But after working nearly sixty hours at the Fork, he was happy to have a Wednesday off, though he had his bi-weekly appointment with Frank that afternoon. The summer was speeding by in a flurry of busyness.

It was nice to have a few hours to *think*. And ponder and wonder. He'd done little of that during his nearly twelve years on the road. Sometimes his mind had been too addled or fleeing hard truths about himself and his life. He'd also spent a fair amount of time working...in restaurants, just like now. But it wasn't at all the same.

Now, he enjoyed thinking and learning. He'd discovered his thirst to learn when he landed at Stephen and Annika's house. They'd had a vast library of Christian life books, fiction, and classics, along with books on many topics in science, finance, and history.

Since arriving in Brenner Falls, he'd found a new book supplier, the local library. He had a card now and was a regular patron when he wasn't at work or at church. A simple life, but one he needed.

"Good morning, sweetie." His mom entered the kitchen and kissed Rick's cheek where he sat at the table. He'd eaten breakfast, but was enjoying a cup of coffee and a new book he'd checked out the day before.

He glanced at the wall clock. "Hey, Mom. Are you running late today?"

"I woke up with a headache, so I called in to say I'd be a little late. The office is flexible, so that was fine." After getting sober, she'd taken some courses and became a legal assistant. For years, his mom had worked at a small law office downtown.

"Flexible is good."

She poured a cup of coffee and sat across from him. "I have a bit of news for you."

Rick met her gaze and pushed his book aside. His mother's eyes sparkled and somehow, she looked younger than she had before. His curiosity flew at full mast.

"I met a man at church a few weeks ago." She smiled and a faint flush filled her cheeks. "I'd gone to that conference they had one Saturday. You were working that day. Anyway, he was at my discussion table, and we sort of hit it off. Then we kept running into each other in the hallways before or after the service."

"That's great, Mom. So, did you go out with him?" Rick leaned forward. "What's his name?"

"His name is Tim, and we met for coffee last week. I didn't have a chance to tell you because you've worked a lot lately. He invited me to dinner this weekend."

He reached out and squeezed her hand. She deserved it, after all she'd suffered. All she'd lost, and all he himself had put her through. "No one deserves a second chance at happiness more than you do, Mom."

She tilted her head. "Oh, you're sweet. I'd like to think I have a chance again. I like him. He's a retired dentist. We'd both lost our spouses to cancer and started talking about that. Then, it went on from there." She let out a bashful chuckle.

"Where are you going for dinner?"

"I don't know yet. He's planning someplace special, I think. I'll let you know."

"You'd better. And you better respect your curfew and stay out of trouble." He winked at her, and she laughed. Suddenly, he realized that his mom was still a pretty woman at fifty-eight. Easy to see how she'd caught the man's eye, that and her sweet nature and sincere faith. That wouldn't have been the case if she hadn't gotten sober. She might not even be alive in that case. He shuddered inwardly. God's grace had rescued their entire family. His throat tightened at the thought, so he kept it light. "Let me know if you need help picking out your outfit." They laughed. Of course, she understood how ludicrous *that* was.

He'd enjoyed being at his mom's, pleasantly surprised by how much fun she could be. Greedily, he drank from the well of second chances.

After she left for work, he decided to take a walk in the pine forest a couple of blocks from the neighborhood. The July morning wasn't too sultry, and the shade of towering pines would drop the temperature a few degrees. He'd gotten into the habit of walking in the forest when he could. Often, he'd stick his dog-eared New Testament in his back pocket, find a rock or fallen tree trunk, and savor the silence as he let God speak.

Rick walked down the cracked sidewalks of Phillips Street where he'd spent his youth, the early summer sun warming the top of his head. He slipped across Brenner Parkway to the forest. The packed earth felt good under his sneakers and the fresh, sharp aroma of pine rolled into his nostrils. He breathed deeply of the scent and continued walking.

His mind went to his mom's news, and he couldn't be happier for her, after all the years of loss, working hard, doing life alone. He'd been home for two months now, so she'd stopped hovering over him with worried eyes that said he could evaporate any moment. Hard to believe he could feel so at home and satisfied in a place of such dark memories. They rarely entered his mind anymore.

He kept in touch by phone or FaceTime with Stephen and Annika, who'd made him promise. As if he could do otherwise. Not only did he love them like family, but they'd literally saved his life and helped him over the threshold into a new one. That evening after supper, he'd call them for an exchange of news.

When he first arrived home, he was hesitant to tell his mom about how close he was with them, though she'd known he'd lived at their house for almost two years. He didn't want her to feel jealous or replaced. He needn't have worried. Instead, she'd clasped her hands and, with tears in her eyes, said, "God answers prayer, son. I prayed for you every day for fourteen years. He protected you, gave you this dear couple to help you when you most needed it, and then he brought you back home."

That was one reason he enjoyed thinking again. As he did, he saw so many pieces fitting neatly together, showing him that although he'd been off the rails in every way possible, God had been watching over him, charting a course to get him back. Like his childhood home, he felt entirely rehabbed.

Following a now-familiar path through the forest, the shade and silence deepened. Only his footfall, barely audible on a carpet of pine needles, and the occasional broken twig sliced the quiet. He spied his favorite boulder with moss on one side, perched alongside a small stream, and climbed on its clammy surface. Through the shadows, a bold stream of light broke through a space in the overhead canopy. He liked to think that was God talking to him.

He pulled his New Testament from his back pocket but instead of opening it, took a breath of the cool, moist air. Though he didn't do it often, he thought about the future, which looked to him like a complete cloud bank. For now, he worked more than full time at The Fork, but what about later? Would he do that for the rest of his life? Definitely not. But what did he want to do?

While he'd been with Stephen and Annika, they'd encouraged him to get his GED. He'd done that. One day, Annika suggested he take some online or in person courses at the community college. Didn't matter that he didn't know what he wanted to do yet, she'd told him. If he got some basic courses under his belt, they'd transfer wherever he went next. He thought that was a good idea, so he did that too. He found he enjoyed business, hospitality, psychology, and history the best, but left with no greater clue about what he wanted to do when he grew up. His mind skipped for a moment to Kelsey's question. What did the future hold? He wished he'd had an impressive answer he could have given her.

"What do you think, Lord? I don't have any big ideas, like most people." His voice cut quietly into the blanket of calm beneath the pines. "I know I haven't been back in town very long. I'm sure I need more time to get solid in the new life you gave me. I guess *you* know what I should do, but you haven't told me yet. Maybe restaurants, maybe youth. Maybe a business. I don't know yet. That's okay, just so you have something in mind."

A passage he'd read recently came into his head and he opened the book he balanced on his knees. The small New Testament also contained the Book of Psalms. He thumbed to Psalm 73 and read a verse aloud. "'Yet I still belong to you; you hold my right hand. You guide me with your counsel, leading me to a glorious destiny.'"

Closing the book, he breathed deeply. "A glorious destiny. You sure you got the right guy?" He chuckled. God was always surprising him. "If that's the case, Lord, that sounds great, my eternal destiny and the one right ahead of me, whatever that is. But...what do you want me to do *now*?"

He pondered, listened. He knew the answer, for God had shown him many times already. Do the *next* thing. The thing that lay right in front of him. The Fork. The youth ministry. Hanging out with Mom and Ben.

Guilt twinged inside. He hadn't spent enough time with Ben, not because he didn't want to. More guilt drove him away. Every time he saw or even imagined his brother's face, it overwhelmed him. He'd asked forgiveness for his past behavior, and Ben had happily given it, pulling Rick in for the longest and richest hug he'd ever received from another man. That should have been enough. But he still lay low, haunted. He didn't even know Ben's wife, Amber, very well. Surely, she knew what he'd done and hated him for it.

Rick sighed. Somehow, he had to shed this shadow and walk into the life God wanted for him. How? Step by step. That was the next thing God wanted him to do, step into his new nature. But he found it difficult to forget the past.

His cell phone rang, and Rick pulled it from his other pocket. Ben must have somehow read his thoughts from afar. "Hey, Ben."

"Hi, Rick. Are you off today?"

"Yeah, been working too much, but it's okay. I'm in the forest now."

"I know the place. It's called Whittier Forest. That's where the mine is."

"The mine?"

"Another story for another day. Are you free for lunch?"

"You're not working today?"

"I am, but I get a lunch break and want to take my little brother to lunch. Mainly, I'd like to see you. We're both busy, so we have to be deliberate about getting together outside of church. That's the only time I see you. Lots of time to make up for."

"Yeah." Rick's insides pinched. Too much time. They could have been close for the last fourteen years instead of making up for lost time now. "That sounds good. You don't have to take me, though. I can pay my way. For a change."

"Aw, cut it out. Past is over, dude. Let's go to George's. It's a good burger bar, if you haven't discovered it. I need to introduce you to Brenner Falls properly. Seems all you know is The Grateful Fork, and there's a lot more here."

Rick grinned. "If you say so. You can be my tour guide. What time?"

"Meet you at George's at twelve, okay?"

"Sure. See you then."

The past was over. If only his heart could get the message.

Once Rick was seated across a booth from Ben, he was happy he came. Didn't matter what they ate. As they talked, he noticed Ben was more outgoing than him. That he, too, liked history. That he loved married life and though it took him thirty years and lots of dating, he'd found the woman God had chosen for him.

It dawned on Rick he was getting to know his brother Ben all over again as an adult, and it was like meeting a new person. That thought excited him, the idea that they could move through a time warp and be close again years later.

"Did you hear about Mom's new guy?" Ben's voice broke into his thoughts.

"Yeah, she told me this morning. When did she tell you?"

"Yesterday. I'm happy for her."

"Me too. She's been alone a long time."

Silence fell for a few minutes as they savored juicy hamburgers which released a combined aroma of charcoal and beef. "Mmm." Rick licked a drop of broth that trickled on his hand.

"So, why don't you come over more, Rick?" Ben's abrupt question broke the flavor fest. "I invited you a couple of times."

Rick squirmed in his seat. Should he be honest or use the *busy at work* excuse? He took a breath. "It's taking time for me to get over the change in myself here in my hometown. I still struggle with how I treated you in the past. I know you forgave me and it's over. I'm a new creation. I get that. But it's taking time."

Ben set his burger on his plate and placed his forearms on the table. He speared Rick with direct but loving brown eyes. "I think you're gonna have to decide to *act* on what you know, bro." His voice was gentle, though his meaning was clear. "Not on what you feel. Amber and I have talked about this. We want you in our lives."

Rick hesitated. A breeze of longing swept through him. "Even Amber?"

"Yes, even Amber."

Rick grinned. "What do I do if she gives me the stink eye?"

Ben laughed aloud. "She won't. If she does, let me know and I'll have a talk with her."

They laughed together and pored through a rich chain of memories until Ben was almost late back to work.

ಌ ಌ ಌ

"Did you enjoy your day off yesterday?" Kelsey asked Rick as he checked salt and pepper shakers and placed napkins on the tables. She'd ventured into his space since she would be in the kitchen all afternoon.

His face brightened when he saw her. "Hi, Kelsey. Yes, it was a *wonderful* day. I had lunch with my brother, who I'm getting to know again, then met with Pastor Frank. Such a wise guy."

Kelsey grinned, enjoying Rick's enthusiasm, which corrected her previous view of him as always reserved. "Yes, he is. You're fortunate to meet with him regularly, since he's so busy. And it's cool you're reconnecting with Ben." After a pause, she asked, "How do you think Danielle is doing? Aggie's popping in a little less often these days."

"It hasn't been very long." His eyes panned the dining room. "I don't mind being Aggie's extra set of eyes, but it's not a long-term solution, in my opinion."

Kelsey nodded. "I had the same thought, though I want to give Danielle the benefit of the doubt." When she remembered *she* could be managing The Fork, the wave of regret that sailed by lessened each day. What was done was done. "Do you know if Danielle put up the specials for today? I didn't see new ones on the chalkboard."

"No, I don't know. I think she's in the kitchen, so you can ask her. Maybe while you're at it, see if she'll delegate anything else to you."

She blinked. As if she couldn't think of that on her own. "I *do* have a list of things to ask her to delegate. But I don't want to be too pushy, or take on everything at once. Then I'll die of exhaustion, and what would be the point?" She grinned, flicking her irritation aside.

"True. We can't have you dying of exhaustion," he said, deadpan.

"I'll go talk to Danielle. Usually, the specials are up by now." She turned and pushed through the metal kitchen door.

Kelsey found Danielle poring over her notebook at a stainless-steel counter. "Hi, Danielle. Do you want me to write up the Thursday specials on the chalkboard?"

Her question met with a blank expression. "Thursday specials? Oh, yes. You can do that."

"Uh...what are they?" Kelsey asked.

Danielle blinked. "I don't know. Doesn't Vince know?"

"He usually knows, but he's off today."

"Ah, right. There's a new chef who fills in, Eric. He might know."

Kelsey glanced at Eric's white-clad back as he leaned over the stove, stirring a bubbling stockpot. "I think Aggie usually consulted with Vince and they decided on the specials a few days in advance. Maybe Vince already told Eric."

"Wait, Kelsey." Danielle held up a hand. "Can't we just put a few regular things on the board and reduce the price a little?"

"Yes, we do that, but people are used to at least one different meal on the board that's only offered that day. Kind of like a special *du jour*. I'll ask Eric."

Kelsey crossed the room and caught Eric's attention over the kitchen clatter. "Eric, we always have Thursday specials, but Danielle forgot about them today. Do you have any quick ideas for a new meal we can present?"

Eric frowned. "I have my hands full of the regular meals, Kelsey. I don't think my staff can whip up something we haven't already planned. All we can do is the meals already on the menu."

"Yeah, that's what Danielle suggested. Lemme think a minute." It wouldn't be the end of the world if they had nothing new that day on special. Patrons were used to a special or two, but most people either didn't know or didn't pay attention.

But what could she do to help? What would she do if it were *her* restaurant?" She returned to Danielle, who looked distressed. "I have an idea. I can call Sophie and see if she has any quiches already made. We can buy them from her."

"It's worth a try. I knew there were specials, but didn't know they were not also part of the regular menu."

Kelsey fished her cell phone from her purse in the cupboard and called Sophie's Coffee Shop.

"Sophie's, can I help you?" Sophie herself had answered.

"Sophie, it's Kelsey," she plunged in. "I'm in a bind at The Fork. Do you, by any chance, have a few quiches we can buy from you to offer for our specials board?"

"Um, I have some extra quiches, but I made them for a special-order pickup this evening. They're spinach and Gruyère."

"Oh, okay." Scratch that idea.

"Wait, if you want, I can sell you six of these, then make more for tonight. The pickup isn't until six o'clock. Thank goodness I just hired Sandra. She can stay at the front with customers while I make extra quiches. I just hope we don't get too busy."

"Are you sure? That would be a huge help. And I'm off at three, so I can come help you."

Sophie chuckled. "Thank you, but I'm sure I'll be fine. *J'ai l'habitude.* I'm used to it. A bit more work for me, but I was going to make more quiches anyway."

"I owe you one. Can we pick them up right now?" She'd ask Rick. He wouldn't need to bus tables yet, since it was still early in his shift.

"Sure. I'll box them up for you after I tell Sandra about it."

Kelsey hung up with Sophie and sighed with relief. She scoped the kitchen for Danielle, but she'd gone to the dining room to hostess. After she seated a family of three, Kelsey pulled her aside. "Sophie said she can sell us six of her spinach quiches. I'll ask Rick to pick them up now, since I'm prepping today and Trina's waiting tables."

"Good idea. Customers are arriving now. Thanks for fast thinking, Kelsey." Danielle offered a shaky smile. "I'm not up to speed just yet. I appreciate your help and experience."

"No problem. I'll go tell Rick."

He was behind the bar filling the ice bin and checking glassware. "Rick, I need your help."

"Sure, what's up?"

"Danielle forgot to set up the Thursday specials. So, I called my friend Sophie, who has a bakery on Warren Street. She's selling us six spinach quiches. Can you go pick them up now? We need to get them heated before the crowd comes."

"I can do that. Do you have the address?" Rick jingled his car keys, ready to bolt.

"I forget the number, but drive to Warren Street and you'll see it on the left. It's across the street from a flower shop."

"I'm on it." Before she could respond, he'd darted out the front door. Disaster averted. Well, maybe not a disaster. Just in time, because customers were arriving. She told Trina, the server, then snatched a box of chalk from behind the bar and headed to the board. "Welcome to The Grateful Fork," she told the couple who entered. Fortunately, she knew them. "Hi Frank and Amy. I'm a little late getting the specials on the board, but Trina can tell you about them."

"Hi, Kelsey. Thanks for letting us know."

Danielle dispatched the couple to a table by the window. Kelsey sighed and glanced around the dining room, where everything looked as usual.

How deceiving appearances could be. Looks like their mission had begun.

Chapter Six

When Rick approached Ben's impressive Victorian home, the driveway was already full of cars. He eased along the curb and parked, grabbed the bowl of fruit he'd prepared, and headed up the flagstone walkway to the wrap-around porch.

The first time he saw his brother's palace, he'd been momentarily mute. He'd seen it years earlier when it resembled a haunted house from a movie, but over the years, Ben had transformed it, one plank, one shutter, one pipe at a time. He'd had no idea his brother was so handy and persistent, having labored for over five years to create the structure before him now. Lights glowed from shuttered windows and painted peaks swirled in attractive designs.

The wide front door swung open. "Rick!"

Amber's enthusiastic exclamation and hug flew in the face of all he'd feared about her when he returned to Brenner Falls. He'd expected disdain, a desire to keep her distance. But no, as Ben had recently assured him, he was family, and she welcomed him in that spirit. Over the last two months he'd gotten to know his pretty sister-in-law, he knew she was genuine and perfect for Ben.

"Hi, Amber. I didn't know what to bring, but you can't go wrong with fruit, right?" They stood in the foyer on dark hardwood flooring, surrounded by mouth-watering smells and snippets of conversation from the adjoining room.

"No, you can't." She grinned and took the bowl from his hands. "Thanks for bringing this, but you didn't have to bring anything."

Ben had told him that. In fact, people always said that, though a contribution was always appreciated. That's what his mom had said as he washed and arranged everything in the bowl. He'd been nervous about coming, since it wasn't just Ben and Amber. A *dinner party*. Meaning other people he didn't know who'd ask a bunch of questions he didn't want to answer. If he was lucky, they'd be self-absorbed and wouldn't ask him anything. No such luck. Ben would never hang around people like that.

Ben appeared around the corner and encased Rick in a bear hug. "Hey, bro." Rick never tired of those hugs, nor of his brother's continued show of love and acceptance. Of welcome and forgiveness.

"Come on in and meet everyone." Ben led him to the living room.

Rick braced himself to meet the nice-looking couple who stood in the center of the elegant room. Open, eager expressions beamed from their smiling faces.

"This is Nathan and Leah Chisholm. My brother, Rick."

Rick shook hands with Nathan and his wife, who looked a couple of months pregnant. "Nice to meet you both." Why was the name Nathan familiar? Kelsey had talked about him. The owner of the restaurant in the Victorian downtown.

"Nathan has been my best friend since we were in junior high." Ben slapped Nathan's shoulder.

Yes, he'd heard the name long before Kelsey talked about him. Nathan, who'd first invited Ben to church.

The doorbell rang and Amber again sailed toward the front door. He had the impression she enjoyed entertaining. Her jubilant greeting to the newly arrived guest floated to where they sat. Another unknown person he'd have to make small talk with.

"Look who's here!"

Kelsey.

She stepped into the living room and greeted everyone. When her eyes landed on Rick, her surprise was clear, though she caught herself and gave him a warm smile. They should have both known the other would be there, since he was Ben's brother, and she was

Amber's close friend. He was the last person to object to her being invited.

"Hi Nathan, hi Leah." She stepped forward and gave each one a warm hug. "Hi, Rick. Glad we're not working tonight, eh?"

He hoped his joy at her presence wasn't too obvious on his face. "Very glad. Everyone needs a night off, so here we are." He hoped she wasn't disappointed to see him. They all sat down again.

"That's right," Nathan said. "You guys know each other because of The Grateful Fork, I guess." He asked Kelsey a few questions about the Fork, having heard about Aggie's retirement.

"Rick's there far more hours than I am during the week."

Rick chose not to contribute much to the conversation about The Fork. He didn't mind working there, but was glad to have an evening away.

Kelsey's responses to Nathan faded as Rick's attention wandered to her thick auburn hair loose and swirling across her shoulders, tucked behind one ear. She wore a colorful tunic and leggings, so unlike the genderless aprons they all wore at work. She'd put on makeup, but hadn't overdone it. Her fresh beauty still shone through.

He didn't want to be caught looking at her, but could barely help it. Kelsey was a powerful magnet for him.

Soon he was drawn into the conversation. "Yes, Aggie left officially about a month ago." He met Kelsey's gaze for confirmation. "Did you hear about her retirement party?"

Leah shook her head. "We weren't close to Aggie, though I met her a couple of times. And we didn't eat at The Grateful Fork often." She turned a grin toward her husband. "Because Nathan's such an amazing cook. I'm really spoiled."

"You might still have your hands full," Kelsey said. "And congratulations, by the way." She leaned forward and kissed Leah's cheek.

Leah smiled and one hand slid onto her belly bulge. "Thanks, Kelsey. We're excited. I have a few months to wait, but it'll be full on after that."

"What about your performances at Seasons?" This from Ben, who'd entered the room with a plate of hors d'oeuvres. He placed them on the table then sat. Amber arrived from the kitchen and perched on the arm of his chair. "Will you still be able to stay active there once the baby comes?"

"I plan to, since the shows are sporadic, though probably not the first few months."

"Are you an actress?" Rick reached for a canape from the tray. Smoked salmon on toast, his favorite.

"More of an astonishingly talented singer." Nathan turned a loving gaze at his wife. "Though sometimes there are speaking parts. We own Seasons Dinner Theater, and along with an ongoing restaurant, we have occasional musicals, plays, comedies, and other types of entertainment."

"Someday, Nathan'll tell you the whole story of Seasons." A wide grin stretched across Ben's face.

"I'll have to make sure to hear about that, Nathan," Rick said. "That's the second time I've heard a reference to Seasons. I'm intrigued now."

"With pleasure," Nathan said. "I'd enjoy the chance to get to know you better, Rick, but telling the Seasons story is always fun for me."

Despite the fact that Nathan and Leah were new to Rick, their warmth and lack of pretense put him immediately at ease. It didn't escape his notice, however, that there were three couples. Two married and two singles. Was Ben up to something?

Not that he'd object to becoming a couple with Kelsey, though that was about as likely as snow in July. No sense in even daydreaming.

Amber stood. "I think we can go to the dining room now. Everything's ready."

As the group moved toward the elegant room, Rick shot a glance at Kelsey, expecting her to have forgotten his presence. Her gaze met his and she offered a shy smile. They sat across from each other, maybe to break any expectation that they were a couple or about to be. Common sense, but a wave of disappointment still echoed through him.

Ben prayed for the meal and Amber started circulating the serving plates. Everything looked and smelled delicious...herb encrusted roast chicken and baby red potatoes and broccoli-cheese puree.

"I invited a couple more people," Amber said as she settled next to Ben. "Dylan Poole, who owns the Tarte Nouveau, was one of them. Neither could come." Her expression seemed apologetic. She probably said this for his and Kelsey's benefit to assure them she wasn't trying to set them up.

Leah leaned toward Rick. "In case you don't know about this, Rick, there's a little abandoned house on the edge of town that Ben and Amber discovered a couple years ago. That's *another* story you need to hear about sometime. It has Art Nouveau architectural features, so the new owner started a brunch place called Tarte *Nouveau*. I think that's clever."

"Sophie told me it isn't proper French, though." Kelsey giggled.

"She should know," Nathan said. "I hope she's not worried about the competition."

"No, she's well-established in The Falls. Everyone loves her pastries." Amber reached for dinner roll. "And it's nice to have variety."

So far, no one had asked Rick about his past or his plans for the future. Most of his life, in fact, was off limits for conversation, leaving him more comfortable asking questions. When would he be comfortable sharing who he was with anyone at all?

Thankfully, the conversation moved on to Ben's job, Nathan's work at Seasons, and a renovation Ben planned to start in a neglected upstairs bedroom. Rick took the opportunity to secretly observe Kelsey, who sat across from him. The thickness of her lashes surrounding her blue eyes, the curve of her full lips, delicate freckles across her small, upturned nose. And the way she clasped her hands or reached delicately for her water glass. Though Amber was a close friend to her, it was the couples who did most of the talking around the table. Kelsey observed, commented at appropriate moments, sent friendly gaze to him, possibly to keep him from feeling out of place. Which he did, but she probably did too.

He enjoyed hearing news about Brenner Falls, about Ben's activities during Rick's missing years, and soaking in more knowledge about his hometown, both old and new. He loved being near Kelsey while she sat serenely across from him instead of dashing around the restaurant. The only exception to that was when Leah asked about her food blog, a fact which made him smile.

After dessert, he glanced at his watch, ready to be alone again. To be free with his thoughts instead of listening and wondering what everyone was talking about. Wondering, too, what Kelsey was thinking as she sat quietly across the table. Everyone did their best to draw the two of them into the conversation, but they were both outsiders. Not because they were the only singles at the table. The two couples had deep friendships with one another that went back for years. Rick couldn't blame them. It had been nice for Ben to invite him.

He found Amber in the kitchen. "Thanks so much, Amber. I'm going to head out now."

"I'm so glad you came, Rick. Sorry you have to leave." She hugged him. "Here's your bowl."

He grinned as Ben entered the room and hugged him. "Someone has to be the first to leave, right?" Rick said. "I'll sacrifice and be the one."

"You're not the first. Kelsey has to leave too."

"Oh, okay." He nodded but wondered if he could intercept her. "She's gone already?"

"No, she's saying goodbye to Nathan and Leah. Maybe she has to go back for Molly." Amber opened the fridge door and put a container in.

Ben pulled Amber close and kissed her brow. "Leave the dishes, hon. We'll do this together after everyone leaves."

"Oh, you're right."

They said goodbye again, then Rick bade farewell to Nathan and Leah. He let himself out into the summer night. Kelsey stood on the front porch holding the dish she'd brought. "Leaving so soon?" he asked softly.

She smiled. "Yeah. I'm not as extroverted as everyone else, though it was great to see them. I told Molly I wouldn't be too late."

"I'm glad you were here tonight. Aside from Ben, I know you the best."

She turned a quizzical look at him under the porchlight then grinned. "Ah, but you only *think* you know me. We don't really know each other very well outside of restaurant stuff."

"What should we do about that?"

Kelsey stilled under the porch light and stared at him, probably in shock. It was their first foray into the personal realm, and she didn't look prepared. Maybe it wasn't even welcome.

He held his breath waiting for her response. "You can tell me while I walk you to your car." He didn't want to start a conversation on Ben's porch with his wife and friends inside.

She stepped from the porch. "I'm parked along the street. I didn't want to block anyone in."

"I did the same thing." Good, a longer walk next to her.

"I'm not ignoring your question. I'm thinking." She turned her face toward him. A glow from the streetlights painted pale light on her cheeks. "What about you tell me something you want me to know."

He smiled. "I noticed you redirected my question, but I'll let it pass for now. There are questions I don't like to answer, but when I get to choose, it's…okay." Then he could pace himself, revealing what he wanted.

They walked together toward the corner, streetlights dimming as they passed a row of trees. They reached her car and stood still, an arm's length from each other. "Did you think of an answer?" she asked.

"I enjoy reading and often spend my mornings at the library or just taking a walk around town."

"What do you like to read?"

"That's two questions." He smiled. "I like business and history. But *you* haven't divulged anything yet."

She laughed. "You're right. I like to read cookbooks and nutrition books, along with fiction sometimes, not that I have time for that. And sometimes when I'm home alone, I put on jazzy music and dance around, either alone or with Molly. It relieves stress and it's fun. And I don't tell that to just anyone."

His brows lifted and he smiled. "I won't divulge your secret." He never would have guessed Kelsey had a wild side. He liked it. It drew him. "Thanks for telling me."

"Did you enjoy tonight?" She asked him after a pause. Her voice was soft, like a firefly in the darkness.

"Sort of. It was nice to be included in Ben's life. Nice to meet Nathan and Leah. Good food. But I have a hard time being myself a hundred percent." He shrugged. "I'm not even sure yet who I would be."

Kelsey moistened her lips. "I know what you mean. I rarely feel like I fit anywhere. I think in general, people like me, but I'm not close to many of them. Amber gets me. We're close. I really like Nathan and Leah, but don't know them well. And I didn't know Ben well before he married Amber, but that's changing." She met his gaze. "Do you feel comfortable around *me*?" Her question was tentative, as risky as his had been.

"Yes, I do, even though, as you pointed out, we don't know each other well. And I don't know your big questions yet."

Her teeth gleamed in the darkness as she smiled. "Little by little, you will. Do you want to tell me anything else?"

"I enjoy walking alone in the forest."

Kelsey's eyes widened with interest. "What do you do when you get there besides walk?"

"I find a big rock and listen to the quiet. I pray. I take my New Testament and read sometimes."

"Cool. I haven't had time to do things like that since my parents left."

"Could it be that you don't *let* yourself find the time?"

Kelsey's mouth twisted. "Hmm. I'll have to think about that. I mean, Molly stayed by herself this evening. She sometimes does, and she's fine. I *should* take more time for myself. For my own projects, and just to...stop. Stop and think."

"Yes, that would be a good thing, since you have a lot going on. Once you start reserving time for yourself, you'll never give it up."

"I need to start." She swallowed and their eyes met. Silence fell between them. His gaze roved to her lips but the idea of kissing her would have to stay on its mental shelf of daydreams.

"Can I ask one more?" He made no move to leave. "How did you get interested in cooking?"

She leaned against her car door and crossed her arms. "I like that topic. I used to watch my mom cook when I was little. When I was five or six, I wanted to make breakfast for my parents. I wasn't sure what went into a batch of pancakes, but I knew there was flour. So, I got the stepladder out and pulled down the bag of flour, which thumped on the counter and made a big cloud." She chuckled. "I saw a few other items in the cupboard and pulled those down. Turned out to be salt, chili powder, and garlic salt."

"Oh no..." Rick brought a hand to his forehead and snickered.

"I didn't get that far, though, because the glass mixing bowl was too heavy and it fell. Woke up the whole house."

"It broke?"

"No, it bounced across the floor, but made a racket."

They laughed.

"But you persisted, and it instilled a lifelong love for cooking."

"Yes, it did."

Silence fell. "You need to write that story on your blogpost."

"What a good idea. It'll be a funny cooking anecdote."

"I can picture you as an adorable curly-haired six-year-old getting into well-meaning mischief. If you have a photo like that, you can add it to your website next to the story."

They grinned together under the leafy shadow that hung over the car. There in the darkened street Rick felt completely at ease. He could probably tell Kelsey anything, and longed for her to feel the same. "Well, we've made a start, Kelsey. We have a long way to go, but we'll save the next episode for another day."

"Thanks, for walking me to my car."

"Anytime." He stepped back as she opened her door. They exchanged a smile, and he watched as she drove away.

ଔ   ଔ   ଔ

The following Tuesday, Kelsey and Molly entered The Fork for the lunch shift. On the days when Molly came, Aggie usually had her work at a corner table prior to the lunch shift, rolling napkins around a set of silverware.

"Why don't you sit at your usual table?" she told Molly. "I'll let Danielle know, since she's the new manager."

Kelsey's gaze panned the room, but she didn't see Rick. Poor guy needed a day off occasionally, but disappointment still pooled inside her. After their conversation on Saturday night, she felt closer to him, but it was like discovering a tiny path when an entire landscape existed. Her thirst to know him more, to simply talk had grown.

Yet it was a bad idea to pursue more than friendship. In terms of potential, some elements lined up while others didn't, like Rick's background being incredibly different from hers. Though she didn't look down on him for his past, with such different life stories, where could it go?

She sighed and went to the kitchen to get an apron. Lately, she'd had more lunch than dinner shifts. The kitchen staff didn't need her for food prep, which she enjoyed more than waiting tables. She spotted Danielle behind the bar, her blond head bent forward as she studied her notebook.

"Hi, Danielle." Kelsey approached the bar. "How is everything going?"

Danielle raised her head and smiled, though Kelsey detected tension in the woman's blue eyes and the set of her jaw.

"Hi, Kelsey. It's going okay so far. I have a lot to learn. It's overwhelming at times, but I'll get it."

Kelsey gave her a reassuring smile. "Yes, you will. You have a whole team here willing and able to help you get your feet under you, so don't hesitate to ask. Your role here is different from what you were doing before. It's natural to have a learning curve."

"Huh. More like a learning *mountain*." Danielle rolled her eyes. "But Aggie gave me some excellent training before she left." She tapped the blue binder sitting on the table. "This notebook is a lifesaver. You can't believe everything there is to do. But there are lots of checklists and calendars of stuff to be done in advance."

The tightness in Kelsey's chest unhinged by a few degrees. Although Aggie could have done better by training Danielle for six months instead of just two weeks, she'd still covered the bases, providing helpful checklists and templates and had walked Danielle through an organized training process. She'd probably be fine. And she'd authorized Kelsey and Rick to keep a watchful eye and fill any holes they observed.

"Rick told me he can organize the sections for the servers the days he's on duty."

"Who was doing that before?"

"I did but gave it to Rick. And he streamlined the drink area behind the bar and organized the walk-in. He's pretty useful."

"Yes, he is." Kelsey smiled, but wondered why Rick hadn't told her, since they were supposedly working together. "By the way, Molly came with me to work today." Kelsey hitched her head toward where Molly sat at a corner table.

Danielle caught Molly's eye and waved to her. "It's always good to see Molly."

"Molly comes with me about once a week to fold napkins or do other simple tasks. She's been doing it for close to a year."

"Does she stay at her table when the dining room gets busy?"

"If I'm still working and there's nothing she can do in the kitchen, she stays at her table and reads. Sometimes she works in the kitchen." Molly had torn lettuce leaves, mixed lemonade, and folded laundered aprons, among other tasks. "She only comes on weekdays if I'm scheduled, when it's less busy."

"Does she get paid for that?"

"She gets her lunch and a few dollars each month. It gives her some skills and a feeling of contribution, along with a bit of pocket money."

Danielle's face relaxed. "That's good for her, and it's good for the rest of us too. Don't get me wrong, Kelsey, I don't mind her coming here. I feel overwhelmed right now and I can't manage her on top of everything else."

"You don't have to manage her. Once I get her the napkins and silverware from the kitchen, she can work on her own. I'm here if she needs anything."

Danielle let out a breath. "Okay, wonderful."

"I'll get her set up and then I'll start."

"You'll be in section five today."

"Thanks. I'll get to it." Kelsey went to the kitchen to retrieve the napkins and tray of silverware for Molly. It was the first day she'd detected stress in Danielle. It *was* a lot to learn.

She chided herself for feeling left out of Rick's initiatives. He was there far more than she was, so it was natural for him to do things on his own. But she thought he'd at least tell her, since they were a team. A team, but not together.

Her disappointment was her fault. She needed to revise her thinking. Getting to know Rick better was not the goal. The Fork's success *was*.

Chapter Seven

Rick's eyes panned the dining room from where he stood behind the bar. He shot a grimace at the other end where Kelsey rang up a customer. Her gaze met his, confirming what he suspected. She was worried.

She approached him. "What's wrong?" Her voice was low.

"Are you seeing what I'm seeing?"

She surveyed the room and turned back to him. "Yes. The dining room isn't as full as usual on a Friday afternoon. And it won't be as full tonight, either, since we don't have a band."

"Danielle didn't reserve the band?"

Kelsey shook her head. "Not in time. We usually do this a couple of months or more beforehand. Aggie would have scheduled them weeks before, but Danielle had to confirm them and send a deposit. Ideally, the dates for the whole summer should be on the website, but there are gaps."

"I wonder if Aggie covered that with her."

"I'm sure she did. But there are hundreds of details, and I think Danielle is drowning. Even with us surveying and helping."

After a moment of silence, he nodded. "The day Aggie announced her retirement I thought you were sad because you'd miss her. But you also understood Danielle isn't the best fit for the job." After nearly two months on the job, that much was clear.

Kelsey nodded. "She's well-meaning and she tries hard." Her voice emerged soft, resigned. "But she lets things slip through the cracks. I worried because I knew she didn't have the experience she needed. She was in IT. Both jobs involve lots of details, but not the same kind." Her frown deepened. "Both Aggie and Danielle must have thought the skills would transfer."

"Not a chance." Rick let out a breath.

"It'll take time for the restaurant to do *badly*, since it enjoyed a long success," she said carefully. "But I'm worried the process is beginning, after just a month. The persona of the owner or manager lends a mood to a place. Maybe people aren't seeing the atmosphere they usually see, so they're going elsewhere."

Rick nodded, stroking his whiskered chin. "You have a point. Atmosphere isn't tangible, but it's a factor."

"Danielle is panicking now because Aggie went on a cruise to Alaska and can't be reached. Or maybe Danielle thinks she should be able to handle it alone. Aggie might also have limited phone coverage." Kelsey shrugged. "Turns out the blue notebook isn't enough."

"It might have been enough for someone who'd had years of management experience or a degree. I've worked in enough restaurants to know this is going to be a train wreck. Eventually."

"I know." Her voice emerged quiet, resigned.

She was silent a long moment, then her eyes rose to meet his, emboldened with sudden...defiance. It sent a jolt through his body. "What?"

"I know Aggie asked us to keep an eye on things for Danielle, but I'm going to try to do *more* than that. I'm going to see if she'll delegate more to me. That'll help her and help The Fork at the same time." Kelsey's jaw hardened. "I'll work more hours if that'll help. I don't know how, because I have a full-time job plus Molly."

"I'm already here a lot, so I'll keep you posted if I see any red flags or other ways we can help. It's what Aggie asked us to do, but a step more."

Then a smile curled her lips. Even though they were discussing saving The Fork, her nearness caused his skin to prickle, taking his thoughts far from the restaurant. In fact, that progression had already accelerated the previous week as they talked at the curb after Ben and Amber's party. He could still picture her face shadowed by the night as she spoke honestly. His heart pounded.

Surely, his feelings didn't go both ways. *Forget it, Russo. She's out of your league.*

"It would be good to get a copy of the blue notebook so we can know *everything* Danielle is supposed to do," she said. "Then we can follow behind her with an actual document to see what she may have missed. That'll be way more effective than just keeping an eye out without knowing what's missing."

He grinned, liking the way she said *we*. "You'll want to ask Danielle first—"

"Of course." Kelsey looked offended.

"I know you've thought of that," he said hastily. "It'll help to see the notebook. Grateful Fork Special Forces to the rescue."

Kelsey laughed. "Fork agents...Fork officers?"

"Undercover Forks," he whispered conspiratorially, relieved they'd moved beyond his gaffe.

They laughed. "This is getting silly," she said, her face pink with humor. That flushed him with a contentment he'd forgotten how to feel.

Rick took on a solemn expression and lowered his voice. "Yet, it's deadly serious, but we must accept the risk. For The Fork."

"For the Fork." She extended her hand, palm down, and he set his on top. Her skin felt smooth and warm. He wanted to keep his hand there for a long time. They shared a final grin, then both glanced around the room at the same time. He saw Danielle glowering at them by the hostess stand.

Kelsey slipped out to the dining room. Back to work, though there was regrettably less of it. Maybe it was simply an off day, but he'd been seeing them more often. It hadn't been long, but the absence of Aggie's energy and spirit was already obvious.

A few minutes later, raised voices caught Rick's attention. Danielle and one of the waitresses stood near the front door, arguing about something. He'd never seen that before at The Fork. The waitress also raised her voice, untied her apron, and threw it at

Danielle's feet before storming out the front door. Danielle watched her leave, then thrust her fingers into her hair.

Rick sighed. Maybe he and Kelsey could do some good there. *Together.*

While Rick was in and out of the kitchen, he monitored Vince, waiting for a lull to ask him a few questions. His mission had begun. When he turned to approach Vince, the man was watching him, a grin on his face.

"I've never seen anyone so efficient with a dishwasher, man." Vince laughed. "You did all that in, like twenty seconds flat."

Rick grinned. "Restaurant work has been my main gig since I was twenty."

Vince gave him a slow nod. "It shows."

Rick knew it was his chance. "Vince, do you have time for a question?"

"Sure, shoot." He crossed his arms and kept a friendly smile.

"Do you know if The Fork uses software to track inventory, orders, point of sale, things like that?"

The big man's brow furrowed. "I don't know. Aggie was kind of old school, but she got things done, so probably didn't see the need."

"Or maybe didn't know how efficient software can be. It streamlines nearly all the tasks in a restaurant."

Vince propped one hand on a stainless-steel worktable. "I've certainly heard about them. But tell me what you're thinking."

"Lots of restaurants use restaurant software to manage everything from food inventory to online ordering and takeout. I haven't worked in many restaurants that *don't* use it. It's not too expensive, and quite honestly, might avoid a disaster at The Fork under its present, uh, conditions."

The chef grew solemn. "I get what you're saying. It keeps me up at night. I've been here for almost thirteen years, but I don't like what's happening. The atmosphere isn't the same. My wife suggested I look for something else."

"No, don't." Rick's voice emerged stronger than he intended. "If some of us fill in the gaps in different ways, we can help Danielle until she gets more comfortable in her role." He wouldn't say Danielle shouldn't even be there. Step one was to help her avoid killing The Grateful Fork. "I'm sure we can help in different ways. For example, what do you think about taking over the planning of the specials? You can plan them and let the wait staff know what they are and the pricing."

He nodded. "I've always thought that should be my role, but Aggie wanted to *collaborate*." He made air quotes on the word, then grinned. "I went along, but I'd be glad to do that. Be a heck of a lot easier."

"Yes, for sure. Thanks, Vince. So, about the software. I'll learn more about it and ask Danielle what she thinks." He paused. "I spoke with Kelsey about all this, and she's trying to see how she can help Danielle, maybe have her delegate a few things. Right now, I believe she's overwhelmed."

"Yeah, I see that. Sounds good, Rick. Count me in."

"Thanks, Vince." Seemed they were building a team.

ೋ ೋ ೋ

Kelsey kept one eye on her watch. She had to pick up Molly at four and wanted to snag Danielle before leaving. In her first few weeks as manager, Danielle showed signs of unraveling. She might be relieved if Kelsey took over some of her tasks.

During her break, Rick had asked for her phone number so he could keep her in the loop when she wasn't there. She swallowed a silent grin. Not only did she want to maintain The Fork's success through this tough season, but she liked being complicit with Rick to that end. Or with anything, even though her brain still shouted, *no potential, Kelsey*!

Danielle sat at a corner table, looking tired and anxious. Kelsey approached her. "Hey, Danielle. Do you have a minute?"

"Sure." Danielle mustered a smile

"I've been thinking about how stressful it must be for you."

Danielle let out a long sigh. "You have no idea."

"I'd like to help if I can. I know I'm only here from time to time, but I could take on planning and promoting the Friday and Saturday bands, if you want me to. I can do that from home, even. Would that help?"

"Yes, it really would. I know Aggie planned some groups for the month, and I didn't realize, with everything else happening, that I needed to confirm at a certain time and follow up. I feel bad that we don't have anyone tonight. It's usually a big crowd here, and I'm afraid it won't be."

Kelsey laid a hand on Danielle's arm. "There aren't bands every week. So, this can be one of those days when there isn't a performance. I'll make sure we have one next week, and no one will know it wasn't planned that way."

A look of relief cascaded over Danielle's face. "Thank you, Kelsey. That would be awesome."

"In fact, there are probably other things you can delegate. Do you want me to look at Aggie's blue notebook and get some ideas of things you can pass to someone else?"

Danielle hesitated then sighed. "Why not? It's not top secret. It's pages of check lists Aggie prepared, so I'd know every task I have to do."

"I'll skim it to see if I and other employees can do some tasks, at least until you get on your feet. It hasn't been that long."

"No, it hasn't. And Aggie's out of town, which freaked me out."

"Remember, we're all here to help. Is there anything else I can do?"

Danielle turned pleading blue eyes to Kelsey. "Would you be able to take a few more shifts in the dining room? I lost Paula today."

"Oh, I'm sorry to hear that. She just quit?"

"Um, we had a little conflict. I've been so stressed, and I didn't handle it well."

"Sure, I can do that in the short run. You'll have to hire more wait staff soon, at least two or three, to cover everything. But let me know in advance when you need me to take shifts, and I'll do my best. I have to work it around Molly, but she's pretty easy."

Danielle gave her a grateful smile. "I appreciate it, Kelsey."

Kelsey felt a sliver of hope as she drove to Treasure House to pick up Molly. While she waited, she rewound her conversation with Danielle, which went better than she'd anticipated. She'd hoped Danielle wouldn't be territorial, but recognize she needed a life raft.

Adopting one task wouldn't be enough. Taking more shifts would help in the short run, but would squeeze the little free time she had left. But she'd told Rick she was willing to do it, so she would. Somehow.

"I'll make us some dinner," Kelsey said when they arrived home. "Then I'll have to work on my laptop tonight. But we'll be together in the living room." Hopefully, the extra help she planned to invest in The Fork would be temporary. Her personal projects faded into the horizon like a mirage. Nevertheless, a flicker of contentment dwelt inside.

"You look happy," Molly pronounced. She didn't miss anything.

Kelsey smiled. "I'm in a good mood, I guess. It sure is nice to see you after a long day. Go change into your comfys, and we'll eat in about an hour."

"'Kay."

Once dinner was in the oven, Kelsey checked her phone. Rick had texted her, which drew a smile and triggered something warm inside.

Hi Kelsey, I talked to Vince today, and he's willing to manage the specials from now on. He'll tell Danielle tomorrow, or maybe he already did. Also, there's software for restaurants that will help a lot. If we can convince Danielle to get it, that'll do the work of six of us. What do you think?

Kelsey grinned. She'd loved the idea of being on a team with Rick to save The Fork, but he was also an incredibly resourceful member.

That's great new! I hope Danielle goes for the software. I said I'd take on finding and reserving the bands and she agreed. She was willing to let me look at the notebook to see what else can be delegated. I'm glad she's accepting help. She asked me to work more shifts, and I said okay.

Her phone pinged.

Great news. I'm glad you'll be around more.

Kelsey paused. A warm flush stirred inside. Did he mean anything by that? A small smile crawled across her face. *Thanks. Not sure how I'll manage with Molly and my full-time job, but hopefully, it's short term. I hope we can do some good.*

She stirred the rice on the stove, but kept one eye on her phone. Just in case.

We will. Or have fun trying. Have a good night!

Kelsey grinned. Was Rick really in the *No potential* category? Her brain argued with the warm flush inside her following his text. Maybe she should rethink that.

The following day Kelsey awoke wondering if she had the day off or not. She craved time to work on her recipes and her blog, but she *had* offered. Danielle would surely take her up on it.

Once she'd washed her face and awakened properly, she saw a text message awaiting her. Rick? No, Danielle.

Good morning, Kelsey. Would you by any chance be able to work lunch and dinner today?

Her gaze went to Molly's closed door. *Hi Danielle. I can do lunch if I can bring Molly. But I can't do both. Sorry.* If she were too available, she'd soon have two full-time jobs. Aside from that, Molly was her primary responsibility. Danielle might not hire new wait staff if Kelsey were too accommodating.

"I know you already folded napkins earlier this week, Molly," Kelsey told her sister as they drove toward downtown. "But I have to work unexpectedly." Maybe Vince or Claire could use her in the kitchen. Usually, they preferred weekdays.

They arrived at The Fork at eleven. Danielle was writing the day's specials on the chalkboard as Kelsey and Molly entered. "Hi, Danielle."

She straightened and offered a smile. "Hi, Kelsey. I'm grateful you could come. And it's always a treat to see you, Molly."

Molly grinned back. "Hi, Danielle."

"No problem." Kelsey scanned the room for Rick but didn't see him. "I wondered if I could have a quick look at the notebook before I start my shift. I'll see what's there and be able to suggest some ways to delegate."

"Oh, sure. It's in my office on the desk. You can look at it there for a few minutes, but please don't move it from there."

"I won't."

A few minutes later, Molly perched on a stool in the kitchen. Before her were heads of washed lettuce, which she'd shred into bite-size pieces. Kelsey slipped into Danielle's office and found the notebook on the desk. She pulled her phone from her apron pocket and took a photo of each page. That notebook was a treasure, the key to The Grateful Fork. Hopefully, Rick would convince Danielle to invest in restaurant software to run the business.

The lunch crowd was larger than it had been the day before, bringing a surge of hope and relief. But it was only one day. Problems still ran like fault lines under the business.

She saw Rick across the room. He gave her a thumbs up and they exchanged smiles, but didn't have a chance to talk before her shift ended. That evening, she would pore over the blue Grateful Fork notebook. Maybe they'd talk or text later.

No doubt, she was drawn to him, with little electric impulses that sprang up inside her whenever he was nearby or caught her eye across the dining room. He invaded her thoughts at odd moments, especially with their current collaboration.

Why did she consider him out of bounds for her? For one, he clearly wasn't interested in her, except as a friend. He might not be ready for a relationship anyway, since he was still getting established in his new life, back in his hometown. He'd been back in Brenner Falls only a few months. They were similar age, both Christians. The backgrounds were vastly different. Was that important? She'd always thought so.

Maybe the barrier was in her, an unknown reason grumbling in the back of her mind, erecting an obstacle. Was she afraid he'd relapse? No, she wasn't. What, then? Did his difficult background scare her, as vastly different as it was from her own? True, she didn't understand what led him to his previous life choices.

Despite the tug of war inside her, Kelsey couldn't deny the magnetic pull she felt toward Rick Russo, as though it were some kind of calling she couldn't shake. All she could do was set her feelings aside and simply enjoy his friendship, his sense of humor, and their joint mission.

She'd be his friend and somehow, that would be enough.

After dinner with Molly, while they cleaned the dishes together, Kelsey heard a beep on her phone. Could be anyone. Could be Rick. She held herself back from checking until later, not wanting to suddenly be obsessed with texts from Rick.

When Molly left the kitchen and Kelsey finished wiping down the counters, she sat at the table and looked at her texts. There were two. One from Amber, and one from Rick. A smile spread across her face. First, Amber.

Can you talk?

Kelsey clicked on Amber's number. "Hey, Amber."

"Hi, Kelsey. I've been meaning to call or text all week. It was great to see you last weekend. I'm so glad you were able to come to the party."

"I enjoyed it. It was good to see Nathan and Leah again. It's been a while. I didn't even know she was pregnant."

"It's great, isn't it? I just wanted to reassure you I wasn't trying to fix you up with Rick. I know there were three couples, so that might have been a bit awkward. The other two people couldn't come."

Kelsey laughed. "No worries. Rick and I are friends."

"Well, if you ask me, he's got more potential than I *ever* thought he would. He's come a long way."

"Oh?" Was her friend aiming at something? She'd used the word *potential*.

"I'm speaking in general, of course." She laughed. "I'm not putting ideas in your head, *but*…it seemed to me he was very aware of you. He watched you all evening."

"He did?" Kelsey's neck grew warm. "He told me, aside from Ben, I was the person he knew the best. Maybe that's all it was."

"Hmm. Not sure about that, Kelss."

"Do you think…I mean. What do I mean?" Kelsey laughed. Amber was her best friend. "Okay, what I'm trying to say is I *am* kind of attracted to him."

"You are? Well, it might go both ways. He's transformed from what he was before, I can guarantee that. And he tries hard."

"He does. I respect a lot of things about him, but we're colleagues. Not even good friends, really. You know how we used to talk about p*otential* or *no potential*, remember?"

Amber laughed. "Yes, I remember. God often has other ideas, though."

Hmm. She hadn't thought of that. "I'm not sure where he would fall in those categories."

"I think you should ditch the categories and let God lead."

"He's warmed up to me lately. He was so reserved at first. But I'm not sure he has any interest in me. Don't say anything about this to Ben."

"Of course not. Keep me posted if anything happens."

"Nothing will happen, Amber. He's not interested in me, I can tell you that. We're friends."

They talked a few more minutes, catching up on what they hadn't had a chance to say during the party, then made a date for breakfast the following week.

Kelsey disconnected, musing on what Amber had said. Had Rick watched her that evening with romantic interest? And what about their conversation by the car?

She clicked on Rick's text. He'd either be finishing up at The Fork or newly arrived at home.

Hi Kelsey, things went pretty smoothly tonight. Danielle wasn't here, but Claire was the manager on duty. I hope you're relaxing at home. Are you?

Kelsey smiled. *Hi Rick. Yes, I just finished supper with Molly and then had a nice chat with Amber.*

What else could she tell him? The other night he seemed eager to know her more, which lent a bit of credence to Amber's observations. *I have to work some at my regular job, unfortunately, but I'll relax after that. I'm hoping for a call from my parents later.*

That must be a highlight. I'm sure they have stories to tell that go way beyond our experience.

I often cringe when they tell me what's happening. I have to entrust them to God every day.

So glad we can do that, whether we're in Africa or Brenner Falls. Don't know how I managed before.

After a few more text messages, he wrote, *I'd better let you get to work. BTW, we're not finished with our questions. The ones we started last weekend. Good night."*

His last phrase stirred anticipation inside. He hadn't let go of his quest to know her better. So far, he hadn't revealed much about his past life. Would he allow her a glimpse into what he'd seemed so eager to hide?

Chapter Eight

The evening sun hung low in the sky as it melted into a well of color. Already early August. Rick liked to go to the church building thirty minutes before the youth group to sit in his car and think. Unwind and review the day, the week. And to pray about his life as well as the evening youth outreach.

He couldn't stop a grin from spreading across his lips recalling Kelsey's abrupt show of activism, which had startled and intrigued him. Prior to that day, he'd wondered what she really wanted in life. There she was, doing a computer job she didn't like, drawing temporary joy from taking shifts at the restaurant. She didn't lack passion, but didn't channel her time in that direction. Why?

Yet, when it came to saving The Fork from Danielle's mismanagement, she leaped into action like an animated doll that had been plugged in. He understood then that there was a lot more inside Kelsey than she allowed others to see. He longed to know more.

Aside from her desire to save Aggie's business, Kelsey herself had drawn him in before they'd even exchanged a word. It started the day he'd filled out his application for the job. He'd looked up from filling in the form and there she was in front of him. Their eyes had locked for only an instant, but the memory of that day hadn't left him since that day. Her fresh, feminine face framed with wisps of auburn curls and intelligent blue eyes that seemed to reach out to him.

Maybe he'd been hallucinating, though he hadn't done that in a long time. A case of wishful thinking, then. She probably had men lined up outside her door, and he was hardly a candidate.

But he loved being around her, for whatever reason. She treated him like an equal, with respect. That was a novel experience for him. He felt comfortable with her, like he could relax and be himself, as he'd told her the night of Amber's party. A rare moment of vulnerability.

Now they tried to stem the hemorrhage of The Grateful Fork, garnering Danielle's express agreement whenever possible. He'd spoken to her about the software, but she'd hesitated due to the cost and learning curve. Though he got her point, it would help avoid the shipwreck of the business. She told him she'd think about it. What damage would occur until then?

Rick glanced at his phone. Time to go. Heading into the gym on Thursday nights was a comfortable routine by now. Even leading the games had become an easy and fun task. He knew the kids by name, though often, there were one or two new ones.

When he entered the gym, some kids played basketball, including Chris and Sal, the new kids, who'd been regulars since their first evening. They all waved or called a greeting as he joined them. The movement energized his limbs after the repetitive actions of his job. The other youth leader, Rhonda, a pony-tailed twenty-something with big round glasses, stood in the corner surrounded by several teenage girls.

That first evening, Chris had shown up as a wary and reserved outsider, but was slowly thawing out. What was his story? All Rick knew was what the guy had told him about having to move across the country following the traumatic breakup of his family. There was more background to that, but Rick wouldn't rush him.

Once Jesse arrived, the group gathered around him, as usual. As the players left the basketball court, Rick turned to Chris. "How's your week been?" A lame opener, but he wasn't yet very good at drawing people out.

Chris shrugged. "Okay. Busy." His laconic response gave Rick enough time to notice the bloodshot eyes and paleness of his face. Alarm rippled through him. Rick knew the signs of drug involvement only too well. Maybe it was a passing indulgence.

Maybe it was more. He'd keep an eye on Chris and continue his efforts at building trust and friendship. So far, none of the kids knew his background. At least *he* hadn't told them. Could his mistakes somehow help Chris? It depended on whether Chris wanted help.

ಌ ಌ ಌ

Friday morning, Kelsey awakened with a new recipe in her mind. A twist on eggs benedict. She had to try it, so she'd do that first and start her online job after. Lately, she'd shifted her online work hours mostly to the evening when she only worked the lunch shift at The Fork. Usually, she felt too drained to be at her best, but at least she had a low-key, undemanding job that still paid the bills.

She opened the kitchen window to let the mild summer breeze fill the kitchen.

"Whatcha doing, Kelsey?" Molly's sleepy voice interrupted Kelsey's concentration at the kitchen counter.

"Good morning, sleepy princess." Kelsey turned and enfolded her sister in a hug. "I'm making something amazing for your breakfast."

"Oatmeal?"

"No, better than that. Do you know what Eggs Benedict is?"

Molly shook her head. "Eggs and bacon?"

"Sort of. Usually, there are eggs, a sauce, and some kind of meat all on an open-faced English muffin. I'm changing up the sauce." Mornay sauce with Gruyère cheese. "And instead of an English muffin, I'm putting it on corn bread. You can be my taster."

Once she'd put everything together, she placed it at Molly's and her place settings in the dining room. "We'll eat in here instead of the kitchen, since it's Friday. It's a special day." Molly heartily approved of Kelsey's adaptation of the breakfast classic. One more for the cookbook and the blog.

Kelsey didn't know why she considered it a special day, except for the volley of text messages she'd exchanged with Rick the previous evening. He'd been to the youth group and messaged her afterward to ask how her evening was. Nothing more. That brought a smile to her and filled her with a tingle of joy which apparently hadn't worn off by the following morning.

She was off that day from the restaurant, so she felt less divided between her various tasks and Molly. It was getting to be too much, since Danielle called on her almost daily to take shifts. Kelsey told Danielle in advance she couldn't work Friday. She needed to rest and catch up on her actual job.

Earlier that week, Kelsey phoned Paula, the waitress who quit, and convinced her to return, pending an apology from Danielle. Fortunately, Danielle was willing to humble herself to avoid having to hire Paula's replacement. One win for the week, but they needed many more.

The customer count continued to ebb, despite an encouraging weekend crowd. *Monday Motivation* even failed to draw in regulars. A pall of dread hovered over the staff of The Fork. Their efforts would not save the ship from hitting the reef, especially since Danielle hadn't yet committed to implementing the restaurant software. Kelsey phoned Aggie after her cruise and hinted things were on a downward spiral after only a month. The older woman claimed Danielle could turn it around once she had more experience. Without the software, that scenario was doubtful.

"I hope you're right, Aggie. You've invested so much for four decades. And everyone in Brenner Falls loves The Fork. I worry a little about it." Though she'd wrapped bad news in gentler terms, Aggie still didn't seem alarmed. Had she detached from her life's work so quickly?

"Kelsey, I *do* hear you." Aggie's words caught Kelsey by surprise. "That's why I wanted you and Rick to keep an eye on things and I hope that helps. I haven't told you this, but I'm having a few health problems I thought might be serious. That's one reason I've been traveling a lot, because I didn't know how much time I'd have."

"Oh, Aggie. I had no idea."

"Turns out it's not that serious, but for a while I didn't know it, so I booked a lot of things. I thought it was now or never."

"I understand." That made more sense that Aggie would travel a lot even though Danielle was learning to run her business. "Let me know if I can help in any way."

"Just focus on The Fork, and we'll take it one day at a time." In the meantime, the staff would continue patching holes.

Following breakfast, Kelsey settled in front of her computer to concentrate on work while Molly read in the living room. She had trouble harnessing her thoughts, which kept bouncing between the problems at The Fork and Rick. At least part of her work was almost mindless.

Before lunch, she stopped and rubbed her eyes. When she reached for her phone, she had a text from Rick. That drew a smile, but it faded when she read his words.

Danielle didn't come to work today. We don't know why yet. She doesn't answer her phone. Will keep you posted.

The clipped tone of the text likely meant he was busy. Danielle's absence caused the most concern. Had she jumped ship after a breakdown of some kind?

Kelsey tapped Danielle's number, and it went to voicemail. What was going on? As she laid the phone back on her desk, it rang. The name *Vince* showed on her screen.

"Hi, Vince. What's going on? I heard Danielle didn't show up today."

"Danielle was in a car accident late last night. She's in the hospital."

Kelsey gasped. "Oh no! Is she alright?"

"Generally, yes, but she broke her leg. Some dude on a motorcycle hit her from behind. I guess it jammed her leg. They reset the bone this morning. Obviously, she can't work for a month or even two. You're the best person to take over for her. Could you do that short-term?"

Her mouth dropped open. "I...uh." She swallowed, and her thoughts raced. "I already work full time, Vince. And I have Molly." How on earth could she do it when she felt overwhelmed already?

Yet, despite Danielle's distressing situation, something inside her percolated. Could she take over Danielle's role and save The Fork just in time? Had God arranged the timing so she could do that? A second opportunity to lead The Fork. *What should I say, Lord? Is this from you?*

"I understand," he said. "Just thought I'd ask."

"Wait, Vince. Let me think about it, okay? I won't say no, if I can arrange something...I'm not sure what. Did you ask Aggie about this?"

"It's funny, but you came to mind before Aggie did, even if she's the owner. But I'll call and ask her what she thinks. Maybe she knows of someone else who can step in, or maybe *she'd* be willing. The staff can hold things together for a day or so, but we'll need a manager soon."

On Danielle's watch, things had begun to unravel to frightening proportions in only a few weeks. Could Kelsey make a difference? If so, how would she juggle two full time jobs and Molly?

An idea crept into her mind. Admittedly, a crazy one, but it might be the only way.

"Danielle is at Brenner Falls General?"

"Yes. She was admitted last night."

"Poor Danielle. But I'm glad it's only a broken leg. It could have been so much worse. I'll go see her. I have an idea I want to run by her."

"Will you be able to come tonight? We'll need you. We have a band and expect a big crowd."

Oh. She'd forgotten. So much for her day at home to catch up. To regroup and relax. She stood and went to the doorway to the living room. "Yes, I'll be there and bring Molly." She caught Molly's quizzical expression. "I'll go see Danielle, then we'll be there around four."

Kelsey disconnected the call, sensing her world had changed in a matter of minutes. "Molly, I need to go to see someone at the hospital. I'll take something out of fridge, and you can microwave it for lunch, okay?"

"'Kay. Who's in the hospital?"

"Danielle. She got hurt in a car accident."

Molly's face fell. "I like Danielle."

"Me too." Not as a manager of The Fork, but otherwise, yes. "I'll go see her and then come back here. Then at four, you and I have to go to The Fork to help."

Kelsey hadn't gone inside Brenner Falls General Hospital in years. She found her way to Danielle's room after consulting with an employee at the entrance. Fortunately, Danielle was awake, but one leg stretched out like a wrapped sausage and was elevated on a few pillows.

"Hey, Danielle." She pulled up a chair beside the bed. "I'm so sorry to see you here. What happened?"

"Hi, Kelsey." Danielle's weak voice seeped out of her pale lips. Her blond hair crumpled in disarray around her face. "I got hit from behind. I wasn't paying too much attention, though. I was worried about stuff..." She took a breath. "I didn't see the guy so close behind me..."

"How long do they think you'll be laid up?"

"They say between one and two months. I need to stay off my legs for a while. I don't know how I'll work."

"I understand. That's one reason I wanted to talk to you, along with seeing how you're doing, of course. Vince asked me if I could fill in for you, but as you know, I have a full-time online job."

"It's a shame. You're such a natural."

Kelsey's eyes widened. "Thanks, Danielle. I...I do like working at The Fork."

"So, here's your chance. You'll be better at it than I was." Danielle mustered a weak smile.

Here was her chance. Would she take it? Was *God* giving her another chance? "I'm willing to do that if I can figure out things with my job and Molly. So...here's an idea for you to think about."

Danielle struggled to keep her eyes open.

"I know you need to rest, but I have to ask you this now. It's a crazy idea."

That phrase perked Danielle up from her sleepy stupor. She struggled to sit upright. "I'm listening."

Kelsey pulled her chair closer to the bed. "So, you're going to be off your feet for a month or two. Let's just say two." Kelsey spoke slowly, seizing on Danielle's momentarily attentive state. "If I take over managing The Fork during that time, I'd need someone to do *my* job. A lot of it is mindless data entry. I know with your IT background, you can handle much more than that, but if you can do that part, it'll be a huge help. It's the only way I could do both."

Danielle's gaze trained on Kelsey, as if she was mulling over the new idea. "Is that legal? I mean, to switch jobs?"

Kelsey frowned. She hadn't thought that far, since it was her one and only chance. "As long as I train you beforehand, then check your work each evening before submitting it to the company, I don't see a problem, since it's short term. We'd each keep whatever paycheck we're used to getting, since it *is* temporary. You'd work at my house during that time, though I have to think about how to get you back and forth from your apartment. I'd also need you to watch over Molly during the hours

I'm at work, and sometime that'll be in the evenings. She goes to adult daycare a few days a week. I can arrange for her to go every day instead during this time."

"I won't be able to drive her for the first few weeks."

"I've thought of that. I can drop her off on the way to the restaurant and get a neighbor or someone there to bring her home." She'd organize a schedule.

"It's actually a good idea and could work." Danielle looked pensive as she bit her lower lip.

"Can you decide by tomorrow?"

"Yes, I will. I know you need an answer soon. Does Aggie know about this idea?"

"I'll let her know. I wanted to talk to you first to see if it was even a possibility."

"I'll think it over, though I already know there aren't any alternatives."

Kelsey reached out and squeezed Danielle's arm. "It's worth a try. And you won't have to worry about The Fork while you're recovering."

Danielle blew out her breath. "It'll be nice *not* worrying about it for a change." Then a smile quirked her lips. "I promise you, Kelsey, I didn't do this on purpose."

They shared a chuckle until Danielle winced.

Kelsey returned her hand to Danielle's arm. "Thanks for being open to the idea. I'll let you rest now."

Her heart thumped as she rushed out of the hospital to her car. Before starting the ignition, she dialed Aggie, praying she'd reach her

"Hi Aggie, it's Kelsey. Can you talk for a minute? It's important."

"Of course, but I'm packing to leave on another trip. This time, I'm going to see my sister. She lives in Florida, and I haven't seen her in a while."

Kelsey's words came out in a rush. "Did you talk to Vince today?"

"No, but I see he left me a voice message."

"Danielle was in a car accident last night. She can't work at The Fork for at least a month. Vince suggested I take her place as manager during that time, but I wanted to check with you first."

"Oh, my goodness! Is she okay?"

"It could have been much worse, but she broke her leg. She had surgery early this morning. If you agree, she and I can switch roles while she recovers. I'll manage The Fork, and she can do my online job and look after Molly."

"Will she be able to do that with a broken leg?" Good question.

"She can't drive at first, but I can arrange transportation for Molly. Also, Molly can make some meals herself. She's more independent than people think. The main thing is my job. I can't do both."

She heard Aggie let out a long breath. "Of course, you can't. Well, you were my first choice for the manager role, as you know. It sounds like a good short-term solution if you can work it out. Thank you, Kelsey."

"I'm glad you're on board with the idea. I need to ask if you'll authorize me to do what I think is best for The Fork." Kelsey couldn't have her hands tied if she were to do any good.

"Yes. Yes, Kelsey," she answered after a pause. "I know your heart for The Fork, and I trust you. I'll admit I had reservations from the start about Danielle, but felt I should give her a chance, since she's family.

"The Fork is your life's work, Aggie. She means well, but I don't think she had enough experience to manage a successful restaurant. I'll do my best."

"I feel guilty leaving Danielle on her own before she was ready. Can she be reached? I'd like to talk to her."

"She has her cell at the hospital. She'll be able to come home in a few days."

"I'll call her now."

"And feel free to call me even while you're gone. I'll give you updates."

"I will. I'll leave for Florida tomorrow, but you can call me too. I won't have any problem with phone reception while I'm at my sister's."

Kelsey disconnected and drove home. She and Molly had only a couple of hours before heading to The Fork. When she entered the house, Molly was at the kitchen table working on a puzzle. "We need a conference, Molls." Kelsey sat across from her sister and propped her elbows on the edge of the table.

"Danielle?"

"I saw her, and she's okay, but she broke her leg. She can't work at The Fork for a while, so I'm going to take her place. And she's going to take mine at my computer job. She'll be here at the house during the day. Is that okay with you?"

Molly nodded. "She will work here? It's okay. I like Danielle."

"Good. I'm glad. Now you'll see her even more."

Kelsey paused, imagining *how* Danielle would come to the house every day when she couldn't drive or walk. She hadn't thought through the mechanics of the switch.

A long pause went by. "Molly."

Molly raised her gaze to Kelsey's.

"Would it be okay if Danielle *lived* here with us for a while? She can stay in the guest room." It would be easier than having to pick her up every day, better for Molly on the evenings Kelsey would be at the restaurant, and better for Danielle, who would need a lot of help for the next few weeks. A win-win.

When Kelsey and Molly drove to The Fork two hours later, Kelsey's new role as manager caused a flutter of nerves for the first few minutes. She didn't have the luxury to let it all sink in, because it was Friday night. Friday, the busiest night of the week, and a concert night. For the next several hours, it would be all hands on deck. Fortunately, she'd pored through the blue notebook over the last week and had a notion of what the job involved.

Kelsey pushed the front door of The Fork, feeling a strange impression of entering for the first time. Across the room, Rick moved quickly among the tables, preparing them for the evening. He glanced at the door, a likely reflex. He stilled as their gazes locked, their silent bond as significant as the news she had to share.

He paused his work as she and Molly approached the table. "Did you talk to Danielle? Is everything okay?"

"I saw Danielle. She has a broken leg and can't work, so…I'm taking her place. As manager."

Rick stilled, and his eyes widened. "You are?" Then his surprise melted away, replaced by a belly laugh. "That's fantastic. I mean—" He sobered for an instant. "Not for Danielle, of course. But for you and for The Fork. God gave you another chance."

"I thought the same thing." Kelsey smiled, despite the huge shift in a short time.

He turned to Molly. "Are you helping tonight, Molly?"

Molly's eyes searched the room. "I don't know."

"No, she's going to stay at her usual table," Kelsey said. "She brought some things to do. I'm not sure what *I'm* supposed to do first going from part-time help to manager."

"I doubt you'll wonder about it for very long. You're a pro, Kelsey."

They shared a grin. "Thanks, Rick. So are you, apparently."

Kelsey hustled Molly to her table in the corner and went to the kitchen. Vince barked orders to the staff as she retrieved an apron. She paused. Did she even *need* an apron that night? She returned it to the shelf.

As she waited for Vince, a wave of uncertainty blew through her then departed. She wiped moist hands on her pants. *Okay, Lord. Please walk me through this evening!*

Vince saw her waiting for him and turned, still eyeing the stockpot. "Thanks for coming, Kelsey. Do you have any news about Danielle?"

"Yes. I went to see her today at the hospital. I also talked to Aggie, and I'm officially on board to be the general manager until Danielle can work again."

He let out a breath, and his shoulders sagged. "Excellent. I'm sorry for Danielle, of course, but I think you're just what we need right now."

Emotion rose in her throat. "I hope I'll measure up to that statement, Vince. Danielle will stay at my house during her recovery. She'll do my online job during that time and watch over Molly."

Bushy eyebrows raised and he nodded in approval. "Good thinking. I know that you're experienced, but you'll still need to learn the ropes. Everyone'll help you. Don't worry and don't hesitate to ask."

"Thanks. I've been studying Aggie's little blue book to see where Danielle could delegate tasks. So, hopefully I'm one step ahead."

He crossed his arms. "So, tell me what you think you should do right now."

Her first quiz. She moistened her lips. "Well, I think getting the overview would be good. Making sure all the tasks have been done before the crowd arrives and everything is ready for them. Making sure the band has what they need."

"Good. Get to it." He grinned at her and winked. "Welcome aboard, Kelsey."

Chapter Nine

As the sermon reached its close, Rick resisted the urge to glance across the aisle where Kelsey sat with a couple of women her age, including Molly. He didn't want to raise suspicion with his mom or Ben, who sat on either side of him on the padded wooden bench of the sanctuary. They didn't need to know he was going to Kelsey's house after the church service to have lunch and talk about The Grateful Fork.

His mind replayed how that situation had come about. She'd come into work for the lunch shift Saturday, the day after officially taking over as manager. It seemed she'd grown in confidence and authority in only one day. Not the arrogant kind, but one that said she was finally stepping into shoes that were made for her.

They'd had a moment to talk after the surge of lunch customers. She had to leave right after her shift to do something with Molly, so she suggested they could talk after church.

"We could grab some lunch," he'd said with what he hoped was an inviting smile. "And you can tell me your vision for The Grateful Fork."

"I'll have Molly." She'd given him a disappointed frown. "So, why don't you come to our house instead? I'll make lunch and we can talk vision afterward. I'd love to hear your ideas too."

He laughed. "My ideas? You're the one who's gifted for this stuff."

"Ha!" She'd given him a playful tap on one shoulder. "You're way too humble." Her eyes had twinkled in a way that transfixed him. Crystal blue, happy, full of humor. "If the truth were known," she'd continued, "*you* should be the manager. From what you said the other day, you have *years* of experience. You could do this."

Huh. She thought he could do the manager job? She *believed* in him?

Rick rebounded from his surprise with humor. "Now I *know* you're overworked. And you've only been the manager for a day. Do you need a vacation already?"

They'd laughed, and it had made his heart sing. He'd always considered laughing together a high-water mark in a relationship, male or female. They were already there, but she still had no idea how he felt about her.

Too bad he couldn't tell her, for lots of reasons.

And now, he had sort of a lunch date with her. Of course, Molly would be there, but there was something so sweet about Molly, it made him want to dance her around the room and finish with a hug. And she was a big part of Kelsey's world, so they were a package.

He hoped Kelsey hadn't told Amber about their lunch plans. The two women were good friends, but he liked keeping his private life to himself, even if they were only meeting to discuss the restaurant. He had no illusions of something more. And he certainly didn't need Ben putting in his two cents about Rick's love life.

Rick snorted. Love life? Far from it.

Everyone stood as the worship band played the final song. He shot a glance at Kelsey's pew, but she and Molly had already left. She'd given him her address, so she'd probably scooted out early to prepare their lunch.

From the church, he drove toward the edge of town and down a long country road where fewer homes sat, spaced out with acreage surrounding each one. As he drove, the tall pines shadowed the quiet streets, casting a layer of peace.

He found the house, a ranch-style building, sprawled out under the trees, and pulled into a gravel driveway. The ground lay under a blanket of pine needles, painted by splotches of sunlight that dribbled through the boughs overhead. A wide wooden deck equipped with a wrought-iron table jutted from one side of the house. The whole sight could only be called inviting.

Rick knocked on the door. Kelsey opened it and ushered him inside. When he saw her up close, he fumbled for words. On an average day, she wore an apron and had a ponytail and limited makeup. In other words, fresh and adorable. That day, her auburn hair curled around her shoulders, and she still wore the pale blue sleeveless dress she'd had on at church. Made him think of a princess.

"Come on in. I'm just finishing up."

She looked slightly nervous, which made him nervous too. He reminded himself it was only a business meeting. A meeting with a regal princess who had him tongue-tied.

A glance through the doorway across from the kitchen revealed a carpeted, sunken living room with a wall of windows overlooking a shady, expansive backyard. What a peaceful place to read. He followed her into the kitchen.

"Nice house."

"Thanks. I like it." Kelsey was already busy in the kitchen.

"You're fast." Rick nodded toward the stove. "The service just ended a few minutes ago."

She laughed. "I confess, I'm warming leftovers."

He went to the counter and leaned against it while she finished up. "I have the feeling *your* leftovers are good enough to deserve a different name."

Kelsey shot him a smile. "Thanks for your confidence. We'll eat here." She motioned toward the table, prepared with three place settings.

"Can I do anything to help?"

"No, thanks. You're my guest. And I suspect you don't get a lot of downtime."

"Good observation. But it was my choice. I figured, since I was new in town, I'd work a lot and get established. I don't mind." His expenses were low, so he socked most of it away in savings. To what end, he wasn't yet sure. Just seemed the smart thing to do. And it was a completely new habit for him that felt good.

"Tell me again when you arrived in The Falls?" She spoke over one shoulder as she tossed the salad in the large ceramic bowl.

"First week of May. Three months ago. Hard to believe." He hoped she wouldn't ask a bunch of questions about his past. He'd probably feel compelled to tell her, unable to put a fence around any part of his life when he was with her.

She pulled a steaming Pyrex pan from the oven and mouth-watering aromas laced with chili hit him in a wave. "Chicken enchiladas," she said. "I just made them last night, so they're not *too* far leftover. Only I sort of tampered with the recipe. I do that a lot."

He laughed. "As in, make it better? That kind of tampering?"

"I hope it's better. I can't leave a recipe alone. I always think, 'wouldn't avocado be good in this?' Or 'I wonder what it would taste like if I add this or that spice.'"

"So, you're inventive. That's good."

She placed the pan on a trivet in the middle of the table, then walked to the doorway. "Molly, lunch is ready." She returned to the kitchen. "We'll eat here because the meal is hot, but we can have dessert out back on the patio." She took a tray of filled glasses from the counter and set it on the table in one swift movement, then leaned over the casserole to spoon an enchilada onto each plate before sitting beside him.

"I saw the deck on the side of the house, and another one out back," he said. "It's nice that you have two. How many acres do you all have here?"

"Five. My parents bought this house years ago when the town was still pretty rural. I loved growing up here. There's lots of space to run around and a forest in back which butts up to the edge of our property."

"Do you have other siblings?"

"No, it's just Molly and me."

Molly came into the kitchen and flanked his other side. She smiled in her heartwarming way, her blue eyes scrunching half-shut. "Hi, Mr. Rick."

"Hello, Molly."

Kelsey prayed, and they all dug in.

"Delicious." It was true. Rick savored the taste before swallowing. "I've had many enchiladas out west, but this is by far the top."

"I'm glad you like it. It's nice of you to exaggerate like that."

He chuckled. "You'll soon learn I don't exaggerate about anything." It was a good time to learn more about Kelsey. "How are your parents enjoying their mission trip?"

"They love it. They've been there for six months, so they have three to go."

He nodded and took a sip of lemonade, which was also the best he'd ever tasted. A guy could get fat like this. "It's cool they wanted to do that. Lots of people probably talk about trips like that. One day they'll do this or that charitable act. But your parents actually *did* it."

"Exactly. They'd talked about it for a couple of years, then it became reality. They're working in a rural village doing agricultural projects and helping with a clinic. My mom has a nursing background."

"That sounds like they're making a huge contribution. Will you stay here once they come back?"

"I haven't thought about it." She sliced into her enchilada, releasing a cloud of steam. "I lived in my own apartment right after college and again for a time when I moved back to The Falls, but I've been back home for three years. It's a big house and I get along well with my parents. Didn't make sense to spend money on rent. Also, I'm able to help with Molly."

"Looks like a great place to live. Where is your home office?"

She pointed to a corner of the kitchen in front of a large double-hung window. "Right there."

ॐ ॐ ॐ

Kelsey projected nonchalance, but smothered an inside grin. How had she managed to invite Rick Russo to her house for lunch? He'd invited her first, sort of a date, almost. But she didn't want to leave Molly by herself on a Sunday afternoon. She didn't mind looking after her sister, but it limited some of her social opportunities. This was the next best thing, and she enjoyed sharing her own food with Rick.

Lunch conversation stayed on the surface, with Rick asking most of the questions. That was fine. They had to start somewhere. Her education, past jobs, whether she liked living in The Falls. Maybe he wanted to steer her away from his own background. Or else he was pursuing what they'd started the other day, learning more about one another.

When they'd finished lunch, the three of them moved outside to the picnic table with bowls of ice cream and cookies. Rick seemed relaxed and serene, especially once they were outside.

Molly licked every drop of her ice cream from the bowl then stood. "I'm going inside to read," she announced and disappeared into the house.

"She always prefers being inside, regardless of the weather." Kelsey knew her sister didn't have a strategy of leaving them alone. But she was glad they were.

"We can move to the lawn chairs. They're more comfortable."

They both pulled away from the wooden picnic table. "You've asked all the questions so far," she said. "Tell me more about you. Then we can talk some about the restaurant."

Rick eyed her. "Tell me what you already know." He suddenly appeared tense, guarded.

She took a breath. How much should she say? How could she avoid driving a wedge between them, just when they were breaking through the surface?

Yet, she'd asked the question and with Rick, she couldn't be anything but fully honest. "I know you left town after high school and moved to Arizona. During that time, you worked in several restaurants, you were involved in drugs and alcohol, and you lived with friends, sometimes without housing." She took a breath. "And by the way, I'm not judging you. Then you met the Lord and now you're a new creation."

For a long moment he didn't speak, but held her gaze, as if deciding how to respond. "That's pretty accurate." His voice had dropped, and his eyes darted away from hers. "There *were* periods when we didn't have housing, but fewer than Ben probably thinks. It was on and off."

"What made you leave Brenner Falls?"

He leaned back in the lawn chair, some of his wariness appearing to slip away. "I was running away from my life. I wanted anything but here. It was full of lousy memories and pain. I numbed the pain with drugs. When the drugs wore off, the pain came back. I didn't like who I was when I was sober. So, it became a cycle."

"I see how that can happen."

His gaze shot to hers. "You do?"

"Not from experience, but I imagine it's an attractively easy way to escape hopelessness and pain. But often there are consequences. Not the least being you have to come back to your life."

That was the sum total of what she knew about drug abuse. It was an article in the news, a side discussion from the friend of a friend about someone neither one knew. It hadn't ever touched her life.

She thrust a bright tone into her voice. "Tell me how you got saved." She'd focus on the now.

His expression softened. "*That's* a story. I was dying under a bridge. I was stoned but had pneumonia. I don't think I would have made it. My so-called buddies left me, thinking I'd overdosed."

"Nice buddies you had there. You could have died, but they didn't get you help."

"Yeah. I thought the same thing later on. So, this couple found me and took me to the hospital. They worried about me like my own parents. Then they brought me home to live with them for the next two years."

"That's amazing. Go on." Kelsey's throat tightened with emotion. She blinked at the sting in her eyes. "What happened during those two years?"

Rick started talking and seemed to relax as he told her his story. How he'd met Stephen and Annika, how they'd taken him to church, how they'd talked to him about the Lord. And how deeply he'd wanted that relationship, that hope. Everything else in his life had become like trash.

"They have two sons, but they were both away at college. Stephen got me a job working at the church doing maintenance, stuff like that. I learned about the Bible, got more solid. Later, I took some classes at the community college."

That was a surprise. He'd packed a lot into the last two years. Kelsey leaned one elbow on the armrest. "What made you come back to Brenner Falls?"

"God." His statement was blunt, emphatic. "I almost audibly heard him tell me to come back. I can't explain it beyond that."

A chill ran down her spine, but she couldn't stop a grin from appearing. "He must have something wonderful for you here."

Rick smiled. "No doubt. Or maybe he just wanted me to stop breaking my mom's heart."

Kelsey swallowed a new lump that had formed in her throat. "What a powerful testimony you have."

"You think? It's a mess."

"Yeah, but don't you think amidst the mess, God's glory shines brighter?"

"That's a nice way to put it. And yes, you're right about that."

"God'll use it in some way, mark my words. I already feel a sense of wonder at what he's done in your life."

"Really?" He seemed to consider her words as his gaze locked with hers. A hum began inside.

"Thanks for your encouragement, Kelsey." He paused. "Lemme ask you something, since I just spilled my life story." His grin held a challenge. "Remember, we're trying to get to know each other. Goes both ways."

"That's fair." She braced herself.

"Why didn't you go to culinary school, but studied computers instead? It's obvious you love cooking and hospitality."

Kelsey sighed. "First, I always loved to putter in the kitchen and invent stuff. I collect my successes for a cookbook I'd like to publish, maybe soon. But culinary school seemed so intense, and I didn't know if doing it professionally would take the fun out of it." And she wasn't convinced she'd succeed, despite her love for it.

"Ah, that's a good point. But maybe it wouldn't have. You could have been a Beard Award winner by this time."

"You know about that? Of course, you do." She nodded in approval. "I still learned a lot with cooking shows and classes, recipes, blogs. Stuff like that. That spurred me to start my blog. It's called *Kelsey's Kitchen*."

His eyebrows raised "Good for you. Can I see it sometime?"

"Sure. I try hard to post regularly, but time presents a challenge."

"Because of your soul-sucking day job?" He grinned.

She laughed. "Yes. That and Molly. And working at The Fork. I kind of feel stuck, since I needed a job that permits me to be here for Molly during this year that my parents are gone."

"I get that. But now, everything has changed. You can try out the restaurant job and see if it's really your thing. Maybe Aggie will make it permanent, and you can quit your other job."

She sighed. "That would be ideal. But when Danielle recovers, she might want her job back."

"Then we'd be right back where we started." He paused. "Does Aggie know things went down as soon as Danielle took over?"

"Yes. I was fairly direct. She wanted to give Danielle a chance."

He grimaced. "Not after forty years of success. You don't hand that over to an amateur just because of family loyalty. She struck me as more savvy than that."

"But *I'm* an amateur."

"No, Kelsey." He leaned forward. Intensity had crept into his voice. "Danielle has no idea what she's doing but you can't say the same thing."

His affirmation brought a smile to her lips. "No, I guess not."

"So, here's your chance to get out of the shadows and live your own life."

Kelsey cocked her head. "What do you mean?"

"Based on what I know of you, you've spent your adult life helping, filling in, serving. That's great, but what about *your* dreams? Your destiny?"

Words left Kelsey. She swallowed. It wasn't like she'd never thought of it before. Her blog, her cookbook, those were efforts. *Sideline* efforts.

Her eyes met his and more electric sparks shot off. This time, he seemed to feel it too, as the truth-laden silence swirled around them. "You're right." Her voice came out softly. "I...I guess I always thought Molly's needs were more important than mine. You know,

I was healthy, and she was born with this thing she had no control over. It wasn't her fault."

As she uttered words she'd never spoken to anyone, a weight pressed on her chest. She hadn't fully known it until Rick pointed a spotlight on her last few years. Maybe even her whole life. She'd developed a kind of comfort living in Molly's shadow. A place she'd subconsciously chosen to stay.

"Her needs don't make you less important. You can help your sister and others without sacrificing your own story. You *have* a story, Kelsey." A smile crept across his lips. "I'm thankful for Danielle's accident if it puts you in your own story... Sorry, Danielle."

They shared a smile. His words had touched a hollow inside her formed by a lifetime of questions about her place. Her worth. He reached out and squeezed her hand, then drew it back. She badly wanted his hand back on hers. Wanted it to stay there, to feel its warmth and texture. "Thanks for saying that. Maybe with all this, God forced me into my own story, as you say. Or at least the opportunity to try. I had to say no the first time, and God honored that by giving me a second chance."

"I'll bet Danielle's relieved to be out of this job."

Kelsey smiled. "I wouldn't be surprised. By the way, she's moving in here tomorrow. She'll stay here while she recovers. It was the most practical solution, since she won't be able to drive. I might need your help to move some of her stuff. And even to help me pick her up from the hospital and bring her here."

"Gladly. Just let me know what time, before or after our shifts. I'm on lunch tomorrow and have dinner off."

"Me too. We can pick her up after the lunch shift."

Silence fell, but it wasn't awkward. His warm eyes found hers, and there was comfort there, friendship...and something else that made her nearly tremble inside. She wouldn't try to define it, since it would leave her empty if there ended up being nothing more than friendship on his side, despite what Amber had said.

"So, do you want to talk about The Fork?" she asked. Seemed to be a good segue for turning to business.

"No. Not really." He crossed his arms, a lazy smile teasing his lips. "I'd like to keep talking about you. But I suppose we should talk about The Fork."

She didn't want to leave the personal level of their conversation, either. They might never get back to it, when Monday arrived and work hit them full force again, along with all her new responsibilities. Managing The Fork, settling Danielle in, overseeing Molly. She didn't want to go back to merely exchanging a smile or a funny face across the room with him. Now, she wanted more.

"When I spoke with Aggie the other day," Kelsey said, "I asked her for her authorization to do what I felt was needed. I had the software in mind when I asked. She said yes. So, can you do the research and find the right program for us? I need to get fully trained with it, and the whole staff. Including you, of course."

Before Rick could protest, she said, "Don't give me the *I'm a humble dishwasher* line again." She narrowed her eyes at him. "You're my ally and my right hand, from now on. Aggie's idea was that we'd work as equals, regardless of our titles."

He laughed aloud. "Sure. I'll try. You don't know what you're asking."

"Cut it out, Rick Russo. Quit putting yourself down and step into *your* destiny, okay?"

"You're right. It's a bad habit I have trouble shedding. I accept."

She extended her hand, palm down, the way she'd done that day when they'd banded together to save the Fork. "The Force for the Fork."

He laid his hand on hers. "For the Fork." They laughed aloud.

Chapter Ten

The next day, Kelsey arrived at The Fork before the lunch shift and went straight to where Rick prepped a table. "Last night I had trouble sleeping," she told him. "I imagined I transported Danielle from the hospital to my house, but broke her other leg by mistake."

He laughed aloud. His eyes emanated warmth and complicity. Since the previous day with him, when he'd shared openly about his life and challenged her about hers, she dwelled in a warm glow of contentment infused with a tingle of excitement. He'd opened the secret door of his life to her, trusted her with his story. They'd stepped deeper into friendship. Wherever it led—or didn't—she was grateful. She'd take what she could get. But was Amber right? Kelsey had almost felt something new in the air the previous day.

She continued. "So, I arranged a medical transport company to bring her over. I was anxious about it."

"I would be too. Are you ready to have her as a house guest for a couple of months? You have a lot going on already."

She sighed. "I won't lie, I think it'll be hard, but I don't see any other way. Otherwise, I'd have to transport her back and forth so she can use my computer and office. I couldn't ask Aggie to do that, even when she's in town. With my new role, I'll have to work late more often. Danielle can stay with Molly, so that'll be a help." She took a breath and met his gaze. "I may still need you to help her get settled."

"Sure. I can be there whenever you need me, or earlier if you want to set anything up."

She gave him a grateful smile. "Thanks, Rick. They're picking her up at three, so anytime around then."

Kelsey turned to report to the kitchen. "Kelsey…" Rick called after her. She turned to face him. "Thanks for yesterday. The great meal and the time after. I enjoyed getting to know you better."

"Me too. Thanks for…for being open about your life. For trusting me."

"By the way, if you're up for it and have time, there's a new place in town that's getting good reviews. We should go and study it one day. You know, get ideas."

Kelsey's spirits soared. It was similar to a date, wasn't it? "That's a great idea. We can see things they do but we don't. This week isn't the best because of Danielle, but next week would be perfect. We'll work lunch and be free afterwards." Heat rose in her neck. "Well, I better git."

As she walked purposefully to the kitchen, her heart raced. Rick had suggested an outing. The first time he'd come to her house, he'd initiated that as well. Maybe Amber was right.

During the lunch shift, Kelsey did her duties with added buoyancy and a multitude of smiles. As general manager, she'd normally work longer hours, but Vince knew Danielle was moving in that day. "I'm leaving now, Vince." Apology laced her voice.

"Go on, get Danielle settled," he said. "I'm glad you both agreed on this temporary solution. Sounds like it'll work in the short run. I'll do my best to hold things together. I can recruit Rick, who's far more capable than he admits."

Kelsey grinned. *"That's* the truth. And thanks, Vince."

She dashed to her car and drove to Treasure House to pick up Molly, who would start attending daily. When she slipped into the car, Kelsey turned to her. "Well, Molls, are you ready for our lives to change?"

"Yes. I like Danielle." Her face showed little emotion, but it would have to work. By the time they arrived home, Rick's car was already in the driveway.

"Thanks for coming," Kelsey said after Rick got out of the car. "I'm not sure whether your brawn will be needed, but I'm glad you're here."

"Glad to help. I'll offer moral support, if nothing else."

The three of them went into the house. "Danielle should be here within fifteen minutes. She just texted me. Want some lemonade in the meantime?"

"I won't say no, especially if it's the same we had yesterday." Rick followed her into the kitchen. "Did you set up a guest room for her?"

"Yes. There are four bedrooms in the house. Fortunately, the spare room is near a bathroom." She turned to Rick. "I hope this idea works."

He laid a hand on her shoulder. "It will. And whatever happens, remember, it's the only solution. You've thought this through."

"Yes, that's true." Just feeling his hand touching her again, as he had yesterday, infused her with assurance. "Thanks for your support and help. I'll need it in days to come."

"I'm here for you, Kelsey. And keep in mind, all this was God's idea anyway, so he's here too."

"Between the two of you, I have top-notch help."

It all seemed so overwhelming. After settling Danielle into her new temporary home and explaining Molly's routine to her, Kelsey would have to make dinner, then spend a couple of hours catching up on her own neglected work. At some point, maybe in a few days or sooner, she'd begin training Danielle to do her job, then dash back over to The Grateful Fork.

The restaurant outing Rick had suggested would take valuable time she didn't have, but she'd never say so. Anticipation already hopped around inside her, being with him, as well as gathering new ideas from a brand-new place. She drew a breath of courage into her lungs as the medical transport vehicle pulled into the driveway.

The crew, consisting of two uniformed men, brought Danielle into the house on a stretcher, detached her, and laid her on the couch in the living room. Her face showed more color than the day Kelsey had seen her at the hospital. One of the men briefed her on what she could and could not do, and for how long. They left a list of instructions, a set of crutches, and the discharge papers from the hospital.

"How are you feeling, Danielle?" Kelsey asked after the medical personnel had left. She handed her a glass of lemonade, then sat in an armchair across from her. "It's probably a dumb question since you just broke a bone."

A smile spread on Danielle's pale face." Better than the other day when I saw you. But now reality is about to hit." She offered a wry smile. "I hope I can pull off this job switch."

"You'll be fine." Rick took a sip. "I hear you already have IT skills. It's actually a great idea to do the job switch, and for you to live here. That'll make life easier for everyone during this month or two. This isn't the time for you to be alone."

"I agree with that," Kelsey said. "And I'll help you as much as I can. Within a week or so, you'll get comfortable with the house, Molly, and the work routine."

"I hope so."

Danielle settled into the guest room and, for the first few days, rested and learned to hobble around the house on her crutches. Kelsey navigated her new role at the restaurant as well as with Danielle and Molly, but sensed God's strength nudging her along through what felt like a three-ring circus.

As soon as Danielle claimed she was ready to dive into training, Kelsey spent a few hours going over the required tasks and surveying her carefully. Fortunately, Danielle was a quick learner with anything technical. Molly enthusiastically took on her new jobs, like heating meals Kelsey had prepared in advance.

Instead of only bussing tables and washing dishes, Rick kept a watchful eye out, ready to step in if Kelsey needed a hand. He arranged for the purchase of the software that would eventually make everything at The Grateful Fork run more smoothly. Best of all, he often sent smiles across the room, linking them together throughout their shifts, despite a non-stop schedule.

Day by day Kelsey was getting it, feeling more at ease, though she wouldn't claim confidence too soon. She followed Aggie's blue notebook to the letter. Once the software and accompanying hardware were installed and everyone including her was trained, some of the load would lighten and she might get some of her free time back.

ଓ ଓ ଓ

Rick glanced at his phone, surveying the time. He still had a few minutes to decompress before entering Brenner Falls Community Church for the youth group meeting, so he stayed in his car, as was his habit, and watched the sky mellow to blues and pinks through the front windshield.

Monday night, after helping Kelsey with Danielle, he'd driven to the basketball court at the local high school to meet a few of the youth group guys for a game. He'd enjoyed the exertion and camaraderie, but learned it was an effective catalyst for going deeper with some of them. Chris had been there, and though he warmed up gradually to Rick, they didn't talk about anything personal. Would Chris open up about a drug problem? Not likely. Not yet. But Rick would keep reaching out, trying to build trust and friendship.

In the previous three days, Rick watched Kelsey blossom as she studied all the aspects of managing The Fork, surveying every category, encouraging the staff, and even coming up with new ideas for menu items or promotions. During her break, he asked how things were going overall with her new life situation.

"It's only been a few days," she'd said. "But so far, things are going like I hoped. Danielle seems up to speed and Molly's gained confidence at helping."

Rick helped her as much as he could, learning the ropes of managing a restaurant alongside Kelsey. As he did, his respect for her grew. As well as his attraction. But where could it go? Maybe he should simply tell her how he felt, but that might destroy the rich friendship they'd built. His background was a fact he couldn't erase. New creation or not, it would be an issue for her, as it would any woman. She deserved better.

A ring filled the quiet car, and he flinched. Jesse was calling, so he must be running late. "Hey, Jesse," Rick answered. "I'm about to go inside the church. Is everything okay?"

"Hi, Rick." A woman's voice startled him. "This is Jesse's wife, Miranda. Jesse needs your help. He can't make it tonight, because we're at the hospital. He ate something that had peanuts in it without knowing, and he's allergic to peanuts. His face is swollen, and he can't talk."

"Oh, I'm sorry to hear that. Will he be okay?"

"Yes, he'll be fine. They've given him some epinephrine, and he's doing better already. He needs you to lead the group tonight, you know, pull together the game and do the devotional. He said he's sorry you won't have time to prepare, but hopefully you can think of something simple to do."

"Sure, I'll think of something. Tell him we'll pray for him to get better fast."

"Thanks so much, Rick."

When he disconnected, his heart pounded in his chest like a timpani drum. He rubbed his hands, slick with moisture, on his jeans. What would he do? The game was not a big deal. He'd been leading the games for a few weeks now. But the devotional? With no time to prepare anything? Should he cover what he'd been reading in his own quiet time? How could he pull something together so fast?

A thought came into his mind, along with physical pressure inside. He drew in a breath. "No, Lord. Please don't ask me to do that."

The pressure continued. Near the end of his time in Flagstaff, he'd shared his story, including some of the raw details of his experience. He linked it to the prodigal son story in the New Testament. God was telling him to share that. *Anything but that, Lord.*

It was time to go inside. The thing God was asking him to do weighed on him like a truckload of concrete. He knew he couldn't say no. The hiding game was over. No longer would he be the nice guy, an older role model. He'd be exposed and his past strewn across the church. So much for new beginnings.

Like a condemned man, he grabbed his Bible, went into the church, down the stairs into the gym. He swallowed the lump in his throat as he scanned the group. "Listen up, everyone," he called to the clusters of kids gathered. "Jesse had a medical problem and can't be here tonight. He's asked me to take his place. So, um, we'll start by introducing anyone who's new."

His terror probably leaked through his words and sent off a warning, though the kids' faces looked like they didn't notice. No new kids had come that night, so he recruited Rhonda, the other youth leader, and started the game. Instead of participating, he observed while his mind combed through vague memories of what he'd shared in Flagstaff. Couldn't he do something different instead? No. The gentle but persistent pressure wouldn't allow him to change course, to save face. He sighed. Might as well let God be responsible for the outcome, as ugly as it might be.

Once the game finished and the group had assembled in the seating area, his perspiration cranked up. During the songs, his mind darted like a trapped hummingbird as he tried to come up with a way to start. He felt the Holy Spirit saying, *I'll speak through you. Don't worry about what you'll say.* It did little to calm his thumping heart.

Finally, it was time to present the devotional talk. He rose from where he sat on the front row and walked to the stand where Jesse usually delivered his message. Rick pulled over a stool and sat, trying to appear calm. He opened his Bible and stared at eighteen pairs of eyes and blank faces.

"So, I heard less than an hour ago that I was supposed to lead the devotional tonight. Right away, God told me what to talk about and you know what?"

He had their attention. Everyone in the room went still.

"I *argued* with him. I said no, anything but *that*. God persisted. He wants me to share my story with you, so I will, in obedience to him." Rick took several breaths. Scanning the room again, he noticed alert faces, students leaning forward, ready to hear him expose his greatest sins. Yet, a tiny thread of energy surged inside, starting deep and spiraling upward. The thread grew wider and stronger, rising like a river about to flood its banks.

"First, I'm going to read you a story out of the New Testament," he said. "Many of you know the story. It's about the prodigal son."

He turned to the passage in the book of Luke and began reading. He finished the section and lifted his gaze to the group. "A prodigal is someone who has faith, but wanders away and gets into stupid stuff. That's my definition. In the story, we see a dad who waited for years for his son to come home. Day after day, he scanned the road for a guy with that familiar walk, his clothing, anything he recognized. Finally, the son returns, and the father runs like crazy to meet him. The kid was broken by his mistakes, so he went home, expecting to be demoted from a son to a servant. As you saw in the story, that's not what the father did.

My story isn't exactly like that. I'm not so much a prodigal as I am a *rescue*. I grew up here in town on Phillips Street. You may know where that is." He continued as the surge of peace continued inside him, spreading branches like a tree. He told of his mother's alcoholism, his father's death, and his departure for the great adventure in Arizona. When he got to the part about drugs, he scanned Chris's face which, like a mask, revealed nothing. None of the kids fidgeted or whispered to the person in the next chair. Every eye was riveted on Rick.

He described how Stephen and Annika had found him, brought him home, shared the truth with him, and helped him take the next steps in his life. "I share this with you tonight for one reason. So you'll understand the father-heart of God. I wasn't seeking him, though I needed him. He sought *me*, a druggie, dying under a bridge. Hopeless. Deserted by those I thought were my friends. But God came after me, just like the father in the story."

Rick paused. His throat ached, but his heart swelled with love for the Lord who'd saved him. "He gave me a new life. He waits for each of us to seek and find his father-heart. God's the perfect father, not like your fathers, even the good ones. Believe me, he can put together all the broken pieces of your life. He specializes in messed-up lives. I can tell you that from experience."

He stopped. The Holy Spirit said it was enough. The lump in Rick's throat had begun out of fear, but returned because of humility and awe.

After the meeting ended, a solemn wonder hovered over the group. Rick scanned the kids' faces. A couple of the girls were crying, and even some of the guys had glassy eyes they tried to disguise. No one looked disgusted. No one had walked out. He'd survived opening the darkest closet of his life.

A few teens clustered around Rick to ask questions or express support, though Chris hung on the edge of the group, looking aloof, then wandered to the snack table. Maybe everything Rick had invested in Chris up to then had just fallen apart, but that was God's responsibility.

Rhonda approached Rick shyly. "Thanks for sharing your story, Rick." A couple more kids gathered around him echoed her words. "I had no idea you'd been through all that, but...wow. God did amazing things in your life."

"Yeah, he did. God gets all the glory." That was why he went through the terrifying experience of sharing his soul with a group of teenagers. What he'd done with his life was stupid, wasteful. Foolish.

What God had done was nothing short of miraculous.

Chapter Eleven

"Do you have another hot date tonight, Mom?" Rick grinned at his mom across the kitchen table Friday morning as they finished their coffee. He knew it embarrassed her to talk about her relationship with Tim, but it was fun to tease her.

His mom shook her head, but a smile teased. "Stop it, will you? Hot is for teenagers. We're mature adults."

"Yeah, sure you are." He winked at her. "I bet you *feel* like a hot teenager, though, right?"

She laughed, and swatted his arm. "Yes, sometimes I do. Satisfied?"

"Very. You deserve it." He stood and kissed her cheek, then took his mug to the counter for a refill.

Rick loved the fact his mom was dating someone regularly. He'd met the guy, who already seemed smitten, and sometimes sat with them in church. She seemed radiant, appearing younger each day. It filled him with joy, but also lightened his guilt.

A few weeks back, Jesse asked him to attend youth church at least twice per month to build continuity with the kids. Rick didn't mind, except that he didn't get to see Kelsey across the sanctuary. He saw a lot of her at The Fork, but Sundays were different. On Sunday mornings, she was more fixed up and her fresh beauty glowed like a sunrise. She looked like a princess whenever they were out of their restaurant box and part of real life.

"Are you working both shifts today?" His mom rose from the table and took her mug to the sink.

"Yes, but I get a break between. I'll be able to do a couple of errands then. Need anything?"

"No, not today. Thanks anyway. You should take a rest or a nap during your break. You're working a lot."

He shrugged.

She frowned. "I guess I'll see you tomorrow, then."

"You will. Behave yourself in the meantime." He narrowed his eyes until she snickered.

After she left for work, Rick continued reading at the table for another few minutes, though his mind bounced around like a rubber ball. Still in a state of wonder, he tried to grapple with what God had done the previous evening at the youth group meeting. He'd never expected words with power beyond him to emerge from his lips, or the impact it had on the kids. Who knew that one messed-up person's story could have such an effect? He'd expected disgust, but received compassion. The main thing he learned was it hadn't been about him. God used Rick's failings to point people back to himself.

Maybe he should stop feeling so ashamed. He'd summarized the evening for his mom when he got home last night and was eager to tell Kelsey as well how God had turned Rick's dread and shame on its head. He chuckled.

His cellphone rang, and he closed his book. It was Jesse. "Hey, Jesse. I was going to call you. How are you feeling?"

"I felt a lot better as soon as I got the EpiPen." He sounded cheerful and chatty. Back to normal. "I usually avoid peanuts like the plague, but a neighbor brought us some brownies she'd made, and they had peanut butter on the bottom layer. I just dove into them without thinking."

"I'm glad you're doing better."

"Hey, thanks so much for filling in for me last night. I felt bad about the non-existent advance notice, but I hear it was amazing."

"You did?" Rick ran one hand over his unshaven jaw.

"Yeah. I spoke with Rhonda, and she said everyone was glued to your talk. I'm sorry I missed it."

"A good thing you did, to be honest. I shared my story, like the *whole* thing. I didn't want to do it, but the Lord told me to."

"I'm glad you shared that, Rick. Sounds like your story really touched the kids. That kind of dramatic change in a person can draw kids closer to the Lord."

"I hope it did. I didn't want to be a bad example for anyone."

"Quite the contrary, Rick. It was a stunning example of a changed life, from what I heard. And not just from Rhonda."

"I'm...I'm glad." Rick didn't know what else to say. "If God can get praise by me sharing my messes, I'm glad to do it."

"The content of your talk blew everyone away, but she said you presented it so well. Like, with power and conviction. No one was bored. I'd like you to start doing the devotional every other week, okay?"

Rick sat up. "Every other week? What should I talk about? That's the only thing I've ever spoken about publicly, and only once before. I have no other experience."

"Well, you're meeting with Pastor Frank, right?"

"Yeah, every couple of weeks."

"I'm sure he can give you some guidelines for preparing a talk. Start with an interesting opener, like a story or example. You can base a whole talk on just a few verses, or even one, then finish with some application."

That didn't sound too bad. "Sure, I'll try."

"You might even think about one day doing some courses online or in person at a Bible college."

"A Bible *college*? Such a thing exists?"

Jesse laughed. "Yeah, it does. Like regular college, but it prepares people to be pastors or for some other kind of ministry. They go deeper into Scripture and stuff like that. It would be perfect for you."

Rick wasn't sure about that. How could he afford it? He'd prefer to stay in Brenner Falls.

"So, would you be able to do the talk week after next?" Jesse asked. "Miranda and I are going on vacation that week, so I'd be happy if you could lead the group again."

Rick swallowed. "No worries. At least I have more notice this time."

"You'll do great."

They disconnected. Rick sat still, pondering what God was up to. He'd known Rick's sordid story would end up encouraging kids, when all the while, Rick had believed he'd be disqualified in their eyes. God's ways were strange. And now, he'd be leading another devotion on an entirely different topic, yet to be determined.

"Okay, God." He sighed. "You're the boss."

ↄ ↄ ↄ

Saturday morning, the house lay in a blanket of silence. Danielle and Molly had been up late watching a movie and would likely sleep in. Thankfully, Kelsey had a slice of quiet to herself, a rare event.

After reading her Bible with a cup of coffee in her favorite armchair near the back window, she rose to work on *Kelsey's Kitchen*. Recently, she'd posted two recipes from her collection of experiments to stay loosely consistent, though she hadn't perfected them. The previous day, she'd developed a new recipe for chicken, covered in a wild mushroom sauce. Maybe she'd ask Vince to try it in the restaurant as a special, though it was fancier than The Fork's typical fare. She'd never presented her own recipes at The Fork before. She could try it that evening on Danielle and Molly, but Rick's opinion counted most for her.

He rarely sent texts anymore, since they were no longer scaffolding Danielle's efforts, and they saw each other practically every day. She missed them, though. She could text him an invitation, though she'd see him during the lunch shift.

Hi Rick, would you be interested in tasting one of my new recipes Sunday evening? Danielle and Molly will be there, and all your opinions will be helpful."

She reread the message. Didn't sound pushy or flirty. It would sound to him like he'd be doing a service, which he would. Even if he wasn't attracted to her, she didn't know many men who'd turn down a good meal. Then next week, they'd go to a restaurant together.

Her phone buzzed. Rick. She couldn't suppress a grin. *I'd consider it a privilege, future Beard Award Winner. Should we all hold up numbers after the meal and give you a rating?*

Kelsey laughed. *Only if you want to. But you'd have to do it before dessert, since maybe you won't get any.*

HaHa. I can't imagine that you wouldn't get straight tens. Maybe you can invite Vince, and he'll be so impressed, he'll add it to the menu.

Kelsey leaned against the counter. His idea mirrored her own, so maybe that was confirmation enough to try.

Yes, I'd thought of that. Not of inviting him, since I prefer our small group. But I can ask him one day to try one of my recipes and see how it's received.

Atta girl. It'll be awesome. Correct that, only God is awesome. But you're pretty amazing.

She was? A grin spread across her cheeks. *It's true that God alone is awesome.* She wasn't sure about the rest.

He responded quickly. *I have something interesting to tell you, whenever we have time.*

That sounds intriguing. We'll have time tomorrow night, if not before.

Good enough. See you soon.

Interesting? What would he tell her? She'd find out soon enough. And he was coming to her house for dinner for the second time, which was all it took to put a grin back on her face.

Sunday evening, Kelsey peered into the oven. Chicken breasts coated with herb breadcrumbs browned nicely while the sauce simmered on the stovetop. She'd tinkered with the sauce that afternoon: melted butter and cream sauteed with wild mushrooms, a pinch of nutmeg and tarragon, and a hint of white wine. As for vegetables, she'd stay simple with garlic green beans and a slivered almond topping alongside mashed potatoes.

Dessert would be chocolate mousse pie, which she'd made that morning in lieu of attending church. She rarely skipped a service, but after working two shifts the day before and having to prepare the evening meal, her body and mind teetered on overload. At least she had the following day off as well, another rare event, though she'd likely spend at least part of it checking in on Danielle's progress with the job.

Kelsey decided to serve the meal in the dining room, since it was elegant, but little used these days. Molly had set the table and folded the napkins, her specialty. Kelsey didn't need Danielle's help with the meal, but thought it might encourage her to contribute. So, she trimmed fresh green beans on a tray in her lap from her place on the couch.

At five thirty, the doorbell rang, and Kelsey's pulse hitched. At least she'd already changed clothes, fluffed her hair, and put on a bit of makeup before Rick's arrival. She wouldn't overdo it. Not only did she prefer understated makeup, but she still didn't know if Rick saw her as anyone besides a good friend.

She opened the door with a welcoming smile. Rick wore a neat short-sleeved shirt. He bore no resemblance to someone who'd previously lived on the street. His wavy dark hair was neatly combed, but long enough to look slightly rakish.

"You look nice, Kelsey. I hope I'm not too early." He thrust a bottle into her hands. Sparkling white grape juice.

"Thanks, Rick. No, you're right on time. You didn't have to bring anything."

He shrugged. "I wanted to contribute something to this stellar event, but I don't drink anymore, so wasn't sure what to bring. My mom suggested this. It's similar to champagne, only without the champagne."

They laughed. "You're mom's a smart one. I saw her in church with a distinguished-looking man." She gestured him to follow her into the kitchen.

"That's her boyfriend, I guess I can say." He grinned. "Sounds weird to say that about my mother, but I'm happy for her. His name is Tim, and he's a retired dentist she met at a church conference a couple of months ago. She deserves it, after all she's been through."

"I'm happy for her too." Kelsey put the juice into the fridge. "She's so sweet. She *has* been through a lot. She lost your dad a long time ago…"

"She's been alone for a while. It's nice to see her blossoming, if I can put it that way." He hesitated. "Do you need any help with anything? You may have done it all, since you're so efficient. But I can set the table."

"I set it in the dining room. I decided to go sort of fancy tonight, since it's a special occasion." *He* made it a special occasion by standing a few feet away from her.

"You can tell me your interesting news after the meal. We'll have fewer distractions then."

He nodded. "Where are Danielle and Molly?"

"I think they're working a puzzle together in the living room."

His gaze met hers. "Molly can do puzzles?"

Kelsey nodded with a smile. "Simple ones. She and Danielle get along well, which is a blessing."

"Things are still going smoothly with Danielle and the job?"

"So far. I'm *so* thankful for that. I check Danielle's work every morning before I send it to my company. There are a few things I still need to do every day, but she's taken a big load off. Then Molly goes to an adult daycare in town every day." Yes, she had much to be thankful for during a complex transition.

After a final peek in the oven, she straightened and removed her apron. "All ready."

"Want me to call in the troops?"

"Yes, thanks."

Kelsey ferried each platter into the dining room. Danielle settled into her chair with Rick's help, and Molly sat next to Danielle.

"Smells fabulous, Kelsey." Danielle lifted her chin and took a deep breath. She grinned at Rick. "Imagine, I get to eat her food every day. I might never go home."

Rick laughed. "Sounds like a sweet deal. Not sure if it makes up for having a broken leg, though."

"It's only been a week, but it's healing well, the doctor told me. I can get myself to the table or the bathroom with the crutches, if I hop on my good foot. Those first few days, I was a complete invalid. Poor Kelsey and Molly waited on me hand and foot."

"And leg," Molly added, and everyone laughed.

"Molly's been a huge help through all this." Kelsey sent a loving glance to her sister. "She learned how to heat casseroles in the oven and microwave, she can make salads, she can take Danielle a drink if she needs one."

"Sounds like she's ready to work full-time at The Grateful Fork." Rick laid a hand on Molly's shoulder. She grinned back at him. He turned his attention to Danielle. "Will you have to do physical therapy once you're ready?"

"Yes, for at least a few weeks. I have to learn how to walk again."

"You should give Amber Dawson—I mean Amber Russo a call. She's my sister-in-law, and she's a PT."

"I know Amber," Danielle said. "Honestly, it didn't surprise me when she and Ben got together. They're perfect for each other."

Kelsey had told Amber the same thing two years earlier. She had a sense they belonged together, even before they'd officially met. Why didn't she have the same intuition for herself?

"Everything's amazing, Kelsey." Danielle's comment broke into her thoughts.

"I completely agree, but wish I'd said it first." Rick lifted his glass. "To Kelsey."

"Hear, hear. We should have real champagne," Danielle said. "This is tasty, but the real thing is too."

"I don't drink anymore, so I brought this." Rick spoke calmly, with no hint of uneasiness.

Danielle leaned forward on her elbows. "How long ago did you stop, if you don't mind me asking? I mean, I was curious about if it was hard or not."

Kelsey froze and watched Rick's face. "I haven't touched a drop in two years. I knew I couldn't handle it, so I stopped altogether. I didn't want to wreck the rest of my life like I'd done the first part."

"Good for you. I heard it can mess up your liver big time too."

"It definitely can. I was headed in that direction. Later, I learned the liver can regenerate. It's one of the only organs that does."

"Kind of like our lives when God gets ahold of us," Kelsey said. Rick was a prime example of that.

He lifted his glass. "Absolutely. Here's to the Healer."

"That's amazing, Rick." Danielle lowered her glass. "Okay, change of topic, I promise. The juice is good, by the way. I'll have to put that on my grocery list, once I'm buying my own groceries again."

Kelsey and Rick exchanged an amused glance. Her respect for him flourished with the way he handled Danielle's blunt question. The rest of the meal and conversation passed smoothly, with a volley of compliments for every course.

"So, do you think I should give this recipe to Vince for The Fork?"

"Yes!" A chorus came from Danielle and Rick.

"Okay, I will." She panned a smiling gaze around the table. "I'll let you know how it goes."

Following the meal, Danielle hobbled back to the couch and Kelsey shooed Molly back to her activities. "I'll bring your dessert soon," she told them. She turned to Rick. "I'll just stick these dishes in the sink and do them later."

Rick rose. "Or I can help you and they won't be waiting for you when you get up tomorrow."

Kelsey sent him a fake frown of disapproval. "I rarely let my guests do any dishes."

But he'd already begun stacking the plates along one arm, a deep chuckle rising from his throat.

He rinsed dishes and loaded the dishwasher while Kelsey put the food away. Working alongside him in a non-work setting triggered flutters of contentment. When they finished, she crossed her arms. "Either you're a professional, or you're eager to eat dessert. That was quick."

He took a little bow. "I'm sure you know it's both. And I had a lovely assistant."

She smiled, though it hadn't escaped her notice that he'd called her lovely and amazing. And when he came to the door that evening, he'd told her she looked nice. Was it courtesy or did it go further? He might be sending a message, too shy to make it bolder. A girl could hope.

Kelsey took the chocolate mousse pie from the fridge and placed it on the granite island. She slid two pieces onto plates, and Rick dispatched them to the living room, where Danielle and Molly watched TV. By the time he returned, she'd cut two more slices for them. "We can stay here in the kitchen."

Once they settled at the kitchen table, they began eating their pie.

"Mmmm..." Rick rolled his eyes theatrically and licked his lips. "Amazing. You might want to add this to your recipes for Vince."

"I didn't invent this one. But I adapted it. I added orange liqueur to the chocolate. And chocolate shavings."

"Adapting something makes it yours. How do you think people invent recipes? They adapt."

Kelsey laughed. "I should know that. I do it almost every day."

"Well, there you go."

After a few seconds of silence and Rick's visible enjoyment of her pie, he pushed the plate away. "I guess you're wondering about the news I wanted to share with you."

"Yes, I was curious." Kelsey licked her fork and pushed her plate next to his. She didn't expect him to admit any attraction to her, because he'd called the news *interesting*.

"Thursday night, I was about to go into the youth meeting, and I got a call from Jesse. He'd had an allergic reaction and was at the hospital, so he asked me to take over the meeting, including the little sermon he does after games. I'd already prepared the game. But God compelled me to share my story that night."

"Oh, wow." Kelsey leaned forward on her elbows, bringing her closer to him.

"Believe me, I didn't want to do it. I thought it would ruin my credibility with the kids. He kept urging me to do it, and you don't argue with God."

Kelsey smiled. "It's not usually a good idea."

"So, I was nervous, but I told the whole story. The kids were real quiet. It seemed like it had a big impact on them."

"I'm sure it did. That was brave of you."

"Not at all. I was anything but brave. God literally forced me to do it. Nicely of course." They laughed. "Then Jesse called me the next day. He said the other youth leader who was there had called it *amazing*. Her word. Jesse wants me to do the teaching twice a month from now on." He sighed. "Kelsey, I don't know beans about preaching to kids. But I had this funny feeling God was speaking through me that night. I hope he'll do that every time, because I sure can't do it myself."

"That's the whole point. He'll help you, though what you experience each time might vary. Sometimes in his obvious power, other times just a peaceful assurance. That's up to him."

"That's what I told him when I thought I was going to expose all my sins to the kids of the church. It's up to him. He's responsible for the outcome, if he's asking me to do it."

"Yes, he is. And maybe he brought you back to Brenner Falls for those kids."

He stared at her. "Funny you should say that. There's one kid, Chris. He's a new kid from outside the church. He's out of school, working. One evening, I detected possible signs of drug use. I wanted him to open up to me, but he never did. Then, he heard my testimony. I don't know if it impacted him."

"You can't ask him, of course."

"No, I can't. But now he knows about my past. And he might not be looking for help or understanding right now."

"I guess, just be available?" She shrugged. "Like you said, it's up to God." Her voice emerged in a whisper.

As she faced him and his dark chocolate brown eyes stared back at her, a wave of tenderness and affection for him gripped her heart, her whole body. His pursuit of God was so pure, so wholehearted. She reached out and squeezed his hand. Then, compelled beyond reason, she leaned toward him and pressed a gentle kiss on his lips. A thrill went through her at the contact until she realized something.

He hadn't responded.

She pulled back, a hot flush of embarrassment creeping up her neck into her cheeks. She'd misread him and had acted on her surge of emotion. "I...I'm sorry, I just felt so close to you..." She leaned back against her chair to get distance.

"Kelsey—"

She held up a hand, her palm facing him "Rick, I like you, but I understand if you don't feel the same way." Her words came out in a rush, matching her heartbeat. Oh, how could she have been so impulsive? She'd ruined everything. "If you only feel friendship for me, I still *treasure* that friendship. If that's all you can offer, that's okay. I don't want you to feel any pressure from me. Just forget this happened."

"Kelsey, it's not that." His voice lowered, laden with sudden intensity. He moistened his lips. "I *do* feel more than friendship for you, and I have for some time. I think you're full of life, smart, funny, beautiful, so many things. I just..." He threw his hands out in a helpless gesture. "You deserve someone great. I'm only now getting my life on track."

She blinked. "You feel the same? You feel more than friendship for me?" Then, why wasn't this the glorious moment she'd dreamed about? "Rick, I happen to think *you're* pretty great."

"Believe me, I'm not great." He lowered his gaze from hers. "I can't be the man you want, as much as I'd like to be."

"What makes you think you're *not* the man I want?" He was everything she wanted. "I care for you." Maybe a lot, though it clearly wasn't the moment to say so. Not with her heart hanging on a precipice.

Amidst the whirling confusion and anguish, a chill of realization rippled inside her, though a hot bolt of frustration lay at its core. "Is it because of your past? The past that God *freed* you from?" She stood, sliding back the chair with a harsh scrape that matched the tension in the room. She paced in front of the table then faced him, arms crossed. "You know your problem? God saved you and made you brand new, but you think you're still sitting on the back porch of heaven on some kind of probation. Forgiven, but not fully a son."

Mild-mannered Kelsey on a rampage, but she couldn't stop, not when her heart and thoughts had been filled with Rick Russo for months, and he felt something for her too. Or so he said.

She lowered her voice, but a thread of steel remained. "You wear your past like a dirty coat. One that was exchanged for a prince's robe two years ago. You don't like the dirty coat, but it's helpful as a shield for whatever scares you, like stepping up in a relationship. You were scared of sharing your story with those youth group kids, but God forced you to do it, and he used it for his glory."

Kelsey set one hand on the table and stared at him. Her shoulders drooped and her fire drained away. "Rick, God has a purpose for you, but you'll never find it if you don't step into your new identity, whether or not that includes a relationship with me or someone else." She held his gaze a moment longer, then turned to gather the dessert dishes.

"You're right, Kelsey," Rick murmured to her back, but said nothing more.

That was the end of the story, a very short story of her heart connection with Rick Russo. Why should she be surprised?

Kelsey rinsed the dessert dishes, staring intently at them as if that could block out what had just happened. Her eyes stung. "Maybe you should go get some rest." She didn't look at him. "You've been working a lot lately. Thanks for coming."

She felt his presence behind her then his hand on her shoulder. She stilled, but didn't turn. "You've given me a lot to think about, Kelsey," he murmured. "Things I know deep inside, but have to let go of. Don't..." She heard him sigh. "...don't give up on me."

Kelsey turned to face him. He stood inches from her, but neither one moved closer. "Never. Because I *believe* in you. You're much more than you think you are. You're not the sum total of your past. The past is over. You're the only one who doesn't know it." She paused. "Goodnight, Rick." She turned back to the sink.

When she felt his warmth leave the room, hot tears of frustration and loss rolled down her cheeks.

Chapter Twelve

Rick sat motionless in his car in front of his mom's one-story Cape Cod brick home as night bruised the sky. He couldn't bear to go inside, couldn't brace himself to hear his mom's eager questions about his evening with Kelsey. He hadn't told his mom about his romantic feelings toward Kelsey, but one day, she'd guessed. Women, his mother included, were attuned to that kind of thing more than he realized. It might have happened the day she came to The Fork with Tim and observed her son following Kelsey's every movement with love-struck eyes.

That story crashed in an unexpected way, and it was his fault. He could have had the woman of his dreams. Might have a date with her, instead of tears on his cheeks. He could have pulled her into his arms and savored the kiss he'd dreamed about, instead of rejecting hers. He could have been the prince she deserved. According to her, and the Bible, he already *was* that prince. Why didn't he feel like one? Why had he let Kelsey slip through his grasp when she'd invited him into hers?

"Lord, what's wrong with me?" His miserable voice rang out in the empty car. "Why do I still feel like that hobo under the bridge?"

He pulled himself out of the car and headed to the house, an evening breeze flicking across his arms. His mom had left the porch light on, but with a wave of gratitude, he saw she'd gone to bed early. She'd grill him the next day, but he'd find a way to evade her until he had more clarity in his own mind.

Rick locked the door behind him and turned off the living room light. His old room welcomed him along with his sorrow as he collapsed on the bed, fully clothed.

He stared at the ceiling, rewinding the evening that, because of him, went off the rails. Of course, Kelsey had spoken the truth in a passionate way that said she'd missed her calling as an activist. Funny how that feisty spirit emerged in moments of truth and passion.

Despite his pain, a bitter smile stretched his lips. She'd been so beautiful during her tirade, with her blue eyes flashing and a bloom of color on her smooth cheeks. How he'd wanted to gather her to his chest and say they should try anyway. The ache inside throbbed through his entire torso. Did he have any hope of fulfilling what they both longed for? He knew what held him back, but he couldn't make it disappear. Not yet.

He'd said his piece, the only one he had. In a nutshell, he couldn't be the man she wanted. What else could he say? She'd wanted him to say God *made* him able to be *everything*...the godly boyfriend, the amazing youth leader. His head told him it was possible according to Scripture. He was a new man. But daily life was another matter, despite how much he longed for it to be different. Despite what he'd already seen God do.

Rick prepared for bed, unable to silence the echoes of Kelsey's words in his head. They were affirming words that should have given him a green light for the dreams of Kelsey he'd held almost since his return to Brenner Falls. He hoped sleep would silence her voice and the memory of her face, but sleep eluded him for several hours. When he did finally sleep, his dreams drew him back to Arizona, to the bridge that was home for a while, and all the wasted years. Faces from the past—*his buddies* who'd left him to die—flared like gruesome phantoms through his sleep, flashbacks invading his unconscious state.

The following day, Rick was off, and he spent it miserable, exhausted, and alone, as he tried to figure himself out. He went to the forest, his usual place of solace, but emerged carrying the same burden. "Why, Lord, can't I embrace my new identity, the one you gave me?" he'd cried out several times beneath the shadow of a towering canopy of pines. But the forest kept its secrets and revealed nothing. It wasn't just for Kelsey's sake he wanted to fully embrace the truth. He didn't want to miss anything God had for him, but he felt the road before him was so long, due to the depths he'd escaped.

His mind went back to his last evening with the youth and the unveiling of all his past mistakes. He'd gone into the church building resigned to his fate, fearful of the consequences, but willing to obey. He hadn't felt ready or even willing, but God used it beyond what he could ever have imagined. It had been *God*, not Rick, at the helm that night. Why then did Rick crumble at this new and *very* desirable challenge before him, embracing Kelsey's declaration of her feelings? That alone humbled and thrilled him at the same time, despite his botched response.

She liked him. She *believed* in him. Why couldn't he grasp this treasure with joy and gratitude and never let it go?

ଔ ଔ ଔ

Voices and clatter from the kitchen scraped Kelsey's nerves. She'd always liked the sound of kitchen activity, voices volleying back and forth. *Table eight ready to be plated! Sides ready for table four!* Not that day. Her head pounded, but she kept her focus glued to her tasks and her mind away from her shredded emotions.

After a week managing The Grateful Fork, many pieces had come together for her and flowed like a steady current. She'd still make mistakes and have much to learn, especially once the software was installed. But she was in her place...physically, at any rate. God had given her that second chance, and she would take the challenge with all she had. But that was work. Beneath her outward competence, waves of regret and frustration frothed, alongside the question, *why, Lord?*

She'd waited years to feel a heart connection with a man with whom she had easy communication and a like faith. And this time, the attraction was mutual. Might even be the first time in her *life* that had happened. Why had it burst into flames? Was Rick too emotionally damaged to sustain a healthy relationship? Or was he not the one for her and she'd avoided more heartache before things went too far?

Sure didn't feel that way.

Amidst a cloud of confusion, Kelsey determined to do her best work at the restaurant, to keep learning, and to avoid Rick Russo. Hard to do, since they passed each other in the dining room or kitchen every five minutes. Naturally, they wouldn't be trying out the new restaurant in town they'd talked about. She'd visit one day with Sophie.

"Can you check the canisters and syrups before the lunch crowd comes?" She asked Rick, who stood behind the counter. He'd probably remembered by himself, but as manager, she had to make sure. She kept her face a mask of indifference, though he probably noted the pain in her eyes. No matter. The apparent longing and regret clearly stamped on his face gave her no satisfaction.

"I just did. They're...they're filled."

She nodded. Of course, he did. Rick was so efficient she hardly had to address him at all. Good news.

Kelsey responded with a curt nod and returned to the kitchen. How would she keep this up for an undetermined length of time? It had been three days since the debacle at her house. Instead of getting easier, it was harder each day. She'd have to find some way to cope...and to let go of her hopes. It would have been so much easier if Rick had told her he saw her only as a friend. If only.

Let go. The words drifted into her mind and as they did, her shoulders released a notch or two of tension. *Yes, Lord, I need to do it.* She'd surrender Rick Russo to whatever God wanted, to whatever process Rick had to undergo. She had her own neglected process to address.

Thankfully, she had the evening off. Once she double-checked everything for the evening shift, she said goodbye to the kitchen staff and headed home. Blessed haven, even though she'd still have to be conscious of Danielle and Molly. She recruited Molly to help with a simple taco dinner. The light banter and fellowship around the table soothed and uplifted Kelsey's mood. Yes, letting go felt good. Mostly.

"I think I'm up to speed on the work." Danielle reached for the bowl of salsa. "It's even a little boring already."

Kelsey grinned. "I knew you'd be quick to catch on. And you're right, it *is* boring. I'm glad you're bored because it probably means you're doing everything right."

They laughed.

"I wish I could do the dishes for you." Danielle gave her a rueful smile.

"No worries. Molly and I can get it done in five minutes. You're already helpful by doing my boring job." She'd started using paper plates and whatever else she could to save time.

"I'm going to spend some alone time on the back patio, okay?" Kelsey stood and slid bowls of taco fixings into the fridge. "So, if you don't see me around, don't call the cops. I haven't been kidnapped by aliens."

Molly let out a burst of laughter, which flushed joy and hope through Kelsey's bruised heart.

Kelsey slipped to the back porch and settled into one of the lawn chairs with her journal, a pen, and a cold drink. Blocking out the memory of being there with Rick two weeks earlier, the day he'd told her his story, she focused on the scene before her. Pine branches towered overhead, their needles etching the pastel sky. She'd always loved gazing at treetops, whether covered with needles or leaves, or barren with winter chill. The sight always whisked her beyond her present life, regardless of what she was experiencing. It reminded her that there was more to her own life and more *than* her own life, more possibilities, more realities. The expanse of sky also reminded her of God's sovereignty and creative artistry. Comfort, no matter the circumstances. Though sometimes hard to grasp, it was there when she slowed down enough to see.

With that singular goal, she gazed, breathed deeply, her eyes tracing the lines between greenery and sky, breathing in the mild summer air. She drew her mind back to the words *Let* Go which had dangled into her thoughts earlier. That didn't only apply to Rick. She wasn't responsible for the world. Her tendency was to be over-conscientious, mindful of everyone but herself. She'd lived her life that way for as long as she remembered. She liked being helpful, as she'd always tried to be with Molly. The neglected piece was *balance.*

What had Rick said that day? Live her *own* life. As much as she didn't want to think of Rick, his words had rung a clanging bell in her soul.

Live her own life. Her own destiny.

What was her dream? "Time to take stock, Lord," she said aloud. "Time to listen too."

What had he put into her heart? Food, of course. But deeper than that, hospitality. *People.* Bringing them together to enjoy, laugh, and fellowship together.

But what should she do with that passion? She was managing The Grateful Fork, so that was something, even though it was temporary. He'd given her a golden chance. What should she learn from it? Experimenting with food and posting on her blog were steps in the direction of her passion as well, but did she have a clear objective?

Truth was, she felt scattered to the four winds. Divided into too many pieces. With Molly and Danielle in her charge, plus the household and The Fork, did she even have a choice?

Or was helping Molly and being useful to her family and to Aggie an excuse for not pursuing her *own* passion in single-minded zeal? Was she simply afraid? Did her helpfulness serve partly as a handy excuse, all the while making her look benevolent and selfless? Were her choices partly driven by fear? Fear of failure, or fear of success?

Kelsey let out a long sigh. She was thirty-one years old, and her professional life had zig-zagged between online work and food service ever since she finished college. Where was she headed? Could she use food and a restaurant to express her passion, earn a living, *and* somehow help people? How?

At that moment, the answers were hazy. But she'd strengthen her grip on her goals, not allocating them to spare moments. And be ready for God to lead her and open each door.

The following day, Kelsey spent the morning in the kitchen. She leafed through her recipes, identifying what she'd added over the last two years. Surprisingly, she had almost eighty recipes in various categories. She hadn't counted them recently, but added one at a time if she approved of the outcome. How many would she need for a cookbook? She had almost enough, plus photos. Might be time to research publishing options.

That morning, she tried two more and tested them on Danielle and Molly. Two more for the cookbook, one of which would also be a blogpost later that evening.

Though Kelsey's world appeared the same, peace had settled in, pushing away some of her pain. She could even see Rick across the room and smile at him, gratified by a relieved smile in return. Something had shifted in her. She'd let go of what she couldn't control, which was most everything, and it felt better. She'd also give more thought to her goals and what she really wanted. Her *own* life. She'd trade her fear for bold surrender.

Kelsey's focus at The Fork seemed clearer too. Often, she quickly perceived what was missing, what needed to be done, and how things could be improved. She visited each table to greet customers and ask how their experience was, but no longer forced herself to appear peaceful and genuine. It simply flowed.

Day by day, it would get easier to be around Rick. One day, they could be friends, like they were before, without the baggage of hopes and dreams. She'd develop new dreams by tightening the focus on her own life, so she could *live* it.

Chapter Thirteen

"Pass! I'm open!"

Rick tossed the basketball to Shorty, one of the new guys in their ragtag pickup basketball group, and the guy launched it perfectly into the basket. Of course, he would. He was six-foot-three. Rick's speed and Shorty's height made them a great pair on a team, leading to numerous wins.

"Game." The word came out as a long sigh from Chris, though a grin accompanied his admission of defeat.

Some of the guys peeled away shouting, "Gotta run", while others crowded the bench for their water bottles, drinking greedily until the liquid splashed down their T-shirts.

No sooner had they vacated the court than a group of teen girls surged in. They started their game without delay. The guys halted their after-game refreshment and watched.

"Woo, look at the blond," murmured Jason. "She's a great player, but cute too. Mmm." He watched for a moment.

"I'm swearing off the female persuasion," stated Shorty with an emphatic nod. "At least for this month." This brought a chorus of laughter.

"Yeah, if one of those gals asked you to join their game, you'd make an exception, is my guess." Brian grinned at Shorty. "I'd give you maybe three minutes to change your mind."

They tired of watching the girls and ambled toward the gate.

"What about you, Rick? You got a girl?"

Shorty's question thrust a dagger in his gut. Yeah, he'd been dealing with it, wrestling all week. "Not at the moment."

"But you *do* have your eye on someone, I'm betting." Jason followed his statement with a chortle of certainty.

Was Rick that transparent? "Uh, yes, actually. But it's not time." Was that response sufficiently vague *and* truthful?

"Ha! I knew it. Not time? Go for it, man. She's not interested and you're trying to woo her, or somethin'?"

Not quite. A bit the other way around, but not that either. "It's complicated."

"Huh." Apparently, Shorty hadn't liked or understood the answer.

Truth was, Rick didn't either.

Throughout a week of torment, he'd suffered numerous flashbacks to the Arizona days, followed immediately by voices telling him he was in no way adequate for anything he was trying to do in his new life, whether with youth or with Kelsey. Was his renewal lacking something?

He'd hinted to Pastor Frank that he was having flashbacks, and the pastor spoke about something called *spiritual battle*. No idea what that was about, though the pastor had given him some verses to read, saying something ominous like there being forces that didn't want him to trust God's promises.

Maybe it was the old nature tugging at him, not that he was tempted at all to return to his old life. He had to figure out a way to step into what everyone said was true.

He should have known Frank's answer would be the same as Kelsey's. Same as Ben's a few weeks back. He was a new creation. The past was gone. As Kelsey had said, he was the only one who didn't know it. And often, he didn't feel it or act on it.

Kelsey. A couple days ago, her demeanor was lighter, less miserable than it had been. It wasn't resigned, but definitely more peaceful. He didn't know how to interpret that. He was afraid she'd simply given up on him in the romantic realm and now felt peace, as if she'd dodged a bullet. Or maybe she was trusting God more, as he should be doing. As he told the kids at church to do. He wasn't following his own words, nor was he a fitting example of anything.

"See you Thursday, guys." Chris was the one who called out.

"What's Thursday?" asked Shorty.

"Youth group," Chris said. "It's not as lame as it sounds, trust me. We meet at the church gym at seven. We play ball, then we hear a little talk about how God helps us out in life. Then we eat. *And there are girls there. Plenty of them.*"

"God?" Jason's brows lifted. "Not sure I'm up for *that*. Snacks and girls, maybe."

"You oughtta come. Check it out."

"Maybe." Shorty and Jason exchanged an undecided glance.

As they returned to their cars, Rick gave Chris a fist-bump. "Great job inviting the guys, Chris." Though it should have been him. Some youth leader *he* was.

Chris shrugged. "I like the group, so maybe they will too. I thought it might be better coming from me, since I'm not a leader..."

Right. Chris had a point. Rick grinned at him. "I'm happy you did that. So, see you next week. I gotta work tonight." The next day was Sunday, so he'd have time to read the verses Pastor Frank had given him.

Evening shift was non-stop. Kelsey wasn't on duty, but he hardly even noticed as he tried to keep from drowning. The band was good, the people numerous. At the end, he drove home, exhausted. And troubled.

He parked in front of his mom's house and cut the engine. He closed his eyes and let the long day roll off him. Basketball followed by an intense shift. During both taxing activities, his mind rolled something around and around. He was still boomeranging back and forth between his old life and his new one. Not because he wanted to, but because each time a new challenge came up—challenging because it was for godly people, not for him—he felt thrown back to his old credentials. Scraping by. Hadn't he seen God work despite his young faith age? Despite the fact that he wasn't *there* yet?

Yes, he had. The youth ministry was proof. Kelsey was another. He let out a deep sigh. "Lord, help me step fully into the new shoes. You're blessing me and I'm not feeling worthy. You never said I was worthy in myself, but you called me to receive this new life. I have trouble with that sometimes."

The front door opened, and his mother's silhouette filled the space, lamplight shining behind her. "Rick, are you okay?" she called.

It was time for that conversation, the one he'd managed to avoid for a week, though maybe it would give him perspective. His mother could rub another kind of balm on his wound, like she'd done when he skinned his knee as a kid, before alcoholism poisoned their lives.

He pulled himself out of the car with a groan. "I'm okay. Just made some mistakes lately."

When he went inside, he saw alarm on her face. "Not *that* kind of mistake, Mom. I'm done with those forever." He laid a hand on her shoulder. "A romantic mistake." He sunk into the couch cushion and she sat opposite him, clothed in her summer bathrobe. "Since you're back in the game now, you can give me your insight."

He summarized his dinner with Kelsey a week before and what he'd said to her. "I don't feel worthy of a girl like Kelsey. I didn't feel I could be what she needs. She sees me as the man I *want* to be." As he spoke, he saw his mother's mouth tighten, and he realized how ridiculous he sounded even to his own ears.

He could guess what his mother would say.

"I agree with Kelsey, Rick." Compassion beamed from her gaze. "She sees in you what I see in you. And Ben, and the kids at church. When you came back from Arizona, you were already a different person. And you've continued to follow the Lord and be transformed day by day. I see it more than you probably can. Having occasional doubts is normal, but it means you have to go back to truth each time. Reread what God says and follow *that*, not your feelings."

Rick opened his mouth to agree in theory and add more lame excuses, but she held up her hand. "I'm not quite finished. One of the things I prayed while you were gone is your future spouse. I don't know if Kelsey's the one or not, but I do believe God will answer that prayer, just like he answered my prayer to bring you back and help you receive his love. But you need to be open to his blessings too and believe it's part of God's plan for you to be happy. You *can* love someone. Stop doing penance for your past." She paused and waited.

He stared at his hands clasped on his knees. "Penance," he murmured. Was that what he was doing?

"If you're waiting to become Jesus incarnate yourself, that'll be a long wait."

They shared a smile. "Being *like* him is the idea," he said. "You're getting through to me, Mom. You women are so smart. Kelsey said I wore my past like a dirty coat."

His mom chuckled. "Very clever. And true."

The women were ganging up on him. Rick fought a smile. "She also said I use it to protect me from anything I'm afraid of." A handy excuse.

"I like this girl. She's perfect for you."

He raised his brows. "Because she told me off?"

"Yes. You need that once in a while." His mother grinned. "What she said about your fear is sometimes true. But I'm proud of you too. You went to the youth meetings, and I know you felt unworthy. You told me that. But you've gotten your rhythm with the kids and now you're changing lives with your preaching."

Rick straightened. "Where'd you hear that?"

She gave him a coy smile, like one with an inside scoop. "Apparently Jesse spoke to Frank, who spoke to Tim. God's going to use you, Rick. If you let him."

His heart and voice grew quiet. "I'd like to let him."

"And having a relationship with Kelsey isn't incompatible with that, in my view. On the contrary. She'll be good for you because she has the same heart."

He considered his mom's words. Warmth stirred deep inside him at the thought of God fully removing his shame and giving him a new mantle to serve him, one of his divine choosing. Another flicker inside related to Kelsey. She believed in him, she'd said. From the beginning, she'd encouraged him. And if that weren't enough, she'd wanted to kiss him as much as he'd wanted to kiss her.

"Thanks, Mom." He rose from the couch. He still had a lot to think about. "God is using you and Kelsey to remind me what he's already done."

"I'll turn in now, but I'm available to talk anytime you want." His mother stood and tightened her bathrobe.

"I'll head out to the back porch for a few minutes. I'm off tomorrow and Monday. Two days, a miracle in itself."

She grinned. "I'm glad to hear it. Maybe I'll see more of you."

"Goodnight, Mom."

He enfolded her in a hug, then she disappeared down the hall.

Rick stumbled to the back door and sat on a lawn chair. The nearly full moon lit up the yard, almost like daytime. Kind of like his heart, basking in new revelation. Or rather, one newly received. "Thanks, Lord," he murmured. "I think you're getting through my thick head. It isn't totally won, but I'm taking a few steps. Help me see myself as the new man instead of the old man in borrowed clothing."

His mind spooled through Kelsey's words. She said he'd never find his purpose if he didn't step into his new identity. His *destiny*.

Finding it was tied to depending on God, not on himself or his record. Missing it was a chilling thought, after all God had done and might want to do in his life. Who was he to argue with God? If he wanted to give Rick a youth ministry and a romance with Kelsey, why should he argue with *that*? He laughed aloud at the thought. "I'm such a bonehead, Lord."

Another thing Kelsey had said. She'd never give up on him because she *believed* in him. He'd spent twelve years with no one believing anything good about him, including himself. Her words took his breath away, humbling him to the core. Knowing everything she knew about him, she still believed in him. God knew infinitely more about him and entrusted him with hearing his voice, with this new relationship, with the future he'd lovingly planned.

It was time that, with God, he started believing in himself.

Before slipping under the sheets that night, Rick spread out his hands and offered everything to God on his altar...his life, Kelsey, any future ministry or job he'd do, everything.

He got into bed and took his phone reverently in one hand. *Kelsey, thank you for your words last week and your patience with me. If it's okay with you, I'd like to see you tomorrow. I'll be at youth church, but could we meet afterward around 1:30 at the River Park shelter? Or anytime you're free? Just let me know.*

She'd probably gone to bed by now, but she'd see his text message the next day when she got up. Five minutes later, his phone buzzed, and he snatched it off the bedside table.

Hi Rick. Yes, I'll meet you at one thirty tomorrow. Sleep well.

Brief and crisp. What could he expect? But she'd said yes, she'd be there. He rolled over and, with a smile, slipped into a peaceful sleep.

The following day after church, Rick waited at the shelter on the edge of River Park. Sparks of sunlight popped like miniature fireworks off the surface of the Susquehanna. It was a sight he'd always loved, until he left town. He hadn't realized how much he missed the river, a point of reference and leisure for all of Brenner Falls. A source of good memories too faded to grasp with clarity.

Along with a gentle late summer breeze, the sight and music of the flowing river brought a surge of peace through his body. He'd arrived early, since that was his new favorite habit. He breathed deeply, yet the anticipation of Kelsey's arrival fluttered inside like an impatient bird. Impatient to see her face.

The parking lot gradually filled with Sunday picnickers. A car approached and parked on the edge of the lot. She walked toward him like a longed-for mirage, her shoulder-length auburn hair blowing in the soft breeze. She wore a print skirt that swirled around her sandaled feet and a pale sleeveless top to match. He walked across the lawn and met her halfway. They stood for an instant, not speaking. He touched a swirl of hair on her shoulder. "Thanks for coming, Kelsey. I'm sorry about last week. Want to walk?"

The weekend crowd thickened around them, families streaming to the grassy areas with folding chairs, coolers, and little kids in tow. Muted voices floated through the air contrasting with the silence hanging between Rick and Kelsey as they walked.

Rick wanted privacy. Near the shelter was a small path he remembered with a few boulders near the bank.

"It was a good service today." Kelsey kept her gaze forward as they followed the path. A random comment, but she must be feeling awkward with the silence and lack of closure from the previous week.

He saw the boulder and a bench beside it. They sat on the bench and after a quiet moment, he turned to her and took her hands, smooth and warm, in his. He linked his gaze with hers, absorbing the intensity of blue he saw there, along with apprehension.

"Kelsey, thank you for your words last week. People have been telling me—Ben, Frank, my mom, and now you—that I'm a new creation with a new identity. God had his bullhorn blaring at me from all directions, and I still didn't think it applied to me. I just felt lucky to slip into God's family, like some kind of street urchin he'd had pity on."

He grinned but Kelsey was already shaking her head, a derisive scowl scrunching her face. "*Lucky*? How about *chosen from the foundation of the earth*? Ever read that somewhere?" Her voice held no harshness, just pleading.

Rick squeezed her hands and grinned. "Yes. In Ephesians. It's easy for me to believe lies, since I had a lot of practice. But the truth is *so* much better. Infinitely better. God's been showing me I have a responsibility, along with the privilege, to step into my new identity, wherever that leads me, even if I don't feel worthy, because *he* made me worthy. My feelings have led me astray on many occasions." He paused. "Except for one." He released one of her hands to trail his fingertips down her velvet soft cheek.

She reached up to cover his hand with hers. The desire to kiss her assailed him, but he held back. For now.

"Kelsey, the moment I first saw you, my heart was yours. That day at The Fork, when I was filling out an application. Remember? You might not—"

"Yes, I do." Her voice emerged silky soft. "I noticed you. Then, after I got to know you, I didn't think you were attracted to me." She shrugged. "I'm not beautiful or—"

"Oh my gosh, Kelsey!" He threw his head back. "You are *so* beautiful. Inside and out. I was so attracted to you, but I was the dishwasher. The busboy. I'd had a past I didn't want to talk about. I had the usual Rick thoughts, like, you were out of my league, if you only knew my story, you'd run away...stuff like that."

"I already knew your story. God opened my heart to you that same day. I never judged you. I was intrigued by you. Then we became friends, and I really *liked* you and respected you for the way your life had changed." A beguiling smile tugged at her lips. "But there was always something more."

Rick swallowed the lump in his throat, unable to believe what he heard, like a dream come true. "That's what I can't get over. You always believed in me, from early on. Since day one, I've loved being around you, Kelsey. You bring out the best in me. I feel totally myself with you, and there aren't many people on the planet I can say that about." He took a breath. "So, all this to say, if you still feel I'm great for you, I think you're pretty great yourself."

She grew still and her eyes became misty. "Oh, Rick..."

"I want to be with you, Kelsey." He took her hands again. In doing so, he felt bound in a sacred union he still couldn't understand. "I was wondering if it would be okay to pick up where we left off at the kitchen table last week..." He gave her a sly grin and she chuckled.

He slipped his hand to the back of her neck, drew her forward, and kissed her, savoring the softness of her lips and the feel of her arms as they slipped around his neck. He drew her closer and deepened the kiss as she pressed into him. How long had it been since he'd shared a pure, heart-driven kiss with a woman? Maybe never. And this wasn't just any woman. She might even be part of his destiny.

ଔ ଔ ଔ

Kelsey sighed in deep contentment and buried her face in Rick's chest. She could stay there on the bench forever, wrapped in his arms, his chin resting on her head. She'd never allowed herself to think about what it might be like to kiss him. The reality far exceeded any fantasy she could have conjured. It was *real*. She still had trouble believing it.

He leaned back and tipped her chin up with two fingers until she was face to face with him. For several seconds, he stared at her with the ghost of a smile tugging at his lips. "So, Kelsey, would you mind telling me why in the world you thought you weren't beautiful? I mean, you have mirrors at your house, right?"

She shrugged, suddenly embarrassed. "Just so you know, I was *not* fishing for compliments."

"Just so *you* know, you don't have to. I'll lavish them on you with no effort at self-restraint."

That drew a giggle. "It's just that things never seemed to work out for me. Several of my gorgeous friends have met people and gotten married, one right after another. Like dominos. I'm happy for them, but figured my strengths were more in being a loyal friend, creative, and warm-hearted."

Rick chuckled. "You are definitely those things too. And the fact that you didn't meet Mr. Right before is because he was still in Arizona. You see, it's simple."

The smug smile on his face was so adorable, Kelsey had to laugh. "I didn't know that before today. I'm glad you explained one of my life's biggest mysteries."

"Glad we got that straight." His voice grew soft, and he leaned in to kiss her again, a slow, lingering kiss that made her feel like warm, melted wax.

He pulled back, but kept her cradled in his arms.

She looked up at him. "So, how'd you learn to kiss like that if you spent all your time with your band of brothers?"

He stilled and she feared she'd opened a can of worms at the worst moment. "Ah, well, they weren't always brothers," he said. "There were a few sisters who came and went during those years too. We met girls at clubs or at the restaurants."

A sharp twinge pinched her inside. "Anyone special?"

"Just one. Her name was Anna. She hung out with us for a few months, and we hit it off. Became sort of an item. Then one day I woke up, and she was gone."

Kelsey's eyes widened. "Gone? Like she was your girlfriend, but she left without saying goodbye or explaining?"

He nodded as a shadow fell across his face. "Didn't matter that much in the end, I guess. At first, it hurt. I felt rejected, but I couldn't show it in front of the guys. I understood it was her, not me. She'd come and gone a few times. She was a drifter, real mixed up. Not that I *wasn't*. She had a hard time staying in one place." He looked away from her as if distancing himself from the conversation and the memory. "So, would you like to come over and I'll make you lunch? I'm not ready to share you with Molly or Danielle just yet."

"That sounds like a perfect idea."

Turned out that Rick was capable in the kitchen and made her a delicious grilled Swiss and avocado sandwich. "Not as elegant as the food you made for me," he said.

"But it'll fill our stomachs."

After the meal, they sat close together on the couch as he talked about his time on the road. She hesitated to ask him any more questions, but laid one hand on his knee. "Rick, I want you to know you never have to talk about that time if you don't want to." She leveled a solemn gaze at him. "I don't mind if you *want* to tell me things, either. There might be things I'm curious about, but you don't have to tell me, if that's what you want."

He reached up and stroked her hair. "I want you to know me, Kelsey. I want to be an open book with you. Right now, there's more past than present to talk about, and I don't like talking about the past. Except for my time with Stephen and Annika."

"I'd love to hear more about those years sometime."

Rick smiled. "I need to call them. They made me promise, and until recently, I kept the promise. I'll tell you about those years. Everything changed as soon as I met them."

"Don't use me as an excuse for not calling them," she teased.

"They're going to be excited when I tell them about you." He drew her back into his arms with his head touching hers. Reality, not fantasy. Finally.

The following day, Kelsey had to come back to earth, faced with a cold computer screen as she checked Danielle's work from the previous day. She fought the mental distraction of her day with Rick, picturing his face, savoring the memory of his kisses and the feel of his arms around her. They'd spent much of the day together, talking, cuddling, and walking. They both understood that after that day, it would be difficult for them to find as much time to spend together.

After leaving Rick's house, Kelsey went home to spend the evening with Molly. The following day, Kelsey would work two shifts and would hardly see her sister. She didn't want Molly to feel she'd dumped her onto Danielle. Kelsey still had responsibilities. A lot of them.

What would a normal day look like now? She and Rick decided to keep their relationship a secret for a while, both at the restaurant and with friends. They'd know the right moment to become public.

Kelsey reigned in her wandering mind as she checked Danielle's work from the previous day before submitting it to her company. How long would she juggle both jobs? Danielle's contribution made it possible for Kelsey to work close to full-time at The Fork. Once she was fully healed, would she want her old job back? Or was her brief experience enough to convince her it wasn't her place?

It would be weeks before Danielle could work anywhere, so Kelsey's role remained safe. For the next hour, Kelsey forced herself to focus and ended up satisfied with what she accomplished. Her eyes went to the time posted on her computer screen and she stood. "Molly, are you ready to go?"

She heard a muffled response from the back bedroom. Thirty minutes later, after dispatching Molly to Treasure House, Kelsey entered The Grateful Fork.

Copies of the recipes she'd prepared lay folded in her pocket. Hopefully, Vince would be willing to try them. When she entered the kitchen, it was already in a busy state of preparation. No Rick, but he'd probably be there soon.

"Hi, Vince," she said to the chef as he stood at one of the prep tables. "Do you have a minute?"

He smiled at her. "Sure, Kelsey. What's on your mind? Did we get the software all installed?"

"It's coming along. Rick arranged for the hardware to be installed at the end of this week, then the software. I thought we could close The Fork for one day so the staff can all be trained. Maybe a week from Monday, if everything's ready by then."

"We'll have to announce that ahead of time."

"I will. So, I have a question for you."

Vince nodded and waited.

Suddenly she felt embarrassed, but pressed on. Rick would cheer for her on the sidelines if he were there. "I've been creating new recipes for quite a while, at least a couple of years. I test them and the ones that work, I keep in a notebook for a cookbook one day."

He raised his bushy brows and nodded appreciatively. "Doesn't surprise me one bit."

"Would you be willing to try a couple of them and we'll see what the response is? I've tested them with other people."

"Sure, whatcha got?"

Kelsey opened the pages she'd printed and explained the chicken recipe and the chocolate mousse pie. As she spoke, Vince nodded several times.

He took an extra minute to reread the recipes and finally looked at her. "I'd be happy to try them, Kelsey. Not tonight, of course.

Since they aren't on the menu, we can feature them on *Monday Motivation* or one of the other chalkboard specials. I'll make a small batch."

She'd passed Vince's test. "That's what I was thinking too. *Monday Motivation* or weekday specials are the ideal time to try new menu items."

"We'll try them next Monday."

Turning to go to the dining room, she almost collided with Rick, who'd just entered the kitchen. "Oh, you're here." As they exchanged wide grins, he touched her arm, and she felt her neck grow hot. Surely, everyone in the kitchen would soon know just by observation that something had changed between them.

"Boy, is it ever good to see you," he whispered, then greeted Vince in a louder voice. "Sorry I'm late. My mom had car trouble, so I had to drop her off at work."

"No worries, pal," Vince said. He seemed not to notice anything different between them, though to Kelsey it felt incredibly obvious and would only be a matter of time before it was common knowledge.

"The feeling is mutual," she whispered with a flirtatious smile, not that she'd been in the least inclined to flirt before yesterday. Rick motivated her to try out new skills.

"I want to go back to yesterday, when we spent the whole day together," he murmured as he slipped into his white apron. "I have a feeling we'll have to fight for that kind of time."

"Do you remember who makes the schedules?" She cocked her head with an innocent expression.

He paused. Then a smile crept across his face. "That's right, you do."

"I'll see what I can do to recreate yesterday, okay?"

"That sounds promising. We also need to do the restaurant date we talked about before I started being stupid."

They laughed. "I'm glad you came around," she said. "We can do it next week."

She looked around, but the cooks were scurrying back and forth. "Oh, I forgot something. I had an idea early this morning, and I'd like to run it by you and Vince."

"Me too?"

"Yes." She was emphatic. "You're my assistant manager, remember? Not *just the busboy*."

"Got it." He grinned. "Do I get a raise?"

She smirked. "We'll see." She pulled on his arm and led him back to Vince as he chuckled. "I forgot to tell you about an idea, so I'll tell you and Rick at the same time. First, a question. Are there meals that aren't as popular and that lose money?"

"Yes," Vince said. "I've kept records of those that people order less often."

"When the software gets hooked up, we'll know that kind of information with the tap of a button," Rick said. "Cost per meal, profit per meal, the right time to order ingredients. Even the highest performing wait staff."

"Ah, I can't wait." Kelsey clasped her hands. "Sounds like magic to me. So, what if we gradually retire some of those less popular items and bring in new ones? We can freshen up the menu. I don't think Aggie has changed anything in years."

"You're the boss," Vince said with a wide grin. "Maybe we'll be doing more of yours."

His comment sent a thrill through her.

"I'm the temporary boss. So, here's my idea. We can welcome fall with a special menu including a handful of new recipes. You know, make it an event, the launch of the new season. We can call it Kickoff to Fall. I have a new band lined up for the second Friday of September, so we can have everything ready by then."

"That's a great idea." Vince nodded. "We had a lull in business and profits while Danielle was here, but since you've been at the helm, things have picked up again, almost without a beat."

Kelsey had noticed the same thing late one night as she pored over the accounts. She'd barely been able to keep her eyes open by then, but had to do it at some point. And she realized even in a sleepy state, that The Fork had regained what it had briefly lost.

"We can eventually print a new menu, maybe by spring," Rick said. "But for now, we'll focus on learning the new software and getting ready for Fall event." He looked at Kelsey. "I like your idea."

Vince grinned at both of them. "Me too."

"Rick and I can work up some menu ideas, with your approval, of course," Kelsey said to Vince. "You're the chef."

"And you two make a good team."

Rick looked at Kelsey with a smile hovering on his lips. "We do, don't we?"

Chapter Fourteen

Notebooks, a Bible, pens, and a coffee cup extended across the kitchen table. Rick stared at the open pages. How to prepare a talk from scratch? The last time, he was inspired—no, compelled—in what he shared. What about this time? It was more programmed. Was that okay?

"Lord, I need your help here. What do you want me to say to these kids tonight? Which passage will speak to them?" He sighed and stared some more. What had Jesse said? A story, a passage, and an application?

He'd asked Frank about it when they'd met the previous day. His comments had been helpful, consistent with what Jesse had said. He could start with the Bible verses, then unfold a few points from there, then finish with a takeaway. Yet, Rick didn't want to limit the Holy Spirit.

Frank had been delighted that Jesse had asked Rick to do the talk on alternate Thursday nights. He'd heard positive echoes about the life experiences he'd shared two weeks earlier. "I hoped you'd one day be ready to share your story," the older man had said, a kind smile crinkling his eyes. "What God did in your life was powerful, even though you feel it's a time you'd rather forget. But it *is* part of your journey."

Yeah, unfortunately it was. One day, the positive part of his life would outweigh the negative. The years would go by, and it would all get mixed into the grace he currently lived. It was so much better already. And he wasn't the only guy to have made crummy choices.

That thought reminded him of another statement Frank had made, one which followed him with a sunbeam of encouragement. He'd told Rick, "You have something to offer people who struggle with their past or their present. They'll know that what you're saying isn't just theory. They'll know you *understand* what it's like to struggle, to fall, and see God bring you out of it."

Warmth stirred inside him at the memory of the man's words. He should look at his life that way instead. Recyclable stupidity.

Maybe Bible college wasn't a bad idea. Jesse had sent him a link to a website the other day, a reputable school he'd never heard of, and a text. *This program would be perfect for you, Rick. Most students are residential, but some study online. Living on campus provides a deeper experience, since you'll study in person with professors, other like-minded students, etc. You can download an application.*

Rick might have an easier time preparing a spiritual talk with more tools, more background. And he'd be more the man Kelsey needed, more at her spiritual level.

A flood of affection engulfed him as he thought of her. She'd been a believer all her life, but accepted him with all his baby steps, his checkered past. Still, it would be nice to have more knowledge about the force that guided his life.

Her questions about his past romances had thrown him momentarily into a dark place. He'd hardly thought about Anna in over two years. He'd still occasionally have to fight the image of the man he used to be, as he had last week. With time, the battles would lessen in frequency and intensity.

Then a truth slipped into his mind, the importance of walking one day at a time, doing the next thing, as he first understood while sitting in the forest weeks ago. Plants grew slowly. Yet, even after a forest fire devastated acres of trees, new life later sprouted there. It took a while, and that strength grew...first sprouts, wobbly plants, then woody trunks. He should be patient with himself but continue step by step on the path. That's what he could share with the youth, and somehow include those who weren't yet believers. The phrase he'd heard in the forest that day resounded in his mind. *Start where you are*. And be faithful to what you know. *Who* you know. And you'll grow.

Rick worked the lunch shift, with barely enough time to catch Kelsey's eye and send a funny face or loving glance. Business was good. But it didn't leave them much time as a couple to build anything.

They stood together behind the bar at the close of his shift as the last of the lunch customers paid their bills and left. They took a breath and exchanged a longing look, which trickled joy down to his toes.

"I miss you," he said. "Seeing you across the room isn't cutting it for me."

"Me either. We'll have Sunday and Monday."

He nodded, then fell silent. "I hope tonight goes okay." The youth meeting wasn't far from his thoughts that day. Kelsey knew he was nervous about leading the entire program, even though he'd done it a couple weeks prior. He kept fighting against the voice inside that hissed, *Who are you to speak to kids about life?* But maybe the real question was, would God lead and equip him like he'd done before? Or was that a one-shot deal?

"Know I'm praying for you." She squeezed his hand and let her fingers linger a moment longer on his. "Call me tonight when you get home."

"I will." Then he headed out, feeling like he'd left a piece of himself behind.

Throughout the evening program—through the game, the announcements, his talk—he felt her prayers and sensed God's divine leading, less dramatic than the previous time, but still with a quiet assurance, as Kelsey had predicted. Seemed once again the kids accepted him fine as their de facto leader in Jesse's absence.

"If you don't get anything else I've said tonight," he told them before wrapping up the talk. "Remember two things. God's character, for one. Whenever you don't understand something or have a bad period in your life, fall back on that, because you can trust him. He's bigger and smarter than us." Rick gazed around the room. "Wherever you are on your journey, if you're simply curious about all this or if you've been a believer all your life, the principle of one foot after the other, doing the next thing, is essential. Talk to someone if you have questions. Get into a small group so you can grow with other people. And if you are a believer, don't neglect your personal relationship with God. Make growing a priority."

After the meeting, a few kids came to him to thank him for his talk, while others told him they were touched by what he'd shared two weeks earlier. He was uneasy with their admiration, their compliments. He wanted to shout at each one, *just don't ever do what I did.*

After most of the kids had gone home, Rick saw Chris hovering nearby. "Hey, Chris. Glad to see you tonight."

Chris gave a nod, probably too cool to acknowledge he'd enjoyed it. "I've been thinking about what you said last time you talked. Dude, you blew my mind. I had no idea."

Rick shrugged. "It's not a pretty story, but God made it a miracle. Don't get me wrong, I'm not perfect. Just on the right road for a change." He gave him an affable smile, but sensed Chris had more to say. "Hey, let me know if you ever want to get together and talk about anything. About life, whatever."

"Yeah, I would. All this stuff is stirring up a lot of questions. Maybe you're the right guy to talk to?"

For an instant, Rick froze in fear. Could he really help Chris with whatever was going on? He relaxed, caught himself. "I don't have all the answers, but it'll be great to talk some."

"Yeah. You free tomorrow?"

"How about Saturday morning?"

Chris offered a rare smile. His eyes were clear. No sign of drugs, but a shadow still dwelt in his eyes. "Not too early," he said. "Eleven would be good. I'll text you my number."

☙ ☙ ☙

Friday evening, Kelsey surveyed the dining room with satisfaction. Seemed the regulars had all returned to The Fork and enjoyed what they'd been accustomed to: a good meal and live music. Her chicken dish had gone over well for *Monday Motivation*, so she risked a new recipe for Friday. She hadn't had a chance to ask Vince how it had fared.

By ten thirty, the crowd had wound down. She poured herself a glass of iced tea behind the bar. Rick bussed tables like an efficient machine. They hadn't exchanged many words during that shift, though they'd spent most of the evening in the same room.

"Why don't you two get outta here?" Vince told her, hitching his head toward the dining room to include Rick, who wiped a table.

"Are you sure?" Kelsey's hopes lifted.

Vince grinned, a knowing gleam in his eyes. Apparently, Kelsey and Rick's secret was out, at least with the chef. Didn't take long, but they were likely more obvious than they realized. "Yeah, I can close. You guys are here all the time, so scoot."

"Thanks, Vince." Kelsey knew she was over-conscientious as general manager of The Fork. Danielle had left quite a collection of tasks for her to catch up. Then there was the new software, bringing another transition, hopefully an effective one.

Content to leave it all behind for a few hours, she said goodbye to Vince and the kitchen staff, and returned to the dining room to give Rick the good news.

"Be right there…" He dashed to the kitchen to tie up his evening's chores, put his apron into the hamper, and wash his hands.

As they exited the restaurant together, a wave of well-being and contentment cascaded inside her. August had arrived, but a trace of chill signaling summer's imminent end wove through the night air, fingering her hair and gliding past her neck.

She took Rick's extended hand.

"Want to take a walk?" he suggested. "I love walking in the evening."

"Even in winter?" They strolled a short distance down Charleston Alley, aka Restaurant Row, and turned down Summit Street toward the center of town.

"All year. I developed the habit in my Arizona days. It was a good way to get away from people and be alone. I didn't have much alone time back then, and I've discovered I like it."

"I imagine you're making a lot of discoveries about yourself, not only having new faith, but a new lifestyle."

"Every day is a new thing."

His words settled into her mind as she imagined what it was like for him to create a completely new life. "I'm glad things went well at the youth meeting last night."

"Me too. I guess it'll take me a while to get into the rhythm and feel more confident."

"From what I've heard, it seems to touch the kids every time you give a talk."

"It's growing each week. Kids are bringing their friends."

"I think you found your niche in youth ministry."

He smiled. "I see myself in a lot of the kids who come. Even the church kids have issues and choices to make. At any point, they could decide against following the faith of their parents. I want to help them own it for themselves."

She squeezed his hand. They stopped walking, and she drew close to him, her arm touching his. "That's one of the many things I admire about you, Rick Russo."

Rick didn't speak for a moment. His gaze roved her face, dipped to her lips and returned to her eyes. He pulled her close and kissed her, a hungry, groping kiss that left her breathless. She slipped her arms around his waist and leaned into his chest.

He drew back. "I can't tell you how many times I've craved this. You've rocked my world, Kelsey. Second only to God."

His words sent a thrill through her chest. "In that case, I don't mind second place." She tipped her head up to renew their kiss, savoring the feel of his arms around her. A month ago, he was a guilty pleasure of sorts, often inhabiting her thoughts, yet seeming impossibly out of reach. And now, their hearts and lips connected them. Each morning, she awakened with the joyful knowledge that they were a couple.

They continued strolling Summit Street past darkened boutiques and offices. A few people walked by on their way to local eateries or the movie theater. The sidewalks gleamed in reflected moonlight as Rick and Kelsey fell into a comfortable silence.

A few days earlier, Kelsey's parents had called from Uganda. As they exchanged news, she'd hinted she was in a new relationship. Of course, her mother plied her with questions, but Kelsey had been deliberately vague, not wanting to divulge Rick's background or situation. Her parents would meet him when they returned, and once they did, they wouldn't care about the rest. Talking about his past might only alarm them. It was more a question of wisdom than shame, wasn't it? The wisdom of keeping Rick's life story under wraps wrestled with her desire to express her feelings for him to the world. It wouldn't likely be the last time she struggled with those questions. Some people would look down on him because of his past, ignoring the strides he'd made in his present life.

Even in her quiet moments alone, uneasy thoughts slithered into her contentment, like the mysterious Anna who'd captured his interest at one time, but had abandoned him. How long had they been together? How serious had it been, and had that relationship left scars behind?

It shouldn't surprise her he'd had other relationships, perhaps many, since he'd been an attractive nonbeliever through his twenties. No wonder he didn't want to talk about them. Sometimes she felt innocent, naïve in the face of Rick's past life. Often, she wondered what else she didn't know. Although these thoughts occasionally hovered in her mind when they weren't together, she had no regrets as she walked beside him. Maybe that was what God had called her to do, be with Rick Russo, regardless of his past, and show him someone believed in him.

"How is Danielle doing?" Rick's voice broke into her thoughts.

"She's made good progress in just over a week. It might only take a month or so for her to get back to normal activities like driving and working."

"And then what?" He cast a worried glance at her. "Do you think she'll want to return to The Fork?"

"I've asked myself the same question, but haven't had the courage to ask her. I have a hard time believing she'd want to come back. She'd have to start from zero."

"If you ask her now what she's likely to do, she might prefer something else. Then you'd have a permanent job managing The Fork. Wouldn't that be good?"

Kelsey had asked herself the same question. "Yes, it would. But I don't want to ask Danielle yet. She's only been laid up for a week and a half, so it seems too soon. Of course, I'd love to get the green light to quit my computer job and work at The Fork." But then, either Danielle or Kelsey wouldn't have income. Another reason to wait.

Rick squeezed her hand. ""You can always ask Aggie what she thinks. This is her life's work, but she's mysteriously vanished from the scene."

"We talked the other day. This might be confidential, but she had a health scare so she decided to travel in case she couldn't later. She called me from Florida, and she's relieved I've stepped in."

Suddenly, Kelsey wanted to talk about something else. The question of Danielle skimmed through her mind occasionally, leaving discomfort behind. For the moment, there was no reason to push the question. One day soon, she'd have to gather her courage and simply ask her.

"Tell me more about your conversation with that guy at youth group," she said.

"We'll be meeting tomorrow at eleven. His name is Chris. I wanted to find a place that wasn't too noisy, something private, in case he wants to talk about drugs, or has questions about faith. So, we'll meet at the river shelter."

"*Our* shelter?" She offered a smile.

He released her hand and slid his arm around her shoulders, tucking her against him. She saw a sparkle in his gaze and upturned mouth. "The very same one where I kissed a princess." His voice took a tender tone.

"A princess?" She grinned at him.

"That's how I think of you, Kelsey. I kissed a princess, but didn't become a frog."

They laughed. His words touched a dark hollow inside her, one inhabited by feminine doubts. She didn't feel like a princess. A scullery maid in the princess's castle, perhaps.

"I know you don't feel like a princess." He must have read her thoughts. "I hope to show you who you are to me. To God. You recently confronted me for not seeing myself the way God and others see me. I'll say the same thing to you."

"I know," she said softly. "My friends tell me that. Amber does." She hadn't planned the conversation to go there, but she drank in his words. *Princess*. Synonym with *special* and *unique*. Those words held a healing salve. Healing the questions her heart sometimes murmured in the dark of night.

"I'll be praying for your conversation with Chris."

"Thanks. I'm only working the evening shift Saturday, as you likely know, since you make the schedule now. So, I'll call you and if you're around, I'd like to see you."

"Maybe you can come to the house. We can discuss the fall event if you want, but I mainly want to be with you."

"Me too. We can tell Danielle and Molly we're planning the event at The Fork."

"I don't mind if they know about us. It'll make it easier to get together if I have to be home."

Though night shadowed his face, she saw him smile.

Chapter Fifteen

Colorful picnic blankets and coolers dotted the grassy expanse surrounding the shelter at River Park. Maybe Rick should have picked a calmer place to meet Chris, since residents trickled from the parking lot, eager to grasp a final family picnic before fall weather set in. But a coffee shop would be worse.

Less than a week ago, Rick's life changed near this very spot. It was here that his status with Kelsey shifted from casting furtive glances at her across the restaurant to holding her in his arms and kissing her. The memory brought a flush of warmth and tugged his mouth into a smile.

Today would be different, but he hoped, just as promising. Like last time, he was nervous, but for a wholly different reason. Would he have answers for Chris? Would Chris talk to him about drug use? Maybe he wasn't an addict but a casual user, which in itself was an issue, since it was illegal, expensive, and could lead to more.

"Lord, I need you to take over this meeting with Chris. I know it's not up to me. I'll just be available and let you do your thing."

His brief prayer was enough to calm his anxiety. "Hey, Rick." The voice startled him. Chris's smile was a rare occurrence and sent Rick a wave of encouragement. He was in jeans and T-shirt, his standard uniform, and wore a baseball cap over wavy blond hair that curled out from under the edges. His eyes looked clear, and he seemed fully sober.

"Hi, Chris." They did a fist bump. "You caught me daydreaming. Want to take a walk? There's the path along the lake."

"Sure. I know the path."

They set out toward the river. "Remind me how long you've been in The Falls," Rick said. He'd expected to be at a loss for words in the beginning, so had prepared something banal to set Chris at ease. He'd also forgotten what Chris had said when they'd talked about it.

"About five years ago. So, it feels like home now."

"I bet it was hard to cross the country. It's nice here, but not at all the same culture as Arizona."

"You got that right. I was a kid. It was the summer before high school, and my dad split. Fell in love with some lady he'd met."

"That sounds hard."

Chris shrugged. "Yeah. You went through hard stuff too."

"So, how did you decide to come here? Your mom had a relative? Her sister?" What Chris had said before slowly came back to him.

"My Aunt Joyce. Worked out okay. I'm glad Mom had someplace to bring me and my little sister."

Rick and Chris walked alongside the river on a hard dirt path, stepping over rocks and gnarled tree roots. Finally, they reached a clearing where two flat boulders stuck out into the water. "Wanna sit there?" Rick extended one hand. He'd discovered the spot on one of his solitary hikes shortly after his arrival in The Falls. One day, before it got cold, he'd bring Kelsey here for a picnic.

They settled on the rock, legs dangling over the side facing the river. Neither one spoke for a couple of minutes. Rick wondered if he should say something, or just let the silence coax out Chris's questions.

"I was kind of shocked by what you shared last week," Chris said, then laughed. "In a way, it made me glad there was someone more messed up than I was. I mean, I know you're not messed up anymore."

He looked over at Chris with a half-smile. "Are you messed up?"

"Not that much. That's just an expression. I get messed up once in a while with certain friends, but I wasn't in the same shape you were in when you lived in Arizona."

"What was it, coke? Weed? If you don't mind me asking."

"Mostly weed, just on weekends, to blow off steam."

Rick nodded. "It's legal in Arizona, but it isn't here."

"I'm careful. And it's casual for me. It's crazy you got so deep into it. I guess you were young."

"Around seventeen. I wasn't even out of high school. I decided to run away from everything, but it didn't get me anywhere. I just lost all those years." It was on the tip of Rick's tongue to say, *So, be careful.* But he didn't want Chris to feel parented when he'd sought him out as a friend. *Tread carefully.* "I'm just glad God didn't let me die. He used my stupidity to help me meet him even when I wasn't looking for him."

"I wasn't either. Not sure I am now, but Rod invited me, and it was nice to get to know other kids."

"I'm glad you've enjoyed it and came back. So, after what you heard so far at the group, where do you stand with your interest in God?"

Chris considered Rick's question a moment before responding. "I have some questions. And I'm interested. But I'm glad no one there pushes things on me. I have to go at my own pace."

"I'm glad you don't feel pushed. The couple who found me were never pushy. They just suggested things. They'd ask me sometimes if I wanted to come to church. Of course, I didn't at first, but kept thinking, why would a couple I don't know save my life by taking me to the hospital, then let me *live* with them? They didn't know me from Adam. These people had something different, and I wanted to know what it was."

"That's wild that they did that. How long did you live with them?"

"Almost two years. Then I felt God telling me it was time to come home."

Chris laughed. "God *talks* to you?"

"Sometimes, but not audibly. It's like an impression. Don't get me wrong, it's not like that all the time. But once in a while, he makes it clear. Like when I shared my story with you guys. That time it was super clear, but I didn't want to do it."

"Why not? It's a crazy story. Everyone liked it."

Rick paused. For an instant, the image of a circus animal doing tricks entered his mind. It had been entertaining for the kids, shocking maybe. Not for him. "I almost died, almost wrecked my life. I'd already lost a big chunk of my youth, the time I should have been building something."

Chris grew still, serious.

"And I just wanted to forget that time. I felt like what God gave me in its place was unbelievably better. A relationship with him, knowing why I was on this earth, future security, and a complete redo from mistakes I'd made. So, that part was good to share, but the human part of me didn't want to be exposed as this dude who'd basically tossed his own life. I didn't want to disillusion anyone."

Chris's eyes narrowed. "But you're not that guy anymore."

"No. And that's why he wanted me to tell you all, I guess." He grinned then. "So, we're not here to talk about me."

"I'm glad to hear more of your story. Puts mine into perspective. I'm doing okay, but I was more messed up in high school. Now it's just occasional."

Rick narrowed his eyes. Time to get to the point. "Are you sure?"

"Yeah, of course." Chris waved at the air. "I get wasted once in a while, but not often."

Rick stared at him a moment, wondering if he was downplaying his drug involvement. "I care, man. I know what I went through, so if at any time you want to talk more about this or about Jesus and what a cool dude *he* is, just let me know. You can even make a list of your questions, and we'll get together sometimes and cover them one at a time." He kept his voice calm. "I hope you feel comfortable enough with me, knowing I will never judge you. Not. Ever." As if he could.

Chris's smile seemed genuine, not just placating. There came a moment when Rick felt he'd shared enough for Chris to think about. He sensed the younger man wasn't ready to reveal or ask any more, and Rick didn't want to overload him with information. He moved the conversation to a more superficial level...Chris's favorite show, what he enjoyed doing on weekends, and what he hoped for the near future.

"Thanks for being willing to talk once in a while," Chris said. "But we can do other stuff too. We should shoot some hoops again before it gets too cold."

"Absolutely."

When they parted company, a swell of satisfaction grew inside him. They'd touched on important topics, but left the doors open for more later. Maybe Chris would digest what he'd gotten so far. The results were up to God.

Time to call Kelsey.

"How did it go with Chris?" She asked when he called her. He hadn't left the parking lot yet.

Rick summarized his meeting with Chris and how open he'd seemed.

"That's great," Kelsey said. "I'm sure you're very approachable, and with what you shared, he knows you've been through a lot of the same things."

"I think he's comfortable with me, and that was a big part of it. Now I can see the wisdom of talking about my failures with other people."

She laughed. "It's easier to do when you've left those failures far behind."

"That's for sure. I don't know what his actual drug involvement might be, but it's probably more than he's admitting to. I'll keep an eye on him."

"Do you have time to come over for lunch?" she asked.

He so hoped she'd ask. "Will it be a problem for you if I come, I mean, with Danielle?"

"Not at all." Her voice was firm. "First of all, I want to tell Danielle about us because that'll give us more freedom to be open at the house. Second, it's my house!" She laughed, a sound he never tired of hearing. "Or rather, my parents' house."

"You're right. It *is* your house. Do what you want. Invite me any time you want." He chuckled. "I don't know if she'll talk about us or not to other people."

"I'm pretty sure I don't care."

He smiled. Didn't look like she was ashamed of him, which *had* crossed his mind. "I don't either. Want me to come right over?"

"As soon as humanly possible."

ಌ ಌ ಌ

Kelsey glanced at the clock and opened the oven to take out her signature mac and cheese casserole. At least, that's what she liked to call it. With three cheeses, chunks of ham, and sautéed green peppers, it deserved a special name.

She'd told Danielle that Rick was coming for lunch, but would wait until he left for his shift before telling her they were dating. She scooped some of the pasta into a bowl for Danielle and took it to her where she sat buried in couch pillows. Her makeshift desk, a wooden TV table, sat to one side.

"I'm sure I'm gaining weight." Danielle took a deep sniff of the cheesy pasta. "But I'm not complaining about the menu. Looks and smells great. Thanks, Kelsey."

"Enjoy. Rick's due here in a minute." The doorbell rang. "See?" She smiled and went to the door.

At least there was no direct view of the front door from the living room, leaving Kelsey free to nestle into Rick's arms and indulge in a tender kiss at the doorway. He clung to her for a couple of extra minutes, as if they hadn't been together in days.

"Smells fabulous, although I'm sure you're tired of hearing that." Rick chuckled as Kelsey led him by the hand into the kitchen.

"It's my special mac and cheese. I already served Danielle hers, so we can have a private lunch."

"Private sounds good." He trailed a hand down her arm, causing a shiver of pleasure.

Rick helped her put the meal on the table. They sat near each other before steaming bowls of pasta. He took her hand and prayed for the meal, then blew on a forkful. With an ecstatic expression, he murmured, "Mmm. Delicious."

They caught up on the news of the day as they ate. "I don't have dessert," Kelsey said when they'd finished.

"Which is fine. I'm stuffed and happy." He squeezed her hand. "Really happy," he added more quietly.

"Me too." Their gazes locked for a long moment. Kelsey still wanted to pinch herself from time to time. Reluctantly, she broke the moment. It had to be done. "Maybe we could talk about the fall event, since you're here and we don't seem to have any time to plan." She refilled their glasses with chilled water.

"Good idea."

"The format won't be that different from a usual Friday night. We'll have a band and some special menu items. Stuff like that. But we can promote it as a launch into the fall."

He wiped his mouth. "Fall décor, maybe. We can think of fall themes…leaves, football. Honestly, I'm inclined to let you do the planning and I'll give my opinion. We all have our gifts, and this isn't mine."

Kelsey smiled. "Fair enough. Vince can help me come up with a menu and you can give me the thumbs up or down."

"*That* I can do. Remind me the date."

"It's the second Friday of September. We don't have that much time."

"And remember, Monday is our training on the new software." He took a long gulp of ice water. "What have you done so far, and how can I help?"

"I've confirmed the band, put an ad in the local Sunday paper, so that'll come out a few times prior to the event. Some social media. I've chosen a few menu specials—"

"Are you including some of yours?"

She frowned. "I'd rather do that on a regular day, like a Monday."

He took her hand. "Kelsey, don't doubt yourself. Your food is amazing. It can stand up to the fall festival...I forgot what you called it."

"Kickoff to Fall," she supplied. "Kind of fits in with the football theme."

"See? You're a natural. I've always said that."

He had. Vince had. Aggie had. Why couldn't she own it? Her intuition about food and hospitality flowed like a natural stream, and it made her happy. And that made customers happy. Becoming the manager of The Grateful Fork was an open door she couldn't have predicted or orchestrated. Yet, there she was. She could use her gifts, her vision, her ideas... all without investing in all the cost and overhead of buying her own restaurant and starting from zero without a customer base. It was ideal, if only she could stay once Danielle was back on her feet.

Kelsey lowered her voice and hitched her head toward the living room. "In a week or so, I'll talk to Danielle to see whether she's planning to take her old job back once she's recovered."

Rick squeezed her hand, which still lay in his. "Hopefully, she'll remember how stressed she was during her short career at The Fork. She'll realize it's not her thing."

"She's doing great at my job here." Clearly, *that* was her niche.

His warm gaze locked on hers. A tantalizing smile curved his lips. "I'm glad you're finding your true destiny, even though you weren't looking for it."

She leaned toward him and matched his tone. "Do you mean that in a double sense?"

"I do." He leaned forward, about to kiss her.

"That was great, Kelsey." Danielle's voice broke the moment as she hobbled into the kitchen, carrying her plate with one hand and clinging to a crutch with the other. "Oh, sorry to interrupt." Her gaze roved from Kelsey to Rick.

Kelsey turned to her and released Rick's hand. Heat rose in her face. "I would have come to get that, Danielle. You shouldn't be putting any weight on your leg."

"I'm not. I basically hopped on the other one. I'm sorry you and Molly have to wait on me."

"We don't mind. That was our arrangement to help you while you heal."

"I know, and I'm grateful." Danielle placed her plate in the sink and clung to the counter. "I needed to move some. It's too easy to stay like a beached whale on the couch." She tittered, but seemed uncomfortable, having walked in on a romantic moment. It would have happened sooner or later.

"I agree with Kelsey," Rick said. "It seems too soon to use just one crutch."

"I'm a little better. I'm looking forward to getting into physical therapy, but my doctor says he'll let me know when I'm ready."

"Give it two more weeks minimum," Kelsey said. "I was there at that appointment, remember?"

"Okay, okay. I'll go back to my couch. See ya, Rick." She turned with a smile and hopped out of the kitchen.

Kelsey sighed and met Rick's amused gaze. "Okay, where were we?"

After Rick left, Kelsey did the dishes. They'd see each other again for the evening shift at The Fork, but in the meantime, she had to pick up Molly and bring her home before heading out again. The roller coaster had begun.

She went to the living room, where Danielle had resumed her morning computer work. "Can I get you anything before I leave to pick up Molly?"

"No, thanks." Danielle stared up from the couch at Kelsey. "Seems something's going on between Rick and Kelsey." Her blue eyes held mischief.

Kelsey swallowed. "You guessed correctly. It hasn't been too long."

Danielle smiled. "I'm happy for you. He's a nice guy."

"Thanks, Danielle. He really is."

"He's greatly reformed from who he was in high school and, apparently, years after."

"He's come a long way. And God has great plans for him." She believed that with all her heart. It didn't stop her from wondering what Danielle *really* thought. Was she wondering about his past and why Kelsey didn't seem bothered by it?

It was too early to pick up Molly, but Kelsey suddenly wanted to escape any further conversation about her new relationship. She hadn't quite adjusted to it herself.

She drove through town and stopped along the curb facing the building. Her mind still spun out questions triggered by Danielle's observations.

Did Kelsey care what other people thought due to their own prejudices? Not usually, though she'd held back information about Rick from her parents, to save them from worry.

Neither her parents nor Danielle knew Rick like she knew him. Yes, their romance was new. But from the first day she saw him, she couldn't deny the effect he'd had on her, one that took root deep inside her. One that wouldn't let go.

Rick spoke often of his gratitude for being saved out of his previous lifestyle. And now, God was using those very mistakes to draw teenagers to himself.

Did she care what other people thought about Rick's past, his lack of a professional career or higher education? For a split second, the thought grazed a hidden and vulnerable place inside her. She'd never felt adequate to attract someone who'd *made it* in life, who looked good on paper.

Did she care about all that?

"No." She spoke aloud and shook her head. "No, Lord. That's not from you. Those criteria are from the world. You yourself said you look at the heart. You've allowed me to see Rick's heart."

She redirected her thoughts from her own low self-esteem to Rick's character and what she knew about him. A wave of certainty coursed through her. She was *called* to be with him, to believe in him. To support him. *Destined*...to use his favorite word. Let people say and think whatever they wanted. She'd stand by him and continue to believe in him.

A smile bloomed on her face as a flood of warmth and peace replaced her tangled questions

For her, there was no *better* than Rick Russo. Period.

Chapter Sixteen

"Any other questions before we go downstairs?" Rick glanced around the rectangular tables which he and Jesse had pushed together to accommodate the ever-growing group of teens. The new school year had just begun, so they'd likely get even more kids.

"No, let's go downstairs," one girl said. "This was cool, though. Thanks, Rick."

As Jesse closed the meeting in prayer, Rick couldn't help but scroll back through the last month in amazement. The youth group had grown in large strides until it had almost doubled. Youth church grew more slowly, but a couple of newcomers trickled in each week so that too had grown.

He and Chris had continued meeting weekly. One day after they finished, Rick got the idea that other kids might be curious or open, like Chris. He suggested to Jesse to launch a casual meeting before the youth group where kids could ask questions about faith or life. Jesse liked the idea, so they started the Discovery Session. The first time eight kids came, then fourteen, then twenty-two. They already had to move the group to a larger room.

He continued to share a teaching role with Jesse, a week on, a week off. A few kids told him he was *speaking their language*. Rick didn't want Jesse's or any other spotlight, and their comments almost made him uncomfortable. But he was thankful to connect with the kids, glad they were receiving something. Jesse just grinned and cheered him on, with no sign of jealousy or territoriality. *Dude, if God is using you to touch kids' hearts, how can I possibly mind that?*

The church was abuzz with what was happening in the youth ministry. Some called it a *revival*. Others said Rick was *anointed*.

He had no idea what either word meant. He just figured God was doing his thing through all of them.

That night, Jesse sat at one end of the table, but had mostly remained silent through the meeting. When he finished his prayer, the kids started talking all at once as they headed downstairs for the main meeting.

As Jesse and Rick followed the kids down the hall toward the stairway, Rick saw Pastor Frank's light beaming from his office. "I'll be right down," he told Jesse and Chris. "Just want to say hi to pastor Frank."

Rick went to the doorway and knocked on the open door. When the older man looked up, a smile spread across his face. "Hey, Rick. You caught me working late. I'm leaving on a short trip tomorrow with Teresa and had a few things to finish up."

"I won't hold you up, Pastor. I wanted to say hi." And ask him for a small favor.

"Well, I'm glad you did. I hear good things about the youth ministry. Seems like it's a perfect spot for you."

"Yes, I think it is." He sat across a wide desk from the pastor. They hadn't met in two weeks. Between their two schedules, it was a challenge to find a common time. "I enjoy the kids. Some of them are asking good questions. A month or so ago, we started another meeting which we do right before the youth group. They come a little early to ask questions, those who are interested."

"Yes, I've heard about that group. It was a great idea and attracts a lot of kids. I'm happy these kids are interested in the gospel. For years, we mostly had kids from the church. Sometimes their parents made them come to youth group, and they weren't excited about faith. That's changing for some of them."

"I'm hopeful the group will help the church kids as much as the kids outside."

Frank leaned forward and set both elbows on the desk. A serious look came into his eyes. "Rick, I'm beginning to wonder if

God has gifted you in a special way for this. You seem to have a larger than usual impact on the kids. I hesitate to tell you this, because of course, you know it's God's doing."

"Absolutely. I'm just a vessel."

"That's right. But he is using you, and it's a delight to see."

Rick smiled. "I appreciate your perspective. Pastor, that brings up a question. I'm interested in being more equipped for this, and so I'm applying to a Bible college. Jesse suggested it, especially since I'm teaching more now."

To his surprise, Frank frowned. "A Bible college? To go away to a school, you mean? Or online?"

"Uh, I don't know yet. I'm not even sure I'd go at all, but I can apply and see what happens." Frank didn't look delighted by the idea. What was that about? "This one isn't too far away. Mid-Penn Bible Institute. I have a reference they want my pastor to fill out." Pastor Frank's response made him add, "You don't think this is a good idea?"

The older man leaned back. His brows gathered. "Going to a Bible college and living away on campus is a perfect idea for certain students. I don't know whether it's good for you for several reasons. None of the reasons put into question your abilities, of course. It's not that. It's just that you're getting excellent hands-on training right here where you are in the context of the church. I *can* see you one day doing online classes and staying in your ministry. You're active with the kids. God is using you here."

"I understand. Jesse suggested it would be good for me to get more Biblical training. I feel pretty ignorant about some things, to be honest. Sometimes I'm scared a kid will ask me something I don't know how to answer."

The pastor chuckled. "I understand the feeling. But no one has all the answers. It's the relationship more than the head knowledge that counts most, especially at their age. Of course, having a solid Biblical background is important. I'm not minimizing that at all. But you can do that with online classes or with mentoring, like we're doing."

"I don't want you to think your mentoring isn't valuable to me. It's my favorite time of the week, and I am learning a lot. But Jesse said living on campus offers a lot of advantages, like interacting with professors, meeting other like-minded students. The downside is I'd be way older than most of them."

"And you'd be gone from Brenner Falls, where your ministry is."

Right. Of course. Frank was making sense. "I could drive back on weekends, if I decide to go." He corrected himself. "Or, if God leads me to go."

Frank paused, as if weighing his words ahead of time. "I'll fill out your reference if you want me to, but be sure to ask God what *he* wants you to do. Studying online would be excellent for you. But be sure it's his leading before you go away anywhere."

"Of course." The words *before you go* stabbed Rick inside as he thought about Kelsey. Ben. His mom. But it wasn't for tomorrow. He'd miss Kelsey if he went away to college, but he'd be close enough to see her on weekends or at least twice a month. It might be a great experience to be surrounded by the Biblical studies atmosphere, especially since he hadn't been to college. She'd understand, wouldn't she?

Realistically, he'd likely never go. How would he pay for it? But Jesse had told him if God wanted it for him, he'd provide the funds one way or another. Rick had built up some savings from working a lot, and his mom hadn't allowed him to pay rent. But it still wasn't much.

He pulled a folded reference form and envelope from a canvas bag he carried and slid it across the desk to Pastor Frank. "Here's the reference and envelope, so you can send it directly to them." He stood. "I'd better get going. I'll see you next week at our Wednesday meeting. Enjoy your trip away. And thank you."

"You're welcome."

Rick returned to the hall, trying to block confusion from his mind over the sad expression on the pastor's face.

ಆ ಆ ಆ

Kelsey reached out to squeeze her sister's arm as guilt tugged at her. "We'll spend some time together tomorrow, okay Molly? I'm sorry I haven't been around much lately."

"It's okay." Molly slipped out of the car and entered the Treasure House building. Kelsey sighed and pulled out in the direction of The Grateful Fork.

Though the new software at The Fork made everything roll more smoothly, Kelsey still felt wound up all the time. When she wasn't at The Fork, she had things to do for Danielle and Molly. She served as a taxi for both of them, and still had to survey Danielle's work daily, as well as add in some tasks of her own.

Then there was Rick, who she saw daily across the restaurant, but they had to strategize and compromise to have time together. Normally on Sundays they managed, if he didn't have a youth activity.

All in all, her life was like a circus.

Danielle was a pleasant enough houseguest, hesitating to bother anyone unless it was necessary, always grateful for the help. But at times the weight of juggling everyone seemed more than Kelsey could bear.

More than a month had passed since the accident, and Danielle's mobility had improved to the point of walking easily on crutches. She still couldn't drive, though she'd begun sitting on the back porch while she could before fall weather settled in. Kelsey was ready to have the house back to herself with Molly, but it might be yet a few more weeks.

One afternoon, Kelsey casually asked her if she planned to return to The Fork once her leg healed. She hoped Danielle would say *of course not*, given the stress and failure she'd experienced there. But she'd merely said, "I'll cross that bridge when I come to it." Which left Kelsey firmly in limbo.

The day finally arrived for the Kickoff to Fall at The Fork. That night, Kelsey would focus all her attention on helping the evening roll out flawlessly. The staff expected a full crowd. Already, the restaurant seemed like a zoo, and it was only four-thirty. Rick had arrived early to prep the tables and drinks and make sure the specials were on the chalkboard. They exchanged broad smiles, but that was all they could manage before customers began piling in through the front door.

To Kelsey's delight, Aggie entered the restaurant accompanied by a woman about her age. Immediately, staff and customers surrounded her to welcome her back. She and her friend settled at a table near the stage. A few moments later, Nathan and Leah came in, followed by Sophie and two girlfriends, then Cooper, Blair, and Jake.

Kelsey rode the wave of excitement and anticipation of the evening. She'd checked everything several times in the days leading up to Friday. Inventory, the band, advertising, the recipes...the list went on. Vince and Rick were a big help, along with the rest of the staff.

She spotted Amber and Ben at the front door and rushed to greet them. "I keep thinking of how much you're juggling, Kelsey," she said. "And you *still* have time to pull this off!"

"This is like a big reunion of new and old friends. I love it."

"I can tell." Ben grinned.

Kelsey seated them and zipped off to seat another couple to help the hostess, who had her hands full with customers pouring in.

The rest of the evening passed in a blur. The dining room filled up well before the concert began. All the available employees were on duty that night and ran back and forth to the kitchen constantly with hardly a break. Finally, during the second set of music following a brief intermission, Kelsey sought refuge behind the bar with a tall glass of cold water.

Soon, Rick stood beside her. "So glad we had a lull at the same time," he said, reaching for another glass and filling it.

"Me too. How are you holding up?"

He smiled at her with a glint in his eye. "I'm holding up, but it helps to look across the room and see you there like a ball of energy. Gives me energy too."

"I miss you." Her hand grazed his fingers though she pulled her gaze away and panned the room. Otherwise, anyone who observed them would guess the truth. She still wanted to be private about their relationship when they were both on duty at The Fork. Unsure of how important or even possible it was, it seemed more professional.

"Excuse me, miss." A man's voice interrupted them. She turned and saw a middle-aged man with blond curls in disarray, with round wire-rimmed glasses perched on his nose. "My name is Lionel Spark. I'm a food journalist, and I was passing through Brenner Falls on my way to Harrisburg for an assignment. I decided to stop here for dinner and never expected such an exciting evening. Are you the owner?"

Kelsey recovered from her surprise. "No, I'm the general manager, Kelsey Brewster. I'm so glad you had a good evening, Mr. Spark. Did you enjoy your meal?"

"Oh, it was fabulous. I had the chicken with sauce, can't remember what it was called."

She exchanged glances with Rick, who grinned. "That was one of Kelsey's own recipes," he said, appearing proud on her behalf.

"Was it, now? Bravo. Your name again…" He pulled out a notepad and flipped it to a fresh page. "Do you mind if I take a few notes?"

"Be my guest. Are you writing an article?"

"I'm doing a piece on various restaurants in smaller towns between Philadelphia and Harrisburg. It's helpful for those on road trips or day trips."

Kelsey grinned. This would be fantastic publicity for The Fork, not that they were hurting for business. "What paper do you write for?"

"The Inquirer." He grinned. "You've heard of it?"

Her eyes widened, and she looked at Rick. "The *Philadelphia Inquirer*?"

"I see you have heard of it."

"Oh, my gosh. You're writing about our little town in the Inquirer? I'm so honored, Mr. Spark."

"The pleasure's mine. I have a contact with your local paper as well, so the residents here will know my high opinion, in case they haven't come yet." He scribbled a few notes on his pad. "Do you have a moment for a few questions?"

How could she not? This was a great honor and would do Aggie so proud. "Of course. The owner, Aggie Durante, was here a moment ago. She's retired now, but ran it for forty years." Kelsey scanned the room for Aggie. She'd spoken to her earlier, but the older woman must have gotten tired and gone home. Too bad Mr. Spark couldn't meet The Fork's owner, but Kelsey knew enough about its history to give him a complete picture for his article.

"I'll keep an eye on things while you two chat," Rick said as he left Kelsey with Mr. Spark. The man asked her questions about the origin of the restaurant as well as current demographics, menu, and trends. He scribbled in his notebook for several minutes. Then he thanked her and returned to his seat.

Kelsey vibrated with excitement, and dashed into the kitchen to catch Vince's attention. "Vince, I have to tell you. I just spoke with a journalist from the Philadelphia Inquirer and he's writing up *our* restaurant. I mentioned your name. Hope that's okay."

Vince's eyes widened. "Kelsey, that's amazing! Of course. I'm honored. We've never had that kind of coverage before. I don't even think the local paper has written anything in recent years about The Fork. You're making a splash."

"No, Vince. *You're* the chef. You deserve much of the credit for tonight's success."

"Don't sell yourself short. You pulled it all together. And Rick was smart to get the software in place. Made a huge difference."

"You probably know Aggie was here for a while. Then, every time I looked around the room, or visited the tables and talked to people, they seemed to be having the time of their lives. They loved the band, the specials, everything."

"Like I said, Kelsey. You're a natural."

Once the restaurant had regained its calm and only a few employees still scurried around finishing up, Kelsey found Rick wiping down the tables. "I know you're probably exhausted, as I am," she said. "But can you come over for a little while? Danielle and Molly will already be in bed, so we'll have the living room to ourselves."

He grinned. "I was hoping you'd ask."

Finally, a small block of time alone with Rick. That was her reward after their intense but successful evening. She drove to the house, aware of his headlights shining in her rearview mirror as he followed her.

Minutes later, they settled on the couch with glasses of cool lemonade. Kelsey leaned against Rick's chest as one arm looped over her shoulders. He bent to kiss her, a leisurely yet tender expression that said he missed her too.

He pulled back and his gaze searched her face. "My beauty. I'm glad to have you all to myself."

She savored his words, the loving glow emanating from his eyes. How did this all happen? She'd almost lost hope. With Rick and The Fork, her life appeared to be headed in a positive, exciting direction. True, it was extremely busy and stressful, but that part was temporary

"Are you happy with how the evening went?" he asked, though the smile tugging at his lips gave away his expectation of her answer.

Kelsey let out a happy sigh. "It was *perfect*. The food, the band, the atmosphere of a party. I love the community feeling when everyone's there enjoying themselves. Like a big family. I love seeing familiar faces coming together. Then, the journalist from Philadelphia was icing on the cake."

"I'm not a bit surprised. You pulled it all together. It was nice to see Aggie there. Did you talk to her?"

"I stopped at her table when I was making rounds chatting with the customers. She said I'm doing a great job. We talked for a few minutes. She seemed happy with the way things were going, though somewhat detached."

"I was surprised she went away so quickly after turning over the reins to Danielle then to you. I would think she'd want to keep an eye out a little longer."

Kelsey shrugged. "Me too. Maybe she was tired of forty years. But in that case, I wonder why she didn't just sell it."

Rick snorted. "The whole *keeping it in the family* thing wasn't rational. I've worked in too many restaurants to understand that mentality. That and not having software to run everything."

"You solved that one." She smiled at him, and he responded by pulling her close in his arms.

Sitting like that with his arms around her was one of Kelsey's greatest pleasures. She felt secure and loved, which was like a brand-new discovery.

"I have an idea I want to run by you," Rick said after a few moments of comfortable silence.

She looked at him expectantly but his face became taut. Alarm rippled through her. "What is it?"

"Well, you know things have kind of exploded at church...in a good way. Kids are coming out in droves and it's exciting, but sometimes I think I need more training. I found out there are these places called Bible colleges that prepare people for ministry. What do you think about something like that for me?"

Kelsey stared at him. "You mean go *away* to school, like to another state or something?"

"No, there are a few right here in Pennsylvania. Is that a bad idea?"

Her mouth opened, but nothing came out. Thoughts scrambled in her head. "Where did this idea come from, Rick?"

"Jesse told me about it. He said it would be good for me to get more Bible knowledge to help me when I give the talk at youth group or whatever."

"You could do it online," she suggested. "That would be a good way to get more training without leaving town. Aren't you still meeting with Pastor Frank?"

"Yeah, we're still meeting a couple of times a month."

"I don't think he does one-on-one mentoring with just anyone. He sees potential in you, Rick, and he's *chosen* to meet with you. You're like his protégé or something."

"But I could also go to school."

Pain rose in her throat. Of course, she was being selfish not wanting Rick to go away. "Would you...want to move away?" She swallowed a lump that had formed.

"No, I wouldn't. It's just an idea. C'mere." He drew her into his arms again and held her tightly against him. She felt his heartbeat through his T-shirt.

Rick kissed the top of her head, then pulled back to look into her face. "It was just an idea, Kelsey. I wondered what you thought. It's not like I'm definitely planning to go. Online class is a good option too."

Kelsey let out a long breath. "You scared me, Rick. I thought you were telling me you were preparing to move away again to become a college student. I mean, if that's what you really want to do, I'd try to be supportive. I'd sure miss you." And they hadn't been together for long, so he'd probably meet someone else while he was there. Another stab of conscience at her own selfishness.

"Stop, Kelsey." His voice was gentle as he tipped up her chin and looked into her eyes. "I want to be with you. I just wondered what you thought." He chuckled. "I guess now, I know."

"Don't you want to give your current life more time to get established? I'm not only talking about us. I mean working, being with the youth. All the things you've built in the short time you've been here should continue, at least for a little while."

"You're right. College sounded like a good way to learn faster and in a concentrated way. That's the part that appealed to me."

"I'm sure you'd learn a lot and it would be great, though faster isn't always better. Spiritual maturity takes time. And head knowledge isn't the only thing that counts."

"That's true, and makes sense. Pastor Frank said that to me once."

"Did you talk to Pastor Frank about this idea?"

"Just this week, I mentioned it to him. I wanted his opinion."

"And?"

"He had the same response as you. He said online was a good option because I didn't have to leave my ministry. And I'm getting hands-on training at the church."

"Well, there you go." Her tension seeped out like a balloon, but her shoulders felt like rubber. "Unless, of course, God is *specifically* leading you there."

"Another thing Frank said. He told me to be sure the decision was God's leading."

"If you kept meeting with Pastor Frank and did online class, you could keep meeting with guys like Chris."

"Don't worry, Kelsey." He pulled her close again. His response should have relieved her, but somehow didn't.

Chapter Seventeen

September sunlight bathed the backyard in a golden glow. Soon, crisp fingers of fall would weave into the air and the transition would begin. Rick breathed in the mellow breeze Sunday morning, trying to settle his nerves.

His conversation with Kelsey Friday night lay like a bad burrito in his stomach. The stricken expression on her face, the glint of tears in her eyes, had cut him in half. Why'd he tell her about Bible college? Had he been truthful when he told her it was just an idea, and he probably wouldn't go?

With her nestled in his arms, feeling like the piece of his heart that had been missing all his life...yes. He'd been truthful. He had no desire to go away from her. In fact, even *aside* from Kelsey, he didn't want to leave Brenner Falls. He'd rediscovered his home as a new man, and it felt good. And all the doors God had opened...

But school was an option he should at least consider.

Why did he feel guilty, then? Because despite what he'd told her, he'd already mailed off the application form. Of course, that didn't obligate him to go. He was covering his bases. That way, he'd be ready in advance, in case he *did* decide to go. And he'd have to apply anyway if he did online courses.

When he looked up the college online and saw their tuition fees, he'd laughed aloud. No way could he afford it unless they gave him some kind of scholarship. At Jesse's advice, he'd told the truth about his past in the essay part of the application without going into details. That alone would likely disqualify him, so he should never have burdened Kelsey with it.

He let out a long sigh. In recent weeks, he'd understood his past was gone, forgiven, and he was a new creature. He stood in God's presence with a clean record. But that didn't automatically equip him for ministry. Maybe Jesse shouldn't have placed him in a teaching role so quickly. Rick often felt he was in over his head. So, the appeal of Bible college was being well-prepared for whatever he was supposed to do. That and being a more spiritual partner to Kelsey, who'd been a believer most of her life.

On the patio table next to his Bible and empty coffee cup sat the Brenner Falls Times. Once he'd found his job at The Fork, he never read the local paper. But that day, he had another motive.

He opened the thin pages to the local leisure section and leafed through to see if there was an article about The Grateful Fork by the traveling journalist whose name he'd already forgotten. He zeroed in on a headline. *A Delicious Landmark to Discover in Brenner Falls,* he read. Maybe that was it.

Tucked in an alley dedicated to eateries, you'll find The Grateful Fork, a popular gathering place with great food and lively entertainment. I was passing through on my way to an assignment in Harrisburg when I happened on this gem. Turns out, The Grateful Fork has been a Brenner Falls landmark for the last forty years. Founded by Charles and Aggie Durante when Brenner Falls was merely a village instead of the small hopping town it is today, the restaurant has endured for decades. That ought to tell you something. Current manager Kelsey Brewster keeps it all flowing smoothly, despite the record crowds that packed out the place Friday night...

In spite of the heaviness inside him, Rick grinned. His girl was making headlines. She probably didn't get the paper, or if she did, probably didn't have time to read it. He took a photo of the article and texted it to her. It would make her smile and feel proud. At least he hoped so. He longed for her to see her value and her giftedness, instead of dwelling on the sidelines of her own dreams.

He included a message. *Good morning, my beauty. Here's the article from that guy. You deserve it! I'll be in church today instead of youth church. Want to sit together? Maybe it's time to go public...*

Rick was ready to tell the world about his feelings for Kelsey. Hopefully, she was ready as well and didn't have any hidden reasons for waiting. Maybe his suggestion would reassure her of his desire to be with her, whisking away his premature statements about leaving for school.

ങ ങ ങ

Kelsey gazed across the table at the sleepy faces of Danielle and Molly. "Did you sleep okay, Molly? I wonder if you guys stayed up too late last night."

"I slept okay." Molly looked glum that day, lacking her usual soft sparkle. Maybe she missed Kelsey as much as Kelsey missed her. And Danielle wasn't a good influence on Molly, who normally kept regular hours and had limited exposure to television. But it was difficult to survey the situation since she worked late many nights. She'd talk to Danielle later about it.

Since becoming manager of The Fork, Kelsey felt disconnected from her sister. Something had to change, but she wasn't sure what. Daily, she dwelt with the conflicting realities of satisfaction and regret. Would things get clearer once Danielle made a final decision about The Fork? Once she moved out, Kelsey would have full responsibility back on her shoulders and it would be even more difficult to juggle than before. But a part of her craved having the house back to just her and Molly.

It seemed inconceivable that Danielle would return to The Fork, taking back the role so perfectly suited to Kelsey. If she were brutally honest, she and the team had salvaged the restaurant from Danielle's lack of suitability. In only a month, Danielle had driven the budget to a downward trend for the first time since Covid. If she'd stayed, it might have been an unrecoverable disaster.

She sighed. Hopefully, that wouldn't happen. Her phone pinged. She didn't normally have it on the table during a meal, but hoped for a note from Rick or one of her friends to cheer her up.

Kelsey read Rick's text and grinned. It had certainly lifted her gloomy spirits. Not only the article by Lionel Spark, but his suggestion for them to sit together. They were finally moving out of the shadows.

"Good news?" Danielle asked.

"The other night at The Fork, a food journalist was passing through and wrote good things about it in an article."

"That's amazing. What good PR for Aggie."

"Yes. Her legacy lives on even when she's off cruising the world." Kelsey didn't even know where Aggie was at that moment. It didn't escape her notice that Danielle didn't mention Kelsey's role in The Fork's success.

At least Aggie had been present Friday night to see the fruit of her hard work and that of the current team. Maybe Kelsey should ask Aggie if she'd give her the job instead of Danielle. Would that be underhanded? If she and Aggie were business contacts instead of long-term friends, she'd have no hesitation. But with Danielle sitting across the table licking her oatmeal spoon, Kelsey couldn't bring herself to do it.

And then there was the bombshell Rick had dropped in her lap the other night. At the thought of Rick leaving for Bible college, a heavy weight sank in her stomach, even though he'd insisted it wasn't a serious idea. It might be a good path for young people headed into ministry, but somehow it didn't seem to fit Rick, who had a burgeoning ministry with youth. Clearly, God's hand was on him in that role.

Was she simply afraid of losing him so soon?

Another thought nagged at her, filling her mind with fearful shadows. When Rick talked about his previous girlfriend, Anna, he'd described her as unable to stay in one place. Maybe that also described him. After all, he'd taken off for Arizona at seventeen and moved around for over a decade. Was he even capable of a stable life? Or would he eventually feel restless, even though things were falling into place for him? Maybe four to six months was his limit. He'd been back for four months. Was he getting antsy to move on, or was his idea motivated purely by his desire to be equipped for ministry?

The whole subject was an overdue reminder to Kelsey to release her relationship with Rick into God's hands and not hold on too tightly. If God was the one leading Rick, she'd be peaceful, knowing he was in the right place.

Once she surrendered Rick to God's will, she felt realigned, calm. Might this be a test for her? There were no guarantees she'd receive what she desired, but she wanted to respond in the right way.

A while later, Kelsey sat next to Rick in church, along with Molly, Rick's mother, and her boyfriend, Tim. Rick cast frequent loving looks toward Kelsey, and her doubts drifted away. Mostly. He took her hand and stroked it with his thumb during the sermon. Amber and Ben weren't there that day. Amber's support of her relationship with Rick meant a lot, even chasing tiny doubts that floated into her mind once in a while.

"Do you want to come for lunch?" Kelsey asked Rick after the service.

"Sure. I could also take you out somewhere. I've been wanting to take you on a real date, kind of like we talked about. Not just for intel, though we could do both."

Kelsey shot a glance at her sister. "I'd love to go today, but I think I've been neglecting Molly. Can we go tomorrow night? Or do you have to work?"

He smiled. "I'm off. Tomorrow it is. For today, we'll do Kelsey's Bistro. Or should I say, Kelsey's Kitchen."

They laughed. "I like the sound of that," she said.

Lately, he came more often to the house, which permitted her to spend time with him *and* Molly without feeling conflicted. Yet, it wasn't sister time. She needed to schedule that too. "It's not quite like being a single mom, but has some resemblance," she said. "I know Molly's in Danielle's care and she's fine, but I sometimes feel like I've abandoned her."

"We can go out for lunch one day and bring Molly," he suggested.

"That's a sweet idea. I'll schedule a breakfast date with her, though generally, she prefers me cooking for her."

"I completely understand *that*."

Soon, they sat with Molly and Danielle at the dining room table enjoying some leftovers Kelsey had pulled together. Though she loved cooking, often she was thankful to have something to heat. One less thing to do. Tension had built between her shoulder blades and her head ached. She needed time alone, but whenever she had a free afternoon, she felt compelled to spend it with Molly or Rick. There simply weren't enough hours in her days.

"Did you hear about the journalist who wrote up a thing on The Fork?" Rick asked Danielle as he passed the bowl of pasta.

"Yes, Kelsey told me about it this morning. Our little Fork is getting famous."

Our little Fork?

"Did she happen to tell you the guy works for the Philadelphia Inquirer?"

Danielle's smile dropped. "Uh, no, she didn't." She turned to Kelsey. "That's amazing. Brenner Falls is a backwater compared to Philadelphia." She chuckled. "Pretty soon, Aggie will have to open up franchises."

"Not sure about that. But it was encouraging." Kelsey sipped her iced tea.

"Kelsey's name was mentioned in the article. And Vince and Aggie." Rick threw Kelsey a proud glance.

Danielle didn't comment, but her expression shifted, with a hardened jaw and cool gaze.

After dinner, Danielle and Molly retreated to the living room. Soon, Kelsey heard the muffled sound of the television. Like every night. She turned to Rick and raised her brows. "Were you trying to communicate something to Danielle just then?"

He grinned and pulled her in for a short kiss. "Of course, I was proud of you. That was my first motivation, but maybe she'll see how ideal the role is for you."

Kelsey lowered her voice. "She might feel you were rubbing her nose in her failure."

Rick's smile fell. "Oh, no. I wouldn't do that. I hope she didn't take it that way."

His contrite frown made her lean forward to kiss him. "I know you meant well. Her response is up to her."

Rick and Kelsey talked on the back porch for another hour, then she walked him to the door. After he left, she poked her head into the living room and only saw Danielle. "Did Molly already go to bed?"

Danielle took her attention from the movie. "Yeah. She said she was tired."

Kelsey nodded. "She rarely stays up past ten thirty. Otherwise, she can be cranky the next day."

"I'll keep that in mind."

"Well, I'll turn in too."

As she turned, she heard Danielle say, "I'd like to say congratulations but my pride's a little hurt."

Kelsey stopped in the doorway. "Your pride? Sorry, I don't understand."

"You got the manager role, then you got Rick, then you got all this recognition. I'm happy for you, but feel a little left in the dust."

Kelsey returned to the chair and sat across from Danielle. "Oh, Danielle. I'm sorry you feel that way. You'd barely gotten started at The Fork when you had your accident." She wouldn't tell Danielle she wasn't cut out for the job. She still hoped Danielle would realize it herself.

"But I was *almost* getting the hang of it when I had my accident." She found Kelsey's gaze. "I do remember you came alongside and wanted to see the notebook. You even took pictures of it."

Kelsey stilled. What was Danielle getting at? "Yes, I came alongside to help. I saw you struggling at first. You'd never worked in restaurants all that much, and there you were managing the whole thing. At the time, you were grateful for all the help. We're a team at The Fork. Aggie said as much."

"I know. I'm just sad I wasn't the one to talk to the journalist that night. It'll be hard to go back and follow your success."

"Danielle." Kelsey's voice was gentle, though her heart pounded with the understanding that Danielle intended to return as manager. "Did you really *like* managing The Fork? I mean, is it your niche as much as IT?"

Danielle fell silent, a frown tugging at her jaw. "Since you put it that way, not really. I didn't know how hard it would be. I kept thinking I'd get it. But then you seemed to breeze right through, so I got a bit jealous." She looked at her hands. "I didn't tell you that, but after what Rick said…"

"I hope you know he wasn't rubbing your nose in my *success—*" She made air quotes. "Of course, it's always a team effort. Rick was proud of me, that's all." At Danielle's silence, Kelsey continued. "You stepped into the role because of Aggie and because you were unemployed. What would you do if you could choose a job for yourself?"

Danielle appeared to ponder. Her gaze met Kelsey's. "I'd do what I was doing before."

"Wouldn't you be happier doing that than struggling at The Fork? I'm saying that for *your* sake, not mine." Though they'd both benefit if Danielle saw her point.

"Yes, I would. But I tried before. Maybe I should try again. I'm grateful for the job swap, though."

"It's been nice having you here. Don't forget you're smart and have lots of gifts. I was amazed by how quickly you learned my job."

"That boring thing? I could do it in my sleep." She grinned.

Kelsey laughed. "See what I mean?"

Chapter Eighteen

The following morning, Kelsey took Molly out for breakfast so they could have some sister time. She'd do that more frequently until Danielle moved out.

When they arrived home, Kelsey called from the hallway, "We're home, Danielle, but not for long."

She stuck her head into the doorway of the living room to see Danielle in her usual spot on the couch, the computer open on the table in front of her. She looked up at Kelsey and offered a relaxed smile, a relief in view of their conversation the previous evening. "Are you working the lunch shift today, Kelsey?"

"Yes, Molly and I are going together, but we won't eat beforehand. We ate a lot for breakfast. I can heat a bowl of spaghetti for you if you like."

"Yes, thanks."

Kelsey heated the spaghetti and carried a tray to Danielle.

"I thought a lot about our conversation yesterday." Danielle settled the tray on her lap. "I think the reason I wanted to try again at The Fork was to prove to myself I can do it, like a personal challenge. Then I remembered how stressed out I was. Picturing myself back in that job gave me a stomachache."

"Because of stress?"

"Yeah. So, I won't go back. I spent some time online this morning looking for jobs. I found a couple that look interesting, so I applied for them."

"That's great, Danielle. You'll be happier, and I'm not just saying that to keep you from going back."

"I don't know how you make it look so easy!"

Kelsey laughed. "I never said it was easy. It's easier for me because I've been doing it for years, and don't forget, I'm a food person."

"You sure are. I've been so spoiled here. I'll miss it when I leave, which I think will be soon."

"Did your doctor say you're able to start doing more?"

"He did. I'm about ready for a boot or just one crutch. I don't know what I'd have done without you, Kelsey. Thanks so much for setting this all up. I'd have been broke *and* helpless."

"Well, you helped me as much as I helped you." Kelsey smiled.

"I'm glad we could help each other. And I'm glad I got a front-row seat to the Rick and Kelsey romance."

They laughed. "I was as surprised as you, believe me."

"He's a good guy. He turned out to be a huge surprise, I'll admit. I'm happy for you two."

On Friday of the same week, Kelsey pulled into the driveway after working the lunch shift and picking up Molly at Treasure House. "We're going to stay home tonight, kiddo. I'll make my super-special pizza that you love, and we'll watch a goofy movie, okay?"

Molly grinned. "I like goofy movies. And pizza." She slipped out of the car. "Rick is coming?"

"No, sadly, he has to work the dinner shift too tonight. He's a busy guy." He was still requesting extra shifts, for some reason. Maybe he was saving money for school tuition. "Or we'll play a game if you'd rather do that."

They entered the house. Kelsey pulled off her cardigan, which she'd started using that week. "We're home, Danielle," she called, then helped Molly remove her sweater.

Kelsey went to the living room and sat in an armchair facing Danielle.

"I have some exciting news for you," Danielle said.

"You won a cruise on a shopping channel."

"No." Danielle grinned.

"You have a date with the mailman. He's kind of cute, as we both noticed."

They both laughed. "Wrong again. Okay, I'll tell you. Otherwise, we'll be here all day. I have a new job."

Kelsey's mouth fell open. "That was quick, but great news. Tell me!"

"I've only been applying for a few days, but the timing was right for this one. It's a financial products company. Investments, insurance. Stuff like that. They loved my resume. I told them I had to work remotely, since I was still recovering, and they said it's a remote position anyway."

"When will you start?"

"I start training on Monday. I think I'm ready to go home now, Kelsey. I'll go home and set up there."

"Will you be able to feed yourself and everything?"

Danielle laughed. "I *need* to fast for about six months, but yes, I can manage. I'm hopping around on one crutch and can put some weight on my bum foot. I'm ready to be more independent."

"I can check on you or help once in a while if you need something," Kelsey offered. "A ride to the doctor or whatever."

"You've done so much already, Kelsey. What'll you do about the online job?"

Kelsey let out a breath. "I guess I'll resign, but may have to give two weeks' notice." And work two full-time jobs in the meantime.

Danielle frowned. "This whole situation would have been smoother if Aggie had been around more. But I can't blame her, either. She hardly took any time off in forty years."

The women fell silent in reflection. The Fork was going to be Kelsey's only job. Something sparked deep inside. It was what she'd wanted, but now was within her grasp. Was she ready to be *the* manager instead of only temporary?

"I should at least let Aggie know," Kelsey said.

"I don't think she'll have any problem with you managing The Fork. For one, she's seen how well you work there. Second, who else would she hire? And third, she really likes you. You're like the daughter she never had."

Warmth flushed through Kelsey's chest. "That's sweet to say. We've always been on the same wavelength about food."

"But she might have just left on a Mediterranean cruise. I hope you can reach her."

Kelsey grimaced. Poor timing.

Working full time alongside Rick...for now, it would be ideal. For the future? No idea.

That evening, once they finished the pizza dinner and cleaned up, they played a board game instead of watching a movie, per Molly's choice. It was more fun and active than a movie. Kelsey hadn't played a board game, read a good book, or truly relaxed in a long time. Now, with Danielle starting her job and moving out, Kelsey would get what she wished for—the house back to herself and Molly. But it would come at a price. She'd have two full-time jobs plus take care of Molly.

She had to get in touch with Aggie, and soon.

As the game wound down, Kelsey kept one eye on the clock. Rick would get off soon. Before the second round began, Kelsey said, "I'm going to take a quick break, but you both start without me."

She slipped back into her bedroom and punched Rick's number. He answered after one ring. "Hello, my beauty. I'm in the car on the way home. In fact, I'm almost there. What are you doing?"

"I just played a board game with Molly and Danielle, but I wanted a chance to talk to you. I never seem to have the time at work. And I have big news."

"I'm going into the house right now where I'll collapse on the couch and listen to your news."

Kelsey heard the keys jangle in the door.

"Okay, I'm officially collapsed," he said. "Feels good to get off my feet."

"I'm sure it does. Danielle found a job and is moving out over the weekend."

Rick whistled. "That was fast. She just started applying a few days ago."

"Yeah, she just hit the right company with an opening that fit her. They rushed her in because they had a big need."

"So, you'll quit your regular job, right?"

"Yes, but I should confirm with Aggie, don't you think?"

"I think you're safe to quit, especially since as manager, you're endowed with powers to hire and fire, even yourself. She wanted to hire you first. And who *else* would she hire?"

"That's what Danielle said. And Aggie has known me for years."

"So, there are at least three reasons she wouldn't mind. But if it makes you feel better, call her."

"I'll try her tomorrow, once I'm sure she's landed."

And since it was Friday, she couldn't contact her boss at her regular job until Monday. Then she'd likely have to give a couple weeks' notice. She'd do her best juggling everything. It was temporary. She could do it.

"Change of subject," Rick said. "I spoke to Chris today. He told me he understands the faith decision better than ever and thinks about it a lot. I hope he'll come around soon."

"Oh, Rick. That's wonderful. You've had a good impact on him, meeting regularly with him."

"He hasn't seen his dad in a couple of years. When his parents split up, his mom moved and eventually his dad remarried and has a new family. I think that's hard on him. He's afraid his dad's written him off. Chris wants to write and ask to visit him over one of the holidays, or even some other time."

"Can't Chris just call him?"

"I don't think they've been in touch lately. It's sad. It's like his dad replaced Chris and his sister when he got remarried."

"How terrible. Well, he should ask. Nothing ventured, nothing gained. I'll pray about that conversation."

"I knew you would. I try to steer him toward God as a perfect father, but he wants his real dad in the picture."

"That's understandable."

"It's a normal desire, but his dad has disappointed him a bunch of times in the past."

Kelsey heard another voice on the phone. Rick's mom had entered the room.

"The lady about town has just come home from her date with the handsome dentist," Rick teased. His mother laughed in the background. "She's in love, Kelsey. My mom's in love. Can you believe that?"

"Stop that, Rick," Kelsey heard his mother say, though she giggled at the same time. Kelsey grinned.

"And she's not the only one," Rick whispered. "Good night, my beauty."

He disconnected too quickly for Kelsey to respond. She stared at her phone. Had she heard him correctly? Maybe he'd disconnected right away because he felt shy telling her he loved her. She savored it in her mind, rolling it around a few times like a delectable hard candy. Was she falling too? Maybe *he* wasn't the only one.

Chapter Nineteen

Rick waited for Chris in one of the less sterile-looking classrooms of the church. A coffee shop would be more appealing to him, but too noisy on a Saturday morning. He'd been meeting with Chris for a couple of months and watched him inch toward spiritual understanding of salvation. Chris was still wary of many people, but for some reason, trusted Rick. Probably because he'd been more messed up than Chris would ever be.

The previous evening, Rick had talked with Stephen and Annika for a long while on Facetime. After the call, he felt like he'd had a shot of vitamins. They'd responded with joy and enthusiasm when he told them about Kelsey. He loved hearing how they were doing too. It made him miss them more. They'd had their youngest son home all summer and had just taken him back to college.

He used the opening to ask them what they thought about Bible school. They assumed he was talking about online classes and said they thought it was a great idea because he could fit it in with his work and ministry. That was hard to imagine, since he worked more than full-time. He didn't mention the option of going away to school, which seemed like a long shot anyway.

Chris walked in and slid into a chair across the table from Rick. "Sorry I'm late. My sister needed a ride somewhere. Her car's busted."

"No worries." They'd just seen each other at the youth meeting a couple of days prior, so Rick launched in. "What've you been reading, and what do you think of it?"

"Your favorite opening question." Chris grinned. "But it works. And knowing you're going to ask me makes me try harder to come up with an answer ahead of time."

Rick laughed. "Good, that was my strategy. Next question will be *what'll you do about it*, but we'll cover that when the time comes."

"So..." Chris thumbed through a spiral notebook. The Bible Rick had given him sat next to it on the table. "Ah, here it is. Luke eight. It was full of crazy stuff, man. Like, Jesus calmed a storm, then he healed this guy...the guy seemed crazy, but it says he had demons." He shook his head. "It was pretty wild. Jesus sent the demons into some pigs."

A smile tugged at Rick's lips. Chris was in for an eye-opening ride, and he'd only just begun. "Did anything hit you when you were reading, like something that might be practical in your life?"

"Yeah. There was the section on the seeds. Some of them grew and others were eaten by birds."

"Do you think God is planting seeds in your life?"

Chris paused. "Lately I think so. I don't want to be the guy whose seeds get eaten by birds." He grinned.

"Me either. Those birds represent all the stuff in life that can pull you away and distract you. Might be temptations, bad company, disappointments..."

Rick feared Chris would hit disappointments with his dad, and suspected he kept negative company sometimes too. "Life can be pretty hard. And it's tough to keep those seeds growing. There are things that'll certainly help. First, we need to water the seeds and let them grow."

They talked for a while longer. Chris had made steady progress week by week. He always had questions and sometimes perceptive observations. Rick felt humbled and honored to have a bond with him, to have earned his trust. He couldn't help but think it was his personal story that had broken the ice for Chris.

"Did you email your dad?"

The light of discovery left Chris's eyes, and they became dull. "Yeah, last night. I asked him if I could come for a visit sometime in the fall before the holidays." He shrugged. "He's a busy guy, but we'll see."

"How long has it been since you've seen him?"

"A couple years. He's got a son, Andrew. He's four. I've never met him."

Rick's eyes widened. "Were you and your dad close before your parents split?"

"I dunno. A little. He always worked a lot."

"My dad was like that too," Rick said. His memory was hazy, but there was a good reason. Not much to remember. "Then after work, he'd fall asleep in front of the TV. Like, every night. I don't remember many conversations with him." Just in case Chris thought having a lame father was unusual.

"Me neither."

"Well, keep me posted."

After his meeting with Chris, Rick drove to Kelsey's house to help her move Danielle back home. When he arrived, Danielle and Kelsey waited outside next to two suitcases and a duffle bag. "Are you ready to fly solo, Danielle?" He grinned as he approached the porch, already dotted with fallen leaves.

"Yeah, I think so. I'll holler for help if I need it."

Kelsey gave a firm nod. "That's our agreement. Ask for help."

Rick took the largest suitcase and slung it into his trunk.

"Once Aggie's back in town, she can help me sometimes too." He and Kelsey hauled everything into the trunk, then Rick helped Danielle gingerly settle into the front seat.

When they'd finished settling Danielle into her small apartment across town, he and Kelsey returned to the house. "Come on in for my special limeade." She gave him a tantalizing wink.

Rick followed her into the kitchen. "Gladly. I'm sure it's as tasty as your lemonade, and about everything else you make."

She poured two glasses for them. Rick took a deep sip of cool, tangy limeade. "Now you have to get used to having the place back to yourself."

She leaned against the counter and sipped her drink. "It's going to be a change. Good, but weird. And hard. For example, I'm working tonight, and I need to take Molly with me. I don't have a built-in helper anymore."

"Can Molly stay by herself sometimes?"

"Yes, she can. I'm just hyper-vigilant, since our parents left her in my care."

"I understand. But you might need to relax a little. Otherwise, you're going to burn out fast."

Kelsey faced him and tears glistened in her eyes. "I'm burning out already." Her voice cracked. "And I haven't even started doing both jobs yet."

He gathered her in his arms and held her for a few moments. "I'd do your online job if I could, but I don't have time either. The only solution is to quit the other one. Have you been able to reach Aggie?"

"Yes, finally today I talked to her. Reception was bad, but at least I got my point across. She said I didn't have to ask her."

"See? I thought she'd say that. So, can you quit your old job?"

"Yes, I'll send my resignation this weekend. They may want two weeks' notice."

He shrugged. "We can deal with that. You'll have to cut down your hours at The Fork for that time, but we'll all pitch in to help you.'"

She smiled and tightened her arms around his waist. "I know you will, and I'm grateful."

The following day, Chris wasn't in youth church. He didn't always make it, but hadn't told Rick he wouldn't be there. Might have slept in. After the service, Rick went to the sanctuary and scanned the crowd for Kelsey. He probably just missed her, but he'd see her later. Once he got to his car, he texted Chris to check on him.

Thirty minutes later, he sat at the kitchen table with Kelsey and Molly as they dug into the lunch Kelsey had prepared. He glanced at his phone. No response from Chris. Since that was unusual, he phoned him, but it went to voice mail.

After lunch, they sat on the couch in the living room while Molly worked on a puzzle on a nearby table. "Seems strange to sit here without Danielle on the couch," Kelsey said. "I'm sure I'll adjust, though."

"Yes, and quickly." He paused. "I'm concerned about Chris. He didn't come to youth church today and I haven't been able to reach him either."

Kelsey's smile dropped and her brows furrowed. "I hope he's okay. Let's pray for him." He took her hands, and they prayed for protection and salvation for Chris, and for his relationship with his dad.

For the next hour, Rick and Kelsey worked with Molly on her puzzle. As the autumn sun mellowed in the sky, Rick's phone rang. It was Jesse.

"Rick, Chris is in the hospital. Apparently, he overdosed last night when he was with some friends. They got scared and called 911."

He was already out of his chair. "When did he go, Jesse? Is he going to be okay?" He thrust his fingers into his hair. Chris had been fine the day before. Rick thought he'd left drugs. He'd been wrong. He should have asked him, confronted him. Why didn't he? *Oh, why?*

"I hope so," Jesse said. "Seems he got to the hospital in time, but I don't know what shape he's in. I couldn't go today, but I'll go as soon as I can tomorrow."

"I'll go. I'm leaving now." His hands shook as he fumbled for his keys.

Rick disconnected the call and turned to Kelsey. Her blue eyes crinkled with worry. He took her hands. "Chris is in the hospital. He OD'd on something last night." His voice rasped and he fought the burn in his eyes.

"Oh, no, Rick!" She bit her lip and fell into his embrace, then pulled back. "Do you want me to go with you?"

"No, stay here with Molly. I'll call you when I have news."

An aching lump weighed in his stomach as he drove across town to Brenner Falls General Hospital. "Lord, why? Why? He was so close to coming to know you. Please protect him, Lord," he murmured as he drove. He prayed it hadn't been fentanyl. Survival rates were dismal. Coke was less lethal.

A nurse gave him Chris's room number. Rick dashed down the hall, into an elevator, and down another hall while the words *why, why, why* throbbed in his head. He peered into the room and saw Chris lying immobile. He looked dead. Rick clenched his fists by his side and stared at the pale face he'd seen only yesterday, but that day it was slightly bluish.

He approached the bed and touched Chris' arm. "Can you hear me, pal? Chris, it's Rick."

When Chris didn't move, new tears threatened to flood down his cheeks. *Lord, don't let him die. Please, he was so close to meeting you. Please protect him.*

Chris's eyes fluttered. He peered up at Rick through slits and groaned. Hope leaped inside Rick. He grasped Chris's hand and squeezed. "You okay, man? I mean, I've seen stupid moves, but this beats all. When you get out of here, we're gonna have a long talk."

He stopped when he saw one side of his lips tug upward. He was smiling? "Wa—ter," he croaked.

"You need water? Sure." A pitcher and cup sat on the side table. Rick poured some into the cup and held it up to Chris's lips, easing a little at a time into his mouth. "When did you get here? Do you remember?"

"Maybe last night. I got messed up...with some friends..."

"I recommend you ditch those friends. I'll introduce you to more people if you need new friends." Relief was making Rick babble. Chris was conscious. That's all that mattered.

"What was it, coke? Fentanyl?"

"Not that...stuff. Coke...bad enough."

"Yeah, you got that right." A hurricane of emotion spun inside Rick. Relief, guilt, sorrow, frustration. "I thought you'd given it up, dude."

"I...did. But then...my dad..."

Oh. "Your dad gave you a negative response?"

Chris nodded at Rick for more water. He took the cup back to his friend's lips. That seemed to help. "My dad said it wasn't a good time to...visit. It was Andrew's birthday and...they were taking a trip."

"So, maybe he wasn't saying no, he didn't want to see you. It sounds like a busy time. Did he suggest anything else?"

Chris shook his head. "That's what...sucks. I told him...I told him he had three kids, not one. That's all I said. I won't try again."

Rick frowned. His insides squeezed with sorrow for Chris. "Yeah, it sucks. I'm sorry, dude. You deserve better. I'm glad you told him that. He needs to be reminded." At least Chris had the last word.

A nurse came into the room. "I'll let you get some rest. I'll come by tomorrow, unless they release you. Jesse said he'd come tomorrow. And I'll stay in touch."

Chris offered a faint smile.

On the drive home, Rick's torment grew like a storm, tossing out memories like dust and debris. Why hadn't he seen the signs? Why hadn't he pointedly asked Chris if he was still using? Chris would have told him the truth. Why had he assumed he'd left his other friends, just because he showed up at youth group and met with Rick regularly?

One thing was sure. Rick had jumped into this youth ministry thing too soon, and now his pride and naivete had come back to bite him. He hadn't been savvy enough—despite his vast experience—to see that Chris was hovering on the edge, still using drugs.

When he arrived at his mom's house, he remembered he'd promised to phone Kelsey. She answered right away. "How's Chris? Is he okay?" Worry laced her voice.

"Yeah, I think he'll be okay."

"Thank God!" She let out a breath. "Will they keep him in the hospital a few days?"

"I don't know. I'll call tomorrow." Speaking required a huge effort. Even to Kelsey. "I'll keep you posted."

"Rick, are you okay? You don't sound okay."

"It's...hard. He came so close...he could have died, Kelsey. I didn't see the signs."

"It's not your fault, Rick. Don't you go blaming yourself."

"But I *know* the signs. I was an expert at that lifestyle, remember?"

Kelsey groaned. "Maybe there *were* no signs. You weren't with Chris twenty-four seven. You told me yourself when he was at youth group, there were no signs after the first time you noticed it. Rick, you're not God. You can't stop people from doing stupid things. If it weren't for you, maybe he'd have overdosed sooner and died! As it is, this kid trusts you enough to meet with you and let you speak into his life. But that doesn't mean you're responsible for him. He's responsible for himself. And don't forget, God is there too."

He let her talk, savoring her words, knowing they were true. Yet, the claws of guilt and regret kept scratching him, making his insides bleed. "Thanks, Kelsey. You're right. Hey, I'll call you tomorrow, okay?"

"Can I see you tomorrow?"

"Um, I don't know. I want to go back to the hospital. I'll call you."

"Please don't go through this alone, Rick. We're a team, remember?"

"Yeah." His voice grew faint, as if he was falling over a cliff. "The Force for The Fork." He attempted a smile, but it didn't take.

"Let's talk tomorrow. You're worrying me now. I want to walk through this with you."

"Okay. Goodnight."

He disconnected before she could say anything else. The anguish in her voice echoed in his ears. She'd been right, but his heart wasn't receiving her words. *Lord, am I really cut out for this stuff?*

༄ ༄ ༄

Kelsey held the warm phone in her hand, feeling something crumble inside her. *Lord, be with Rick in this crisis. Help him to see it's not his fault. Comfort him, please!*

Fighting tears, she rose and pushed out a cheery question. "Ready for a simple dinner, Molly?" She didn't have the leisure to lock herself in her room to cry and pray for Rick. Not yet. Of course, he was disappointed and worried about Chris, who'd shown such a thirst for God. It was a setback, but Rick would be okay. Wouldn't he?

She forced light conversation over dinner. When they'd finished, she stood. "I need some time alone, okay? I'll be in my room if you need me. I might even go to bed early."

"Okay." Molly's large eyes searched Kelsey's face. Kelsey knew Molly sensed trouble descending in the room, felt her despair. Molly reached out her hands. "Kelsey."

Kelsey drew Molly into a hug and held her tightly for a long moment. She drew strength from the physical connection with her sister, who didn't understand everything, but knew intuitively something was wrong. With her face over Molly's shoulder, she blinked back tears. "Rick is discouraged." Her voice broke. "We need to pray for him, and for his friend who is in the hospital."

Molly murmured simple but heartfelt words and Kelsey added her own. "Amen," they said together. Kelsey's burden lifted slightly.

Kelsey didn't see Rick the following day, though they usually saw each other at some point every Monday. He'd told her on the phone he wanted to go back to the hospital and had some other errands to run, but she felt uneasy. Normally, he'd want to see her. And she deeply wanted to walk with him through the crisis, sensing he was taking it personally. She spent most of the day working on her online job, though Rick's state hovered like a dark cloud over her all day. She also sent her resignation to her boss, lacking the satisfaction and sense of closure she'd hoped to have when she pushed *send*.

By Wednesday, Kelsey had only seen Rick across the room at The Fork, working with a stoic set on his face. He'd called a couple of times, to let her know that Chris was doing better and had gone home. That was a relief. Yet, he hadn't suggested they see each other. He was spiraling into a crisis she didn't understand, but why, since Chris was on the mend?

Finally, she texted him. *Rick, I miss talking to you and I'm concerned for you. I don't know what's going on in your head, but please don't shut me out. Let me walk through this with you. Please.* She almost added, *I love you*, but stopped herself. She knew she did love Rick Russo, but didn't know where she stood with him anymore. How could he shut her out like that? What was going on?

He'd texted back, *Don't worry, my beauty. I'm just working through it in my way. I'll be okay. We'll talk soon.* His words lifted a portion of her burden, but not all. Something still wasn't right.

That evening, she called Amber. The day Kelsey told Amber of her relationship with Rick, she'd been supportive, seeing Rick in the present instead of the past. *He needs someone like you in his life*, she'd said. *I think you're good together.*

Kelsey wasn't doing Rick any good now, though.

"Amber, I need to talk to Ben. Something's up with Rick. One of the guys from the youth group overdosed, and he's taking it hard. Maybe it's reminding him of his similar experience. I don't know. But he's blocking me out, and it's not like him."

"Oh, I'm so sorry, Kelsey," Amber said. "I'm sure you're really worried about him. Ben isn't here now, but I'll let him know and he can reach out to Rick."

They caught up on a few other pieces of news, then disconnected.

Hopefully, Ben could reach his brother in a way that Kelsey could not.

Chapter Twenty

Garbled noise from customer conversations and clanking silverware rose to the ceiling, rubbing on Rick's nerves. He tried to block it out and stay focused on his work as he went back and forth to the kitchen, carrying more and more plates and glasses. He ought to use the cart that was available for that purpose, but it was an old habit to do it by himself.

What was harder to block out than the noise was the awareness of Kelsey across the room visiting each table to check in with customers, or circulating around surveying everything. He knew her well by now. He could see the despondency that saturated her, down to her gait, her facial expression, how she held her shoulders...though she faked her way through each smiling conversation with diners.

Guilt lay on him like a heavy blanket, along with a longing for her that went down to his bones. Despite Kelsey pleading numerous times to let her walk alongside him through his struggle with what had happened to Chris, he held her at arm's length too. For what reason...he wasn't exactly sure. Except that he knew he wasn't the man she thought he was.

That was the reason Bible college seemed a better and better option to him. He'd go there for a while and come out a *better* man. Transformed. Full of knowledge, experiences, input from other believers. No longer would he misread situations that could lead to disastrous consequences.

But where did he stand with Kelsey? Had he broken up with her? Certainly not, though she probably felt like he had. But the more time he spent with her, the harder it would be to go away. Not that he'd be very far. He wanted to do the responsible thing, with her and with himself, but had no idea what that was.

After his shift, he tossed his filthy apron into the bin. Fortunately, Kelsey was busy, so he was able to slip out without her miserable gaze gutting him. He'd also dodged several texts and phone calls from Ben. Guilt seemed to be second nature anymore. Kind of like breathing.

He inhaled a deep draught of fresh air untainted by odors of oil and condiments. The crisp autumn day embraced him, and right away he felt lighter, more hopeful. A flawless powder blue sky stretched out above him. He drove toward the river, where he could be far from anything or anyone that would trigger more guilt and confusion.

Without meaning to, he ended up parking at the shelter. A painful twinge cut him inside as he thought of Kelsey, that day when he first told her how he felt about her. The day he first kissed her. His breath and heart became heavy, so he shifted his thoughts away from her, away from how he was hurting her even now. Since they'd been together, he'd never left The Fork before without saying goodbye or telling her he missed being with her.

This section of the river was also where he first met with Chris. Fortunately, he'd been discharged from the hospital and had gone home to the hovering care of his mother and sister. The day Rick saw him again at the hospital, Chris had been more alert and able to talk.

Hey, Dude. You had Jesse and me scared out of our heads, Rick had told him. *I thought you'd given up on that junk.*

I mostly did, honest. When I got that response from my dad, I don't know. It just hit me real hard. It wasn't so much what he said, it was the fact that he'd said the very same thing the last time I asked him. Every time, I ask him if I can see him and he tells me it's not a good time, instead of him wanting to see my sister and me. Like he's written us off.

I'm sorry, man. That's really tough. It's his loss, but he still hurt you.

Yeah, I felt like I wasn't worth anything to him. Then it spiraled, you know? Goes from there to I'm not worth anything, period. Got together with some friends and felt better for a while. Then they started getting stoned and the temptation was too strong. He'd given Rick a sheepish shrug. *But I'm done with that stuff.*

I hope so, but I'm not judging you. I was worried. I'm glad you're okay. It was a close call.

Their conversation had lifted Rick's spirits. Chris wasn't blaming him. So, why did Rick blame himself? Chris's crisis had passed, and he'd survived. Rick's crisis got deeper every day. *Lord, what's the story with my life here? What do you want me to do?*

Silence met his question, which was fueled more by frustration than a desire to know. One option was to continue what he was doing. Youth, Kelsey, The Fork. It was a good life for now, unless he found himself over his head again. Who was he kidding? He'd be in over his head before he went to bed that night. At least he wasn't doing the talk at youth group later on. His mind was still in a dark place, not ready to share inspirational truth with teenagers.

He'd already embraced his forgiveness and his new nature. But that didn't mean he was equipped for ministry. He was a baby, a beginner wearing big boy shoes. He'd only been a believer for two years.

Though he savored the sight of the sun on the water's surface, he left the park with no distinct direction. The days of God clearly speaking to him seemed to be over. The thought deepened his anguish.

When he arrived home, he snagged a fistful of mail from the box. His mom wasn't due home for a while, so the house was quiet and still. Most of the mail was for her, but one thick envelope was addressed to him. An envelope from the Mid-Penn Bible Institute.

Rick ripped into the envelope, almost hoping for a regret letter. As he skimmed it, his eyes widened. They'd not only accepted him, but offered a partial scholarship based on the content of his essay and his financial situation, with an option for a part-time work-study job on campus. He sat still like a statue, letting the realization flow over him. Everything had fallen into place. The scholarship, the acceptance. Even his mom was settled in her new relationship, freeing him to move on. God might not have spoken to Rick clearly at the river, but wasn't he speaking now? Wasn't this proof enough of what he wanted?

ঞ ঞ ঞ

Friday night, there was no band, but the Grateful Fork was every bit as busy and noisy as if there'd been rollicking country western music blaring through the room. Kelsey hadn't stopped moving all evening, not even taking a break. Part of that was by design. She couldn't bear to look at Rick across the room or chance running into him in the kitchen. It wasn't a break-up, really. But she had no idea what it was, aside from absolutely miserable.

On top of that, she still had a week left of her previous job. She'd cut back her hours at The Fork for her sanity's sake, not only with her double responsibilities, but with Rick's behavior. It had been a matter of survival and nearly constant prayer.

As the dining room emptied and the evening wound down, Kelsey looked at the clock. Might not be too late to watch a movie with Molly with bowls of ice cream. Anything to occupy her mind and rediscover a normal rhythm at the house.

She pitched her apron into the bin and turned, nearly running into Rick. "Want to take a walk?" he asked softly. Warmth flickered in his eyes. "It's not too cold out."

"Uh, sure. That would be nice." A thread of hope leaped inside, but his expression didn't confirm it. Though friendly enough, the soft, loving look she loved hadn't returned.

Would he explain his thinking and tell her why he'd gone off the rails as her boyfriend and even as her friend? Kelsey said goodnight to Vince and the last few servers, put on her jacket, and left with Rick.

The evening air, laced with chill, refreshed her after the constant running all evening. The pace had made time go by quickly, but it was often physically exhausting. At that moment, however, her senses were on high alert as she and Rick walked side by side. He didn't speak and didn't take her hand. Her hope that things would revert to normal between them seeped away.

Their footsteps echoed on the empty street as they walked toward the park where the weekly market took place, now empty and eclipsed by the night. "Are you feeling better?" she ventured into the silence.

"I feel better about Chris. I've talked to him about what happened, and I think he was spooked enough to not let it happen again."

Kelsey frowned. Though his words were positive, they weren't the words she'd hoped to hear. Instead, his statement could have come from a neighbor or a friend. "And you?" She stopped walking and threw up her hands in frustration. "Do you want to tell me what happened to you this week, Rick? Or are you only going to tell me about how Chris feels better and everyone's glad he didn't die? Yes, of course, we're glad. But does this explain why you haven't spoken to me in a week? Was I somehow at fault?"

His mouth fell open at her outburst. "No, of course not. You had nothing to do with it."

Then the veneer of anger cracked, and tears squeezed from her eyes. She turned away from him and crossed her arms. "Is this the way you deal with hard things? Is this how you face trials and setbacks and disappointments?"

He touched her shoulder. "I don't really know how I deal with those things, Kelsey. When I was young, I got high and drunk. Then eventually, I'd just leave and start over somewhere else."

"And those responses weren't productive, as I'm sure you know. So now, you're thirty-one. A grown man living a responsible life for a couple of years, right? So, what do you call this?" She held out her hands. "What do you call shutting out everyone who cares about you and not even *talking* to them?" Her tone had risen again while the tears flowed freely. The geyser of despair and frustration had finally exploded.

"I call it...wrong. It's wrong. I'm so sorry, Kelsey. I couldn't deal with anything else."

She took a breath. "It's upsetting, what happened to Chris. I agree. But he's okay now. You did your best for him, and he acted like an idiot. So, let's move on."

They approached a wooden picnic table, and he sat on a bench. He thrust a hand through his hair and turned his anguished face toward her. "I felt like I'd failed Chris. I'd gotten in over my head playing youth pastor." His jaw tightened.

"You did *not*. You stepped out by faith and God blessed your efforts. He used your past failures and bad choices to draw kids so you can help them. He showed you the gift he gave you. *He* did that. It's not about you, Rick. It's about being available to God."

When he didn't answer, she continued. "You're still led by guilt. That's not going to get you anywhere. It's going to block you until you can let it go and believe the truth."

"Everything you're saying is right on. But I think I need more background. More training before I do all this."

Kelsey sighed. "Maybe you do. We've talked about this, remember? You're meeting with Pastor Frank, with Jesse. They give you opportunities and training. Mentoring. That's fantastic. Why isn't it enough? Just take it a step at a time, like you've been doing. If you want to pull back, pull back. You can even quit the youth ministry for a while or permanently. Just don't stonewall everyone when you have a setback."

Rick rose from the bench and faced her, his hands in his coat pockets. "I shouldn't have shut you out, Kelsey. I had a lot to think about. And I..." He sighed and glanced away from her. "I need more training," he said again. "I'm...I'm leaving for Bible college in January."

Kelsey stared at him as her insides splintered. "Bible college." She swallowed. "I thought you weren't serious the other night."

Darkness shadowed his face, but she saw the stubborn set of his jaw. Gone was the peace and openness he had before. "I need more education," he said dully. "The campus isn't that far from here, a little over an hour. I'll come back a couple weekends a month and we can see each other."

"Why can't you do online classes? That way, you don't have to leave at all. And you can keep working with the kids. Chris needs you even *more* than before. What do you think he'll do when you leave? He'll feel like you abandoned him, just like his dad did." Rick winced, but didn't respond.

"I have news for you, Rick. Bible college isn't some kind of box you go into and come out the other side transformed, with guarantees to never fail, never lack an answer, never disappoint anyone. All of that stuff is called *life*. And it's what helps us grow, because each step of the way, we have to respond according to our faith. We have to *choose* to follow God, and he teaches us along the way. You've never had to do that before. And now, you're running away, just like you did when you were seventeen."

She stopped herself, completely out of steam. Kelsey couldn't convince Rick of anything. She'd said her piece, probably more than she should have. He'd have to figure it out on his own, since her feelings and all they'd shared didn't appear to weigh much for him.

Kelsey softened her tone. "If you've prayed about this and you're sure it's *God* who is leading you rather than your feelings of guilt an inadequacy, then you have my blessing."

She turned and left him standing near the bench. With her face moistened by tears, she walked back to her car through the lamplit darkness.

Chapter Twenty-One

Was it too early to pack? Of course, it was. It wasn't even November yet. But Rick felt antsy in his mom's empty house that Saturday morning. She'd just left for the grocery store. He couldn't yet bring himself to tell her he was again leaving her life, this time to go to Bible college.

Normally, he would have met with Chris that morning, but had told him he had things to do. In reality, he was putting off telling Chris he was leaving town in a couple months. That news could wait. He'd read more about the school online, hoping it would spark some excitement, but the result was more guilt. Maybe by the time he left, he'd feel better about the decision, instead of the conviction that, once again, he was letting everyone down.

He should put Chris first right now instead of himself. He should be over there picking up where they'd left off the day they talked about scattered seeds. Maybe his close call had made an impact on him. Were those birds eating *Rick's* seeds of understanding?

Rick returned to the kitchen and opened some cupboards, searching for distraction. He wasn't hungry and hadn't been for several days. He shut the cupboards, and his thoughts returned to his conversation with Kelsey the previous evening, though he'd never actually *stopped* thinking about it. Her words boomeranged several times during the night as he awoke from a troubled sleep. She'd been completely right about his skewed motivation for going to school. One hundred percent. Why, then, was he still thinking of leaving?

The weight of expectation, that was why. He'd been dodging the truth for days. The longer he stayed, the more people—Kelsey, his family, the teens at the church—would *depend* on him, and the more likely he was to fail them. But could he do worse by staying than he'd done years earlier when he left Brenner Falls the first time?

Kelsey said he was running away. Running from guilt, from fear of failure. Where was God in all this? Had he forgotten? *Lord, what am I doing? I knew you were leading me, ever since I landed at Stephen and Annika's house. You orchestrated all that. So, why am I trying to swim through this on my own? My emotions alone are guiding me, but I can't seem to stop myself.*

What else had Kelsey said? That Bible college didn't guarantee he'd avoid mistakes, growing pains, failures. All the things he was trying to flee. No guarantees. God's leading was the only guarantee. This should be easy.

A knock on the front door startled him. He rose from the couch to open it. His handsome, confident brother filled the doorway.

"Ben," was all Rick said. He stood aside and his brother strode in, his face like an approaching storm.

"Bro, you haven't answered my calls or texts." Ben's voice held an edge of accusation. "Would you mind telling me what's going on here?"

Rick blinked. He didn't want to explain it again. Each time he did, he felt more confused and less able to convince even himself. He turned away and rubbed his unshaven chin. "I'm sorry, Ben. Didn't mean to worry you. Um, sit down, please. Do you want anything to drink?"

Ben didn't respond, but only stared at Rick, waiting for an answer.

Rick let out his breath. "I had a setback with this guy, Chris, who I was meeting with. It was a lot like my story years ago. He overdosed and ended up in the hospital, just like I did. There should have been something else I could have done."

"Rick, this guy's decisions aren't your fault. You're carrying around guilt for his mistake? Is that why you're leaving town? You can't face it?"

"How'd you know I was leaving?"

"A few days ago, Kelsey called Amber to ask us to pray for you. That's why I've been trying to reach you all week. And Kelsey mentioned something about it, not to break confidence but because she was upset. Amber and Kelsey are close friends."

Rick nodded. Of course. "It was like seeing myself all over again, and it triggered me. It was like I had a wake-up call to how completely over my head I am. I'm not ready for the things happening to me, the ministry, Kelsey, anything."

"So, you're afraid? Is that it?" Ben waited a second. "Join the club, bro. Life is scary. But you know what? When we don't walk it alone, it's a lot better. First, with God. He goes before you in everything. Especially if he's called and gifted you for something, which he clearly has in your case. You can run away from that, like Jonah did in the Bible. Remember? You know how that turned out."

Rick smiled then. "Yeah. Don't want to smell like the inside of a fish."

"Right. First with God. Then, look at the people you have. Kelsey's a gem and she believes in you."

Yeah, she did. He'd forgotten about that. Warmth rumbled inside him.

"I have a confession for you," Ben continued. "After you left way back when, I blamed myself. All those years you were in Arizona. If I'd been a better brother, if I'd been a better example..."

Rick's eyes widened. "You did? But you tried so many times to bring me back. Said you'd help me get a job, help me get on my feet... It was completely *my* mistake. My stubbornness."

"Bingo. You're doing the same thing with Chris. I know you've been meeting with him for a couple of months, probably the best moments of his life, since he likes and respects you. You have no reason to feel guilt or inadequacy. Shoot, it was your *failures* that opened the door for him to trust you. And I had no reason to feel guilty about *your* decisions, either. Amber helped me see that. So, don't make the same mistake. Whatever you do, don't let guilt drive you. That's never God's way."

"One reason I didn't come back to The Falls for so long was to avoid facing what I'd done to you and Mom." Rick scratched his head. True confession time. "I didn't want to be confronted with my guilt, so I just didn't come. I escaped by staying away. Now I'm here, and it's tempting to escape for the same reason. Kelsey told me I was running away from the possibility of failing. But I'm also running from how I've *already* failed. Sounds so lame to say it now."

"Yeah, it's lame. Gotta be truthful here. Your being here brings *healing* to Mom and me for the past. Ever think of it that way? It *restores* what we lost." Ben's eyes grew moist. He blinked. Swallowed. "Living takes courage, bro. But you know God makes a difference. I'm back to that. He changes everything."

He *had* changed everything. What was God saying to Rick now? Through Kelsey, through Ben, through Stephen? Through Pastor Frank? God *was* speaking. He cared enough to repeat himself until Rick got it.

And he was getting it.

Ben's words reached a bruised place inside Rick, touching him, healing scars. By staying in Brenner Falls, he was healing his mom and his brother from the past, by remaining in relationship with them. Maybe it would be the same for Chris and other teens struggling like he did. He bowed his head, humbled by the realization.

"You've given me a lot to think about, Ben." He could barely murmur the words. His heart knotted, but for once, it felt good.

His brother grinned. "I'm glad. Know I love you and Mom loves you. We want the best for you. Know also that Bible college doesn't rewrite your past, if that's what you're after. Jesus did that already. It's enough."

Jesus's work on the cross was enough to erase Rick's guilt *and* his bad record. His daily presence was enough for whatever scary *or* exciting things came along. Ministry, Kelsey...a glorious destiny.

Rick stepped forward, and Ben met him in a tight embrace. "Thanks, Ben." His voice was thick, and his throat ached. "I love you too."

ଔ ଔ ଔ

Kelsey awoke Saturday morning, unrefreshed after a fitful night...one of a series. Memories of her conversation with Rick the previous evening assaulted her, and she winced. His coldness and distance squeezed her inside until tears flowed from her eyes. Couldn't she just sleep for the next few days and avoid what her life had become?

No. There was always something to do, and she couldn't indulge herself. The fact that she rarely did was beside the point. She hauled herself out of bed and trudged to the bathroom sink to splash away the facial signs of despair. It was the best she could do.

Rick hadn't said they were breaking up. He'd said he'd return twice a month to see her. That was something, wasn't it? Shouldn't she be glad he'd saved her a bit of room in his new academic life?

Her heart wasn't buying it, because the whole thing felt wrong. Rick was making a mistake because his *reasons* were wrong. Not the worst one he could make, but still. It seemed clear to everyone but him. And what made her heart ache most was the distance she felt from him, the loss of their closeness. He'd become like a stranger. A troubled stranger.

Another red flag, he'd asked for the whole day off. True, he hadn't had a Saturday off in four months. Whatever the reason or circumstances, he deserved that. And yet, it wasn't the Rick she knew, and it added another layer of tension. What was he doing that day? Hopefully, going to see Chris.

Once in the kitchen, Kelsey felt only a trace better. She'd do a food experiment for Molly's breakfast that day. She and Molly had the house back to themselves, which she savored. Though Kelsey attempted to return to their previous pre-Danielle lifestyle, nothing was the same. Tinkering with food in the kitchen was a distant memory.

That day, she'd try avocado spread on flatbread with feta cheese and a sprinkle of oregano. By the time she'd scooped the soft avocado from its shell, Molly filled in the doorway, her strawberry blond hair poking in messy spikes from her head.

"Good morning, sunshine." Kelsey forced a cheery greeting and hugged her sister, who looked as sleepy as she felt. "I'm making a special breakfast for you. I don't know if you'll like it, but it's an experiment."

Molly didn't have exotic tastes, so the flatbread likely wouldn't go over too well. "'Kay," her sister murmured and slipped into a chair. Kelsey quickly finished preparing the meal, then sat next to Molly. When she prayed for the meal, she included Rick in her prayer, which had become a frequent habit.

"Rick is coming?" Molly asked.

Molly's question was innocent, yet her words struck Kelsey's chest like a weapon. "No, he can't come today. He's been busy lately. That's why you haven't seen him." Impossible to explain the situation, even to someone who didn't have Down's Syndrome.

"I'm working at The Fork today at lunch, but I'll be home this evening." Kelsey took a bite of her creation. Hmm. Needed something. Cheese? "You can either stay home this afternoon or come with me to The Fork."

Molly grunted and pushed her plate away. The twist of her mouth told Kelsey everything. "I want oatmeal. Please."

Kelsey sighed. "Okay, I guess this won't be on your list. Well, I did say it was an experiment, and some experiments don't work out." It *was* bland, but if she tried pumpernickel instead of flatbread... "I'll make your oatmeal in a minute."

After cleaning up breakfast, Kelsey spent a couple of hours on her online job, which, thankfully, would finish Monday. Then she prepared herself for her lunch shift at The Fork, actively pushing away any thoughts of Rick and what he was up to, how he was feeling, and the ways he'd shut her out.

When Kelsey was ready to leave at ten-forty-five, Molly was still in the living room in her pajamas. "I guess that means you've decided to stay home, right?" Kelsey stood in the doorway while Molly ignored her, absorbed in her puzzle. "So, I'll be home around four. Okay?"

Molly looked up then. "I want to go to The Fork."

"No, Molly, you're not ready and I have to leave now." Kelsey's voice emerged more harshly than she intended. Molly's eyes widened and teared up.

"Oh, Molly, I'm so sorry!" Kelsey threw down her purse and gathered Molly in her arms. "I'm so sorry I yelled at you. I'm stressed out, but I shouldn't have done that." She pulled back, tears filling her own eyes. "Do you forgive me, my Molly?"

Molly nodded as a tear rolled down her chubby cheek. Kelsey squeezed her again in a tight hug.

Kelsey hated to leave Molly with tears on her face. She hated leaving her alone without clear instructions and a plan, but the morning had slipped away. "I have to go now. I can't wait for you to dress, okay? You can come next time."

As she drove to The Fork, tears slid down her cheeks. She was losing it, falling apart. Already, the load of carrying two full time jobs and Molly had shredded her nerves and eroded her patience. Add to that a lack of adequate sleep as she worried about Rick's state and his decisions... It was too much for her. Now she was snapping at Molly, in out-of-character exasperation.

Her lunch shift at The Grateful Fork distracted her, thankfully, for a few hours. Normally as manager, she'd spend more time there on a weekend. Her conscientious nature tugged at her each time she left the building after a shorter-than-usual shift, but she simply couldn't do more. Vince bridged the gap, understanding her predicament of having two jobs, and perceiving what she hadn't said...that things weren't going well with Rick.

༺ ༺ ༺

Rick knocked on the red wooden door. Paint peeled around the edges, but on the stoop sat two terracotta pots of mums in bright yellow and fuchsia, extending a cordial welcome.

His heart and chest still tingled with the impact of Ben's visit. The fog that had surrounded him for the previous few days had cleared, leaving behind the sense of being washed clean after a storm.

True, he felt like an idiot who'd been lost in a misguided stupor. The worst part was the people he'd hurt, especially Kelsey, but God had pulled him back onto the path before he did anything too dramatic. A far more satisfying conviction was that of getting back on track with his life. He knew with startling clarity what that was, which was why he stood on the doorstep at that moment.

The door opened and a plain-faced woman with a pleasant smile faced him through the screen. "You must be Rick," she said. "I've heard a lot about you. Good things." She opened the screen door so he could enter.

"It's nice to finally meet you, Mrs. Thompson."

"Chris is doing much better, day by day, thank God. We were really afraid for him." Her voice broke, and she forced out another smile.

"I can imagine. I was afraid too." Rick wondered if Chris's mother knew he'd experienced a close parallel in another life.

"Please, have a seat." She extended her hand toward the tidy, homey living room. "Chris," she called to the back of the house. "Your friend Rick is here."

Rick sat at one end of the couch. A few minutes later, Chris came through the doorway. He held his hand out to Rick for a fist-bump, then sat in the armchair next to the couch. Except for being paler than usual, he looked fully recovered.

"I didn't think I'd see you today, but thanks for coming."

Rick knew he should have come by sooner, but at least he had his head on straight now. "How are you feeling, dude?"

Chris blew out a breath. "The short answer is better. But it would take me a while to answer that question in detail. It blows my mind that I came this close—" he held up one hand with a small space between his index finger and his thumb, "—to dying." He swallowed and his eyes reddened. He glanced away. "I wasn't ready to die, Rick. I'm young, but I could have died just like that. But I hadn't met God yet, so I wasn't ready in that way either. I'd listened to your words, I'd read about him, but thought I had time. I never knew..." His voice broke and continued in a rasp. "I didn't know it could be gone just like that."

Rick let him talk, watched the range of emotions pass across his face as he viewed what could have been a movie of his own life. His throat ached. *Thank you, Lord, for saving his life. Thank you for saving mine back then.*

"Sounds like you've been thinking a lot since everything happened." Rick leaned against the back of the couch as an invitation to Chris to continue talking.

He did. He talked about some of the dreams he remembered while he was unconscious. Seeing Jesus. Feeling like he was falling. Feeling like it was too late. "Even while I was unconscious, I remember asking God to give me a chance...to live." His eyes filled, but he didn't hide his tears. He swiped one wrist over his eyes. "There were some crazy dreams too, ones I couldn't make sense of. Others I didn't remember. When I woke up, I realized I was *alive*. I was thankful and prayed."

"You did? What did you pray?"

"I thanked God that I was alive. That was first. I told him I didn't know what to do next, but thought he'd show me." He smiled then.

"Are you more ready to meet God than before? On *this* side of death, I mean." A smile tugged at Rick's lips as he waited for Chris to respond.

Chris leveled a gaze at him. "Yeah. I'm about ready."

"Just ask him. Just tell God you know Jesus died in your place and you want to believe."

"That's all?"

"Belief is first. Humbling your heart to know you need his help and his forgiveness, that's key. You're receiving something he's offering. The words aren't so important. After that, it's like..." He paused.

How to explain? A week earlier, he'd have berated himself for not knowing, and that would have been another point for Bible college. This time, he waited until the words came, imperfect as they'd be. After all, it wasn't up to him to convince Chris. "It's like a poor kid who's adopted into a rich guy's family. He has to learn how to act and think like a rich kid instead of a poor one."

Chris grinned. "Sounds good to me."

"I can pray with you or for you, or you can do it on your own."

"I'll do it on my own."

Rick had expected Chris to say that. "Soon?"

"Yeah."

Rick grinned. "Okay, I'll ask you about it. Maybe tomorrow or in a few days."

Chris nodded. "Alright."

His mom came into the living room. "Rick, would you be free to stay with us for dinner, or do you have to work? Chris said you work a lot on weekends."

"No, I took today off. I'd be happy to stay. Thank you, Mrs. Thompson."

ೞ ೞ ೞ

Kelsey tried to make up for her impatient attitude by making Molly's favorite for dinner, macaroni and cheese with sausage patties. Not very gourmet, but it put a smile on Molly's face. She glanced at the wall clock. "If you can finish within ten minutes, you'll be ready for Mom and Dad's phone call."

In response, Molly took a large spoonful of pasta.

"On second thought, *don't* hurry, you'll choke yourself! Or you can wait, and I'll heat it up after the call."

"I'm done." Molly stood and carried her plate to the sink.

Minutes later, they waited in the living room for the monthly phone call. Sometimes her parents managed a second call in the month, but it depended on transportation, demands on their time, flooding near the village, outbreaks at the clinic or tension in the region...any number of things. Thankfully, they'd stayed safe so far.

When the landline phone rang, Kelsey answered. Her mother usually talked first, then put their father on the line. "Hi, Mom. It's good to hear from you." Though Kelsey had grown used to not seeing or hearing from her parents often, her mother's voice was a balm for her frayed nerves.

"How is everything going there?" her mother asked.

Difficult question to answer. "How much time do you have?" Kelsey let out an unsteady chuckle, though her heart felt like lead. She'd summarize. Anything else would be too painful, and she didn't want to blubber on the phone. "Here, I'll let you talk to Molly first."

That was their usual routine. Molly always had a brief conversation first, then Kelsey filled them in on the happenings. She turned to Molly at the end of the couch. "Say hi to Mom and Dad."

Molly leaped up and took the phone. She exchanged simple sentences, answering questions her mother then her father asked for a few minutes. She returned the phone to Kelsey.

"What's been going on, Kelsey?" Concern threaded her mother's voice. "Sounds like a lot is happening. Hopefully, good things."

Kelsey bit her lip. "Well, you know Danielle was living here for almost two months while her leg recovered. You might remember we'd swapped jobs, since she was laid up. She's better now and decided to get a different job. She won't be returning to The Fork so I can continue as manager. I just resigned from my online job and am nearly finished my two-week notice period."

"While you're working at The Fork? At the same time?"

"More or less, but I've cut back from The Fork a little until I'm fully finished."

"When will that be?"

"I'll finish on Monday. I have some accounts to tie up, so I'll be working all weekend on those. I worked lunch today at the restaurant."

"Sounds like an awful lot, Kelsey. I didn't know you were juggling all of that, plus Molly. And what about the young man you told us about?"

Kelsey's breath hitched. "He, um, he's going through a tough time right now. So, it's not super, but it should get better soon." There was no possible way to summarize her status with Rick, especially since she didn't know.

There was a brief silence on the phone and Kelsey thought they'd been disconnected, since occasionally, they were. "Just a minute, Kelsey. Your father is saying something." She heard her father's muffled voice in the background.

"I'm back," her mother said. "Kelsey, you know, we're due to come back in a month, but your father suggested we shorten our commitment and come back now. I agree with him."

Kelsey's brow furrowed. "I don't understand. Why would you do that? Because of me? Or Molly?"

"Because we're your parents and we want to support you. We didn't realize how much you had on your shoulders. It sounds like so much, Kelsey. We've served almost our whole commitment, so it's not a big problem to cut off a few weeks."

"But your mission—"

"Kelsey, we *want* to do that." Her father's voice had come on the phone. "We've been away for eight months and left you holding down the fort. It didn't dawn on us how much you have to deal with all by yourself. We're sorry, Kelsey."

Kelsey smiled. "That's sweet, Dad. But I'll be okay."

"We know you'll be okay." Her mom's voice again. "Because you're smart and strong and a wonderful daughter. But there's something that we both want to tell you loud and clear. We don't only have *one* daughter. We have *two* daughters. We're grateful you took care of Molly for all these months, but you have needs of your own. Let us step in and help *you* for a change, Kelsey."

Before Kelsey could respond, her father took the phone again. "Kelsey, sweetie, you don't have to agree." He chuckled. "We'll be there by next weekend if we can get a flight out of Kampala by then."

Tears pricked Kelsey's eyes. *She* was their daughter too. Not the hired help. She hadn't even realized, since Molly required extra focus and care, how often she forgot that. How often she overrode her own needs and desires. Maybe her parents even forgot sometimes. "In that case, I'm really glad. I can't wait to see you. Please let me know the date as soon as you can."

After they hung up, Kelsey turned to Molly and smiled. "I have news for you. Mom and Dad are coming home early. They might be here as early as next weekend."

Molly let out a squeal followed by a huge grin and a seated dance on the couch. Kelsey slid over and put her arms around her sister as warm tears flowed freely from her eyes. They'd be a family again. And Kelsey would be a daughter.

Chapter Twenty-Two

Rick scanned the sanctuary for Kelsey, but didn't see her. He glanced at the hour on his phone several times. If she was coming, she'd be there by now. So, he slid into the pew with Ben, Amber, his mom, and her boyfriend, Tim. The five of them took up half a row. Contentment surged inside, just being among them. Part of them. His family.

The only part missing was Kelsey. He *had* to see her.

During the service, his eyes kept wandering to the spot where they'd sat together a few times when he wasn't at youth church. As if she'd arrive late, which she never did.

After the service, Rick filed with everyone else toward the doorway leading from the sanctuary to the big hallway and entrance doors. Pastor Frank stood at the threshold shaking hands, asking questions, responding to the people who passed by. When Rick reached him, the man's face brightened. He took Rick's hand in both of his and warmly shook it.

"Hi, Pastor. Good sermon today."

"How are you, Rick? Feels like I haven't seen you in a little while." The man looked worried for him, and with good reason. He'd shut Frank out, along with everyone else in the last week.

"I've had a tough week, but I'm doing a lot better. I need prayer for something, though."

Pastor Frank's gaze traveled to the trickle of members headed to the doorway. "I can pray with you now. Can you come to my office?"

"Sure." Rick waited for a couple of final handshakes, then Pastor Frank nodded at him and led the way down the hall to his office.

"Tell me what's going on, Rick," he said once they were seated. "After our last conversation, which seems like a month ago, I sensed something had taken a bad turn for you. I've prayed for you and called once, but unfortunately, didn't make time to reach out more than that. I'm sorry."

"No worries, Pastor. You've got a lot on your plate."

Rick summarized all that had happened with Chris and his own tailspin as a result. He finished with a long sigh, as if he'd done a couple of rounds in a boxing ring. "In the past, I'd had experiences where I knew God was leading me. That wasn't the case for the Bible college. But that was because I was trying to run away."

All the while, Pastor Frank's eyes crinkled with compassion, and he nodded without speaking. "I understand feeling in over your head. Bible college can certainly be helpful, but not if you're going with the wrong motivation. I'm proud of you for recognizing that. Rick, if you'd had any qualifications in yourself, you'd be completely unqualified."

"Come again?"

"God loves to work through our weaknesses, because then it's *his* work, not ours. And he strengthens us by our dependence on him. He loves those kinds of contradictions, you see. Take a look at the disciples. Totally unqualified men, but they started a movement that changed the world. As we make ourselves available to him, he works through us. Of course, I'm not saying education and experience aren't important. There are many ways to get that. In my opinion, the kids here need you. Chris needs you. And stability in your current life is important for you now, considering your past experiences."

"Yeah, that's what my girlfriend said." He felt a stab inside. "She wasn't in favor of the school idea because she knew my motives were wrong."

Frank smiled. "Smart girl. Hang onto her."

He fully intended to, and never let go. But he had to talk to her first. That was his next stop.

"Let's continue meeting together, but more regularly," Pastor Frank said. "Then you can do some online classes with the college. I know they offer whole degree programs online."

"They gave me a partial scholarship plus work-study. I don't know if they require full-time attendance for the scholarship or not. Do you think they could apply that to online classes? They're still expensive. And I'd like to keep working."

"I can make a phone call for you to see if they'll apply the scholarship to your online program, even part time. I'll let them know we need you in the youth program here as part of your training, which is true."

A wave of peace flowed through Rick. All the broken pieces were settling back into place, one at a time. "I'd wanted your advice and prayer for wisdom, but I think I've got all that now."

"Doesn't mean I can't pray with you."

The pastor prayed for him, including gratitude for Rick's presence in the church and his godly heart. Rick hadn't expected *that*. Frank also prayed for his future wherever he was led, into ministry or elsewhere, and included Kelsey. The prayer felt like a protective covering as well as a consecration of his life. A wave of otherworldly joy flushed through him for a few moments, then faded, leaving peace in its wake.

Pastor Frank stood, and Rick followed. The older man gave Rick's shoulder a firm pat. "The scholarship shouldn't be an issue. I'll call them tomorrow and let you know what they say."

Rick couldn't get to Kelsey's house fast enough. Her car sat in the driveway, a good sign. His hands were moist as he stood in front of the door and knocked. When the door opened, the sight of her took his breath away. She wore sweatpants and a fleece top. Her hair was loose and curled around her shoulders, and her face was clear and fresh, with no makeup.

"Rick, come in." Her expression gave nothing away.

"Hi, Kelsey." They stood in the foyer, facing each other. "You weren't in church today."

"I was exhausted. Plus, I had several hours of work to do before tying up my other job. Thank goodness it'll be over tomorrow."

As she spoke, his eyes roved over her smooth face, her plump lips, her authentic beauty. He held back from kissing her right then. "I know you'll be so relieved to only have one job." He swallowed. "Kelsey, can we talk?" He had so much to say.

"Yes. We'll go to the back porch." Her voice was soft, though wary. That was understandable. She didn't know what he was going to tell her.

They sat on folding chairs on the back deck, covered with a layer of pine needles and a scattering of colorful fall leaves. Rick pulled his chair to face her, but was close to her too. "Kelsey, I have three things I want to say to you." He shuffled his chair even closer.

Her face softened. "I'm listening."

"The first thing is, I'm sorry. I'm sorry I stonewalled you. I know in a relationship, talking about things is really important. Especially when bad or confusing stuff happens. I can only imagine how you felt." He took both of her hands in his. "Shut out and abandoned. I never want you to feel that way and I never want to do that again, no matter what happens."

Her dark blue eyes stayed riveted to his, but moisture gathered around the edges.

Kelsey hadn't spoken yet, so he continued. "The second thing is I'm not going to Bible college. Not away. I'll take a few classes at a time online and stay in Brenner Falls. I was running away from people's expectations and the possibility of failing, like you told me. Kelsey, you were completely right about everything." He reached up and moved a lock of hair from her cheek, then smiled. "That was the second time you've confronted me since I've known you, and you were right both times. My mom told me I needed a woman like you who cares enough to tell me the truth. I agree with her. I *do* need you in my life."

Her face was still stoic, but more tears had escaped and rolled down her cheeks.

"I'd like to keep working at The Fork and with the youth. But there's something else I'd like even more, which leads me to the third thing."

He made sure he held her gaze in his. "I love you, Kelsey. I'd like to keep dating you, being with you. Remember when I told you as soon as I saw you that my heart belonged to you? That's still the case, so if you'll forgive me for being a misguided jerk, I'd like to pick up where we were before things got messy."

The edge of Kelsey's mouth quirked on one side amidst a trickle of tears. "Of course, I forgive you."

With her words, he knew he couldn't wait another second. He leaned and pulled her toward him with both hands, covering her lips in one swift motion, her tears moistening his cheeks. He kissed her as if it were the first time and the last time, for all the moments reserved for them in the future. Her arms curled around his neck, and she fervently pressed into him. It was heaven to be in her arms again, to have torn away all the barriers and reclaimed his love for her.

He'd loved her from the very first day, knowing nothing about her or how exquisitely they'd fit together. He'd sensed it, then doubted it. After all, why would a woman like Kelsey give him the time of day? Until she said she believed in him. He thought he'd been mistaken, but she'd said it clearly. Oh, how he'd needed someone to believe in him. And not just anyone, this woman in his arms. This woman made for him. Part of his destiny.

Their kiss expressed many moods and covered varied terrain...tender, ferocious, bonded. When at last they pulled away, their gazes refused to unlock from one another.

"Rick," she breathed. A delicate and angelic smile pulled at her lips. "I love you too. I love you forever."

A sting began in his eyes. It was too much. Too good. Nothing else to do but kiss her again.

ಌ ಌ ಌ

Attention Customers: The Grateful Fork will close after the lunch service on Monday, October 21st for a private party. If you are friends or acquaintances of Mr. and Mrs. Dennis Brewster of Brenner Falls, you are invited to attend a Welcome Back party in their honor, following eight months of missionary service in Uganda, Africa.

Festivities are from 6 pm until 8:30 pm.

The last week was a complete turnaround from the week before. Kelsey floated on air, or felt like it, even though she'd been putting in long days at The Fork since the official end of her other job. Having just one job changed her focus and schedule, and having Rick back changed everything else.

Her parents arrived on Saturday. It seemed like a long-deferred dream to embrace them again, with plenty of emotion and joy, eight months after saying tearful goodbyes at the airport. Anticipating their return revealed to Kelsey how much she'd missed them. During the year, she hadn't allowed herself to think about it, since they'd needed her to hold down the fort and take care of Molly. But now she savored their physical presence. They talked for hours until jet lag took over.

When she explained her idea to throw a welcome-back party in their honor at The Fork, they enthusiastically agreed, but requested a few days of recovery to regain their bearings in their home culture, so different from rural Uganda, and catch up on lost sleep. The rest of their adjustment would take more time, but Kelsey wanted to celebrate and let all of Brenner Falls know their hometown missionaries had returned.

"Kelsey, I'm glad you had the idea for the party," her mother said after they returned to the house from church the next day. "It'll be nice to see so many friends all at once."

"Exactly what I had in mind." Kelsey preheated the oven and took a lasagna casserole she'd made the day before from the fridge.

"Can I help you with anything, dear?"

"No, it'll take thirty minutes or so to heat up the casserole. Go change into something comfy and we'll meet in the living room. I'm guessing you and Dad'll need another nap by this afternoon."

Her mom came to Kelsey for an extended hug. "It's so good to be with you. I didn't realize how much I missed while we were gone." She pulled back and gazed at Kelsey with misty eyes.

Kelsey swallowed the lump in her own throat. "No regrets, right?"

"No, no regrets. You know, your dad and I talked about the mission for a couple of years before he retired. Then when it came up again, we got serious about it. But it's so good to be home too, to see my girls again." She placed a kiss on Kelsey's brow. "I'm looking forward to meeting Rick soon."

Kelsey smiled. "You will."

She hadn't told her parents about Rick's background yet, preferring for them to meet him first. She'd invited him to join them for lunch that day, but he had plans with his mother and Tim to go to a restaurant. He hadn't spent much time with his mother and her boyfriend lately, so she was glad for him.

He also hadn't wanted to crowd her reunion with her parents too soon. A legitimate point, but she hoped he wasn't putting off meeting them and facing the possibility of their disillusionment with the man their daughter had chosen. She'd invited him for dinner or dessert as well, but he said he was spending time with Ben and Amber, but would call her that evening.

Kelsey enjoyed her day with her parents and Molly, but she missed Rick. They usually spent time together on Sundays and Mondays. They'd only been back on track in their relationship less than a week, and she was still nervous when she sensed or feared him backing away for any reason.

At eight that evening, Kelsey waited for his call in her bedroom, craving the sound of his voice. The phone rang at eight o'clock, right on schedule.

"Hi," he said, tender affection lacing his voice. "I miss you."

"I miss you too. Did you have a good day with your mom and with Ben and Amber?"

"Yeah, it was really good on both counts. I'd been neglecting all of them already with working so much. Then, with the problem I had with Chris, actively avoided everyone."

"So glad that's over."

"No more avoidance, especially of you, my beauty. I'd give almost anything to be there now and hold you in my arms, maybe steal a couple kisses..."

Kelsey giggled. "Which I'd gladly return. I'm looking forward to my parents meeting you."

"I'll be honest, I'm a little nervous about that," Rick said after a brief silence.

"I understand your feelings, but once my parents meet you, they'll see the man I see. A man with a different life and a new direction as well as a wonderful heart for God and for teens. Rick, remember how you felt when God told you to share your story? You feared the worst, and it ended up being a blessing to everyone who heard you."

"I guess you're right. As usual."

"Keep thinking that way and we'll get along just fine." They laughed. "I haven't told them anything either because I wanted them to meet you first. Also, it's your story to tell."

"And they'll ask me a bunch of questions about my life—"

"They'll ask because they're interested, and they'll do it with grace, Rick. They won't judge you. I know my parents."

She heard him sigh. "I hope you're right, Kelsey. Because I'm not going anywhere."

"Music to my ears. So, you'll meet them tomorrow night before the party."

"That's perfect. There'll be so much commotion, they won't be able to ask me anything, but they may get a good surface impression."

"Please don't worry. I didn't schedule you to do any service for the party, by the way. You're going to sit with us at our table like a member of the family."

"Oh? As your significant other? I think I like that."

She laughed. "Exactly. Extremely, immensely, wonderfully significant."

On Monday afternoon, with Rick's help, Kelsey hung a banner over the bar and put up decorations consisting of streamers, artifacts from Africa—masks, fabrics, utensils—and a large collage of photos her parents had emailed during the previous year.

A portion of the staff had agreed to work that night for the party, including Vince. Where would Kelsey be without Vince? Without his support, filling in the gaps, and, of course, his skillful cuisine? The two of them created a special Africa-inspired menu they'd serve buffet-style to about forty people.

Thirty minutes ahead of time, Kelsey's parents arrived with Molly. Kelsey went to the door to greet them. "What do you think? Is the décor authentic enough for a small-town representation of Uganda?"

Her father laughed and kissed her cheek. "It's perfect, Kelsey. Everything looks great."

"And wait till you taste the buffet. Mom sent me some recipes over the last few months, which, of course, I tried at home. I got others online." She scanned the room for Rick and cocked her head toward him as an invitation.

"I'm sure it'll be delicious," her mother said.

"It's Rick!" cried Molly as a smile spread across her face. She dashed toward him and met him halfway across the room as he approached. He gave her a warm hug, and she led him by the hand toward her and Kelsey's parents.

"Mom, Dad, this is Rick Russo." Kelsey tried to see Rick through her parents' eyes, and saw a handsome, well-mannered and well-dressed thirty something man with dark eyes and longish wavy hair. True, they didn't know much else about him, except that he worked at The Grateful Fork.

"My parents, Dennis and Penny Brewster."

Both of Kelsey's parents grinned broadly and shook Rick's hand.

"It's nice to finally meet you both," Rick said.

"I can't believe how much we missed being away." Kelsey's mom echoed what she'd said the previous day. "So much has happened. You're part of that, Rick. We're so thrilled to finally meet you too. Are you originally from Brenner Falls?" The questions had begun, but there was little time to cover more than the basics. Kelsey relaxed.

"Yes, born and raised. I was away for several years, but I've been back since last spring." To his credit, Rick looked fully relaxed. Maybe he'd made peace with his own life story.

"Do you have family here?" Kelsey's dad asked.

"My mom and my older brother live here. I have an older sister who lives in Hershey with her family."

"We'll have time to get acquainted over dinner," Kelsey said. "Why don't you all settle at your assigned table here?" Kelsey extended one arm to a specially decorated table on one side of the room. "It's for the guests of honor and their loved ones. Rick and I still have a few things yet to do."

Which was a true statement, but it seemed good timing to avoid further questions before an optimum moment. Her parents complied and the three of them sat at the reserved table as people began filing in for the party. "I'll bring you some cold drinks," she told them. Rick grinned, likely in approval at her artful diversion tactic.

"It'll make quite the statement to all of Brenner Falls if I'm seated at the same table with you and your family," he murmured with an entrancing smile.

She smirked. "Oh, gee, I hadn't thought of that." Then she bumped his arm lightly with one shoulder. "That's because you're a *loved one.*"

Chapter Twenty-Three

"You're working tonight, aren't you, Rick?"

Rick looked at his mother over the rim of his coffee cup. "I'm actually working a double today. Friday's a big day at The Fork. We often have a band. I'll be off for a couple hours between, though. Do you need anything?"

His mother frowned. "That's a shame. Tim's coming for supper, and I thought it would be nice to have you join us."

Rick eyed her. "Are you trying to break me into the new stepfather, Mom?" He grinned at her, and she blushed.

"No, I'm not. I'd like you to get to know him better. Since…things *are* moving in a kind of serious direction."

Rick lifted a fist in the air. "Woo hoo! That's great news, Mom. Though, it's not really news since I saw it coming, like the first day I met the guy."

"You did? You never said."

"I observed that you're good together. He seems in love with you and hopefully it goes both ways."

"It does." Her tone softened and before his eyes, she looked seventeen.

"Like I said before, Mom." His throat thickened as tenderness and gratitude surged inside him. "You deserve it." He stepped forward and hugged her.

"Not to change the subject, but how was the youth meeting last night?" she asked when he pulled away.

"Amazing. I don't know what's going on over there, but we average twenty or so kids at Discovery Session. That's over double the number we started with almost two months ago. You might remember, that's the meeting we do before youth group when kids can ask questions. Jesse had to get us a bigger room for the second time. No one minded the inconvenience."

His mother smiled. "I bet. You're having such an impact, Rick. I'm glad you didn't go away to college."

Yeah, him too. What he would have missed. No doubt, Bible college would have been a fantastic opportunity, but it was clearly not where God wanted *him*. Rick planned to start online classes in January, but at least he'd be on site to take part in the momentum that kept brewing among the youth.

"God made it clear, that's for sure. The church kids like coming to *Discovery*. They all call it that now, and it has some of the kids at school curious. They say, *Hey, are you going to Discovery tonight?* Then the kids that overhear them are dying to know what it is. Fear of Missing Out." He laughed.

"How wonderful. Make the FOMO work in your favor."

Rick chuckled. "Oh, we do. The church kids like Discovery too, because when they ask questions at home, their parents either get worried or start preaching to them. Or both. This group gives them a safe place to express questions or doubts."

"That's wonderful that the group is good for both church kids and town kids."

"Then they usually stay for youth group, so it's a win-win."

Another amazing event had occurred a week and a half earlier. Chris had sent a text to Rick two days after he'd dropped by to see him. The same day Ben helped Rick get his head on straight. Chris's text had simply said, *Did it, Rick. I'm with God now.* Rick's flood of joy hit a new level.

He'd texted back, *Welcome to the family. Let me know when you want to meet. I have important stuff to share with you about next steps.* He decided to meet with Chris twice weekly, initially. It would be tough to manage, along with The Fork and Kelsey, but he considered it a top priority. Come January, he'd have to add online classes to his schedule. He'd figure it out by then.

So much was going right in his world. Being back on track with Kelsey was high on the list. He'd see her all day that day, since they were both working a double shift. They didn't have a chance to say much to each other on those days, but he still enjoyed being in the same building with her.

He hadn't yet had the courage to come around her parents too much, but had to do it sooner or later, or they'd grow suspicious. He was preparing himself for what he didn't want to say about his life.

Rick stood and gave his mom a hug. "I have to get ready to go, but I hope your dinner with Dr. Tim is very romantic." He grinned and she swatted his shoulder.

"I won't tell you if it is."

They laughed.

He walked into The Grateful Fork a few minutes early for the lunch shift. The room was already buzzing with early patrons, and the new wait staff Kelsey had hired. He slipped behind the bar and into the kitchen through the swinging metal door. He saw Kelsey in the far corner of the room consulting with one of the sous-chefs. She was *so* in her place. He tried to catch her eye but didn't succeed.

"Hi, Vince. How's everything?"

The burly chef put out his hand for a fist bump with Rick. Made him feel even more like one of the gang. "Good, good. I'm trying a new Kelsey recipe today. She's all nervous about it. We gotta convince her how awesome she is."

Rick laughed. "I'm working on it. I already think she is." In every way. Vince chuckled and cast him a knowing smile. "So, what band do we have tonight? I'm not too up to date on Brenner Falls talent."

"It's a group out of Lewisburg. They've been here before and the Brennerites seem to like 'em."

"Brennerites? Haven't heard that one." Yet, Rick was one too. And lately, he was increasingly glad about it. He grinned and slipped on his apron. He'd start with some dishes left from the morning prep.

"Hi, handsome." He looked up from the sudsy water and Kelsey stood beside him.

"Hey, my beauty." He kept his voice low. "Looks like I'll have to content myself with seeing you across the room all day and night, eh?"

"Afraid so. But I've scheduled us to have tomorrow lunch off."

"Just lunch? Oh, right. It's Saturday."

Kelsey crinkled her nose. "Yeah, but we'll get Sunday."

"How are things with your parents working out? It's a big change, even though you're glad to see them."

"Slowly they're getting their bearings again. It's like reverse culture shock for them."

"What about you? You're used to having the place to yourself. The lady of the house, so to speak. Now you're *merely* a daughter." He emphasized the word, knowing how precious it had become to Kelsey once she understood that's what she truly was.

Kelsey fell silent and nodded. "Being a daughter is wonderful. But the house...I'm not sure yet. It's kind of weird, but getting more and more normal. I'm so glad to have them back."

"Good."

Her gaze met his. "They still need to get to know you."

"Yeah, I guess so..."

"Rick, you're nervous about it, I can tell. Please don't worry."

There was a sudden flurry of greetings as the door to the kitchen swung open.

"Aggie!" Kelsey left his side and dashed to the doorway to give the older woman a hug. She hadn't been to The Fork in a month, the same day the food journalist came through town. Seemed like a year had passed since that time, so much had happened, with Danielle, Bible college, Chris...

Drying his hands on his apron, Rick approached the small crowd of kitchen help gathered around Aggie. She held onto a table with one hand, looking older and frailer than when she'd worked daily at The Fork not so long ago.

"I haven't been actively involved here," Aggie said. "But I've loosely followed the goings-on, and I'm pleased and proud of every one of you." She looked pointedly at Kelsey. "And you, young lady, are a *rock star* as the kids say." Everyone laughed and a few voiced agreement while Kelsey's face pinkened. "You've been amazing as the manager of The Fork. And Danielle is happy at her current job, so it's a win for both."

"Are you home for a while now?" Kelsey asked.

"Yes, in fact I am. I wasn't planning to travel as much, but the opportunity arose and suddenly, there was nothing to stop me." She laughed. "At my age, tomorrow is not a guarantee. Imagine, a cruise on the Mediterranean! I'd never dreamed of such a thing in the past. And now, I've done it. Retirement suits me." She chuckled again and several employees joined her. "I don't want to hold you up from your duties, folks. But I do have important news for you. I just need your attention for a few minutes."

The chatter dropped and everyone waited for Aggie's announcement.

"This is hard for me to say." Her voice grew solemn, and the silence thickened as every eye riveted to Aggie. She took a long breath. "I've decided to sell The Grateful Fork." This brought a collective gasp followed by silence, as many likely wondered how that would change their lives and jobs.

Aggie sat on a stool with a groan. "I've only recently come to that decision and haven't started looking for a buyer yet. Naturally, I'll try my hardest to make sure your jobs are secure. I'd like to see as smooth a transition as possible, though I can't guarantee at all what the next owner will do or change here. That's just the honest truth."

Rick watched Kelsey, who stood across the circle from him. She appeared to be in shock, standing deathly still with furrowed brows and tightened lips. Now that she had her perfect niche, was her job in danger? What if a new owner came in with his or her own staff? Rick wasn't worried about his own job. He could bus tables anywhere, or get something else. Amber's brother, Cooper, could even hire him on a construction site. It didn't matter, as long as he could still see Kelsey and keep up with the youth group.

But Kelsey...she'd invested. She'd given hours and her heart to this place. He blocked the pain for her that wound up from his heart into his throat.

"I can't answer any questions now," Aggie said, "because it's a new decision. I probably should have told you all when things were further along, once I had a buyer, but I'd feel dishonest withholding the news from you. Now, please don't go quitting or anything. I'm only at the beginning of this change. I expect you all to work with your hearts as you always have."

"Will you stay in Brenner Falls once you sell?" asked Veronica, one of the line cooks.

"Yes, I will. I'll travel from time to time, but I'm staying here. I'll probably come in for lunch more often." She grinned, seeming unaware of having dropped a grenade in the room.

"We hope you'll visit often, Aggie," Vince said. "Now for the rest of you, let's get back to work. I hear the dining room is filling up."

The chefs and waitstaff snapped back into action, returning to their tasks. Kelsey stood a second longer, then caught herself and did the same. Rick came alongside her. "We can talk about this later, Kelss. I'd like to hear your thoughts, but I can tell they're not peaceful. It'll be okay. God and I are both in your corner." He offered a gentle smile he hoped brought her comfort.

She nodded. "I know." Her gaze met his full on. "I'm so glad you're still in Brenner Falls."

The next morning, Kelsey awoke to the aroma of bacon frying and bread baking. For the first time in eight months, someone was making *her* breakfast. She burrowed deeper into the covers but hazarded a glance at the clock. Almost eight, much later than she usually arose. Normally, she'd be up before seven getting breakfast started for Molly or reading her Bible with a cup of coffee in front of the living room window.

But the previous night, sleep had eluded her for hours as she rewound Aggie's announcement in her mind. After all she'd done to patch up damage from Danielle's short stint as manager, and to pull the restaurant back on track afterward. And after *finally* stepping in as the general manager of The Fork without a secondary job hovering like a cloud in the background...

Now Aggie was selling.

Kelsey should have known it was a possibility, since the woman had just retired. There was no reason for her to keep it, really. Maybe she realized it was still a source of stress, and it might as well become someone else's headache instead of hers. Yet, it seemed surreal to Kelsey. Aggie had owned The Fork for forty years.

What changes would result in new ownership? Would it cease to be a gathering place for locals, a place to share news and see old friends? Would it no longer resemble a family but become merely a business guided by current demands and a bottom line? Of course, those things were important, but The Fork always had something else. It had the soul of invitation, warmth, and comfort.

Kelsey pulled herself out of bed, washed her face, and put on a sweatsuit. She went into the kitchen where her mother stood at the stove, spatula in hand. "Good morning, Kelsey." Her mother smiled at her as she flipped fried eggs.

"You're making breakfast. How nice." Kelsey hugged her.

"I missed doing this while we were gone. I need to find my bearings again, so I thought we'd start with a nice breakfast."

"Sounds great. What can I do?"

"You can set the table if you want. I'll call the troops when the eggs are done."

Kelsey had cooked breakfast for the family a few times since her parents had returned. Having all four of them at the table was a treat, but it would still take time to get used to. She still had a subconscious expectation of her parents picking up their suitcases and departing any minute, leaving her alone with Molly.

If she were honest, she hadn't yet found her footing, simply as the *daughter*. Though the blessing of being part of this family was solid, she no longer knew where she fit. Slowly an understanding dawned on her, that the feeling wasn't only recent, but reached further back than that summer. That could be one reason why The Fork represented home and family to her.

Once they were settled at the table, her father prayed for the meal, including thankfulness for being back home with his daughters. It surprised Kelsey more than it should have to realize how much her parents had missed her and Molly, as they expressed many times since their return. Though Molly had grown accustomed to not seeing her parents every day, their presence filled her with joy, which she expressed as only Molly could, with exuberant, childlike celebration. She'd found her new normal quickly, but it was more difficult for the rest of the family.

"That was delicious, Mom. Thanks for making it," Kelsey said. Having someone cook for her was so unusual, it almost added flavor to the whole meal.

Molly took her plate and a few other dishes to the sink then went into the living room. Kelsey's dad was about to rise. "Could you both stay here for a little bit?"

"Sure, honey," her dad said. "Is everything okay?"

"Uh..." Her eyes filled and tears trickled down her cheeks.

"What is it, Kelsey? Is everything okay?" Her mom reached for her hand as alarm filled her voice.

Kelsey sniffed. "Yes, everything's okay. I just need us to... *talk*. Just us. There are things I want to talk about, but we also need to...reconnect, I guess." She shrugged, unsure of how else to express the sudden storm inside.

"Of course, we do." Her mother turned compassionate eyes toward her. "I want to fill in all the gaps of your life we've missed over the last year, or at least hear about some of them. Is there anything you'd like to talk about?"

"Probably lots of things." Kelsey let out an awkward chuckle. She didn't have an agenda, but still needed their attention to hear whatever would come bubbling out of her mouth. "First, the time you were gone went fine, everything was fairly smooth, at least for a while. I had routines with Molly and with work. I occasionally worked at The Fork. You know, similar to before your trip. Then lots of things started happening. I told you about some of them."

"Yes, you did. With Danielle's accident and swapping your jobs." Her dad patted her arm. "That was very smart, because it ended up helping you both. You're very resourceful, Kelsey."

She smiled. "Thanks. I did my best. I sometimes felt like I was juggling a lot of balls at once, and that was before Danielle even got here. Then it was worse. Then there was Rick in the middle of that, but he's the good part. It was just...a lot." More tears flowed but she couldn't stop them. "I don't know why I'm crying now."

"It's normal, Kelsey," her dad said. "Sounds like you've been through a lot. Those are probably stress *and* relief tears coming out. That was one reason we came back early. Don't get me wrong, you did a wonderful job running the house, taking care of Molly, and all the other things you're doing. But we recognize it was a lot."

"And now there's even more, because Aggie's going to sell The Fork." Her voice broke, followed by shuddering sobs. "After *everything*..."

Her mother slid an arm around Kelsey's shoulder and drew her close. "I'm so sorry, Kelsey," she murmured. Felt so good to have her mother's arm around her. She'd felt so...responsible for her world and alone with the burden. "She just told us yesterday."

Her mother pulled back to meet Kelsey's gaze. "Will she keep you on there as manager? Is that what is worrying you?"

"It won't be her decision once she sells. She doesn't have a buyer yet, since she just made the decision recently. So, where does that leave me? Already, I don't know where I fit *here* anymore."

"Oh, honey..." Her father said, and the sad look in his eyes triggered more tears. "I guess we all have to redraw our boundaries and roles. We can do it, because we're a family, but it'll take time."

"You know, Kelsey," her mother said. "You've always been such a big help with Molly and with the house, even before we left for Africa, but especially while we were gone. You're such a faithful, responsible woman, putting everyone first except yourself. I admire your selfless nature, but I wonder if it's time for you to live your *own* story. Have you thought about that?"

Kelsey cocked her head as her mother unknowingly repeated Rick's words, words that hadn't left her heart since the day he spoke them.

For an instant, something fresh and hopeful surged through her. She'd begun researching her own story a month or so ago, before her life went out of control. "You mean like The Fork? That's kind of my story, but it's in jeopardy right now. I can't make that my story."

"I'm thinking broader than that." Her mother caught her eye and smiled. "Your story is unlimited. The Fork isn't the only option."

"You know you can trust God with that, don't you?" Her dad's eyes were gentle as they linked to hers. "He has a path for you going forward. I agree with your mother. You may have dreams that go beyond The Fork. Like your recipes and your cookbook, and I don't know what else. And you don't have to stay here at the house. You're always welcome to, of course, but you can also get your own place, decorate it like you want." He smiled.

"A place with a big kitchen to do your experiments." Kelsey's mother challenged her with a grin. "We want you to spread your wings and fly the way God is leading you. You don't have to put us and Molly first all the time. We appreciate your help, but *your* needs and desires are important too."

Kelsey sat still, receiving their words like fresh rain into dry soil. Words she'd never internalized before, whether they'd been said or not. She had for years put helpfulness as her first priority. Had she been hiding from the challenges her own dreams would bring, fearful of them? Or simply trying to do the selfless thing? Or maybe both? Her own desires were there, but often waited in the wings until she had ten minutes to give them, which wasn't often. What did it mean to live her own story? Was God nudging her away from The Fork so she could do that, whatever it was? And what was Rick's role in that story? In her *destiny*?

She took a long breath. "Thanks, Mom and Dad. Thanks for saying that. I need to think more about *my* story. I'm happy working at The Fork, but I need to be willing to let it go, if it comes to that. I could manage another restaurant, I guess, but The Fork is special. It has always been." She swallowed the thickness that had formed in her throat. "But maybe God is telling me to move on."

"You don't have to know right now," her mother said. "You have time, since you said Aggie just made the decision recently. Then there's Rick. I can tell you care for each other, and it makes my heart happy."

Kelsey couldn't suppress a smile. "I love him." Her eyes met her mother's. "I need to tell you he's hesitant to let you get to know him because he had a difficult background."

"That doesn't matter, Kelsey," her father said. "It's the man he is now that counts."

She smiled. "That's what I told him. And he's a completely different man than he was even three years ago. He's afraid to tell you his story, so I'd like to do it for him. I don't think you'll judge him, and once you know, we can go forward. He can come around knowing you know everything, and he'll be more comfortable around you both."

"Was he in prison?" her father asked. "Because we can handle that."

"No, nothing like that. His mother was an alcoholic, and his father died when he was fifteen. He left home at seventeen and moved out west. He got into drugs and alcohol, and lived that lifestyle for over ten years. At times, he even lived on the streets with a group of friends."

Kelsey watched her parents' faces as she spoke. They showed no judgment, but instead, compassion. The tight knot inside her began to unfurl, one thread at a time. "So, one day this Christian couple found him unconscious under a bridge. He was high on drugs but also sick with pneumonia. He would have died, but they took him to the hospital. When he was better, they brought him home and he stayed with them for almost two years."

Her mother's hand went to her mouth. Her eyes widened and filled with tears. "How amazing! What a wonderful couple to take in a stranger."

"They were Jesus to him," Kelsey murmured. Her throat grew tight thinking of what Rick went through and how God pulled him out of it. A couple more tears fell. "He became a believer and got a job at the church doing maintenance. He got into the Word, took some classes, got on his feet. Then God called him back here. He's been working at The Fork since then, bussing and washing dishes. He could do a lot more, because he has a lot of restaurant experience from his years out west, plus he's really smart, but that's the opening we had. He's also very gifted in youth ministry. The kids know his story and are drawn to him."

She smiled and looked back and forth between them. "I know he doesn't have a bunch of credentials that would impress parents, but he loves God and follows him. And God called me to love him. That may sound crazy to you, but it's true. I believe in him, regardless of what he's been through in the past."

Kelsey's mother reached across the table and enfolded Kelsey's hands in both of her own. A few new tears tumbled down her cheeks. "I'm sorry for what Rick went through. But I'm *so* looking forward to getting to know him better."

"Kelsey, you're not a child." Her father's gruff voice showed that he, too, was moved by her account of Rick's past situation. "You're a grown woman and you have an exciting life ahead. We support you in whatever you do and whoever you fall in love with, because *we* believe in *you*.

Chapter Twenty-Four

Rick texted Kelsey at eleven that morning. They'd both work the evening shift at The Fork, but he wanted to see her beforehand to walk with her through Aggie's news, which must be a shock. And he wanted to simply *be* with her.

Good morning, my beauty. I want to see you. We need to talk before work. Can I come over and can we talk privately?

Moments later, he received a ping of notification. *Please come as soon as you can. We can find a private spot, maybe take a walk.*

My thoughts exactly. See you in fifteen minutes. I love you.

And I love you.

Her response made him smile and humbled him all at once. She loved him. She loved the likes of Rick Russo. He couldn't get over it.

Fifteen minutes later (he was always on time or early) Rick parked in front of the sprawling ranch house under the pines. He liked this place, but now it had changed. Kelsey's parents now lived there, not just Kelsey and Molly. And Aggie was selling The Grateful Fork, after forty years. Everything had changed once again in such a short time.

It was nearly November, and the crisp air no longer hid that fact. He tightened the scarf around his neck, though it wasn't yet too cold. His first winter in Pennsylvania in fourteen years might be a challenge after living in Arizona. He was no longer used to frigid winters or biting wind. He'd get through it, because he knew he belonged here.

Before he could cut the motor, Kelsey appeared on the porch wearing a short jacket and gloves. He joined her on the porch and tipped her chin to kiss her. She grasped his jacket to pull closer. If her parents saw them through the window...too bad. Let them see. He missed Kelsey too much to let the moment pass.

"Want to walk? We can go down the road there." Rick pointed to a deserted road that vanished around a curve.

"Or wander through the acreage behind my parents' house. Doesn't matter to me." She tossed him a coy smile. "I have what I want now." She slid her arm through his.

"Is that right?" He smiled back and laid his other hand on her arm. "I have *everything* I want right here."

They walked in silence until he could no longer see the house, nor any house. "So, tell me what you're thinking about The Fork." He'd start there. For sure, they had lots more to talk about.

She stopped walking and faced him, placing her hands on his chest. "First, I need to tell you something, and I hope you won't be angry with me." Concern hovered in her blue eyes. "I...I told my parents about your past."

At her words, his smile fell, and a fist gripped inside. "You did? What'd they say?" He braced himself, but kept his face calm. Receptive.

"I did it because I knew you didn't want to. It was your story to tell, so I'm sorry if I betrayed you. I thought you'd be relieved that it was done. I hope I'm right."

He narrowed his eyes. "What'd they say?" he asked again, not sure he wanted to hear, yet part of him was relieved it was done.

Kelsey offered a soft, inviting smile that lessened the pain in his stomach. "They were very compassionate. I told you they would be. They understand you're a different man than you were then. You have a different direction, commitment, everything. And they trust my judgment about you."

He let out the breath he'd been holding, then reached up and touched her cheek. "Thank you, Kelsey. I'm actually glad you did that for me. Now I can get to know them without dreading what they'll learn. It's already on the table."

"Yes, it is. No more fear. You can get acquainted with them knowing they already accept you and trust my judgment about you."

He grinned. "They didn't ask how a dishwasher's going to support their daughter and our children?"

Kelsey laughed, surprise and joy ballooning inside her at his question. "You're getting ahead of yourself, aren't you? But I *really* like the way you think." Her face flushed.

"Of course..." The phrase lingered on his lips as he caught her deep blue gaze in his. "I won't always be a dishwasher."

"A foregone conclusion." Her words were a whisper and enticed him to pull her in and kiss her with the force of relief and love intertwined.

They pulled apart. He took her hand, and they began walking. "So. New topic. How did you feel about Aggie's news yesterday? I saw it on your face, but I want to hear it from you."

She sighed. "Aggie's news surprised me, though all along, I knew it was possible. I never thought it would happen this soon, though. I felt despondent, thinking of all I'd done, all *we'd* done so far to rescue The Fork and now I'm the general manager. And for what? All that so she can sell it? I admit, I had a pity party for a minute."

"There's no guarantee you'd lose your position. The new owner might want an experienced, savvy, adorable general manager." He touched the tip of her nose.

"They might just as easily see me as an obstacle to get rid of. They might have their own staff. And if I didn't lose my job, what might a new owner do to the restaurant itself? He or she might destroy what The Fork is to Brenner Falls by changing the whole culture of the place, so it might become a bad place to work." She frowned, then her gaze found his and suddenly lightened. "But I talked with my parents this morning and they helped me to let go and see that maybe my story is bigger than The Fork." She grinned. "They even used your words. *My own story...*"

Rick cocked his head. "Huh. I guess I'm wiser than I thought? Or else we're both plugged into the same Holy Spirit, and he has a message for you."

She nodded slowly, a smile still etched on her face as well as a new serenity. "Yes, I believe he does."

"So, you can wait and see what happens." He shoved his now-cold hands into his pockets. "Then you'll know whether you'll stay or move onto a greater adventure."

They continued walking in silence for a few minutes. Rick blew out a breath, cloudy with cold. "It's too bad you can't just buy The Grateful Fork yourself."

Kelsey stopped dead in mid-stride without speaking. She turned to Rick, a strange look on her face.

"What's wrong?" he asked.

"Maybe I can, Rick."

"What?" His voice pitched up along with his brows. Surely, he'd misunderstood.

"I might be able to buy The Grateful Fork."

"Uh, please explain that to me."

She grabbed his arm and started walking again, propelled with sudden energy. "I need to look at the numbers. I haven't done that in a while."

"Kelsey, tell me what you're talking about."

She stopped again and faced him. "When I graduated from college, I got a job as an analyst for a pharmaceutical company. I was good at my job, and I kept getting promoted. In other words, I was well paid. I never really had a fancy lifestyle, so I saved and invested. I did that for a total of six years, though in the last three, I haven't paid rent, so I was able to save even more. This past year, I had to take a simpler job which didn't pay as much, so I could juggle that plus Molly. Since I'd invested the money, it grew. I don't even know how much there is now, but it might be enough to put a sizeable chunk down on The Fork. I could get a loan for the rest."

Rick put his hands on her arms. "Kelsey, that's amazing. Is that what you want to do? Own The Fork?"

She paused as a look of wonder passed across her face. "I...I think so. Of course, I need to pray about it. But I don't know what else I'd do with the money. I was saving it for...whatever. I didn't know. Retirement, I guess."

"That's the last thing I expected to hear, Kelsey." Rick laughed aloud with surprise. "I have no doubt your heart is in The Grateful Fork. I bet Aggie would love to sell it to you as opposed to anyone else."

"I bet you're right."

On the way back to the house, they talked about what it might look like for Kelsey to buy The Grateful Fork. "If Aggie sells it to me, the culture will remain the same. Of course, I'll improve things too. I'll put my stamp on it."

"Naturally." Rick could tell Kelsey was getting excited. He was excited with her, without asking himself where that would leave him. She'd be his employer? He chuckled silently. Why not?

"And you'd give your input," she said. "You have a ton of experience. You can be the new manager, even."

They laughed.

"Don't get ahead of yourself, but know I'm with you whatever you do."

ଔ ଔ ଔ

Soon, they arrived at the house. "I need to tell my parents about this," she said. "They have *no* idea." Why hadn't she thought about this before? She knew the answer to that question. She'd made a deliberate practice to *not* think about the money because she didn't want it to become important to her. It was there and it was growing. That's all. One day, she'd be surprised at how much was there.

When she was old, she might need it for something, or as a cushion of some kind. It was there for a rainy day.

The rainy day just might have arrived.

"Let's go talk to my parents. They're good sounding boards."

"Okay." Rick seemed hesitant, but didn't back away. He was ready to face her parents or at least stand by her while she told them her idea.

They entered the house. "Mom, Dad," she called.

"We're in the living room." Her mom's voice reached them in the front hall.

They went to the living room, where her parents sat on the couch.

"Hello, Rick," her mom said. Her smile was as warm as it had been before she knew about Rick's past. Hopefully, he noticed that and took comfort.

"I need to talk to you about something." Kelsey pulled a chair over so she and Rick could both sit facing them. She wanted to include him in every step. His comment about supporting her and their children still rang in her heart in waves of joy.

Her parents waited eagerly for what she'd say. Kelsey moistened her lips. "I'd like your input. We were talking about the sale of The Fork, and I realized I have almost enough money to *buy* it."

"You do?" Her father leaned forward, and his graying brows rose.

Kelsey explained to them what she'd told Rick.

"We didn't know you'd saved all that money, Kelsey," her mother said. "How wise you are."

"I just left it to grow, and so it did. I have to look at my account online and find out how much is there. I don't know Aggie's asking price for the restaurant. Hopefully, I can put down the majority and get a small loan for the rest."

"Maybe we can help you too," her father ventured while her mom nodded. "That way, your loan will be smaller.

"Really? Are you sure?" She looked from her father to her mother.

"Of course," her mother said. "We'll do what we can."

Her dad chuckled. "We can't take it with us, and don't need to."

Kelsey wanted to jump up and down like Molly sometimes did when she was excited. "I'll give Aggie a call as soon as I have time within the next couple of days and tell her I'm interested in buying it. I'll find out her price, if she's settled on one." She blew out a breath, trying to grapple with the new opportunity that had come out of the blue.

"It's a lot to think about, sweetie," her mother said. "We'll help in any way we can, both financially and with all the moral support we can give."

"That'll be our new mission," her father said, and they laughed.

"Mine too." Rick cast a loving glance her way and reached for her hand.

A while later, Kelsey and Rick rose. "Thanks so much, Mom and Dad. I really appreciate your support. Think and pray about it and let me know if you have any reservations. I want to look at all the angles before making a huge decision like this. Of course, Rick and I will continue to talk about it as I get more details."

"Before you two go, Rick, are you able to join us for lunch tomorrow after church?" Kelsey's mother asked.

Rick grinned. "Yes, thanks. I'd love to."

Too soon, it was time to prepare for the dinner shift. Kelsey walked Rick to his car so he could stop at home to change clothes. They stood beside the car as the chill air chafed Kelsey's neck. Late afternoon shadows darkened his face. "I really want your input too, Rick. This isn't just my thing."

"I'll be glad to support you. I'll ask you questions you might not have thought of, things like that. But it *is* your thing. It's your money, your decision."

Kelsey faced him in the mellowing sunshine, a smile pulling at her lips. "Yes and no." She grasped the edges of his open jacket and drew him close. "What if you're part of my future, Rick Russo? That means you *do* have a say. I'm not trying to be pushy, but I have a strong feeling about your role in my life. And vice versa. Don't you?"

Rick slipped his hand around her waist and drew her even closer. "Be pushy all you want, my beauty, because I'm *determined* to be part of your future. And yes, I have a strong feeling about that too. Since the first day I laid eyes on you."

"So, we're a team?" She whispered and brushed his lips with hers. "For The Fork?"

A chuckle emerged from deep in his throat. "For the Fork. And for everything else." He whispered back then kissed her.

Chapter Twenty-Five

Three Months Later

A hum of conversation hung in the church sanctuary as people settled into their seats and greeted friends. Rick squeezed Kelsey's hand beside him. He looked to his other side where Chris sat, wearing a hoodie that covered a T-shirt. Beneath that were cargo pants, warm enough for January, but quick drying.

"I'm proud of you, bro," Rick told him. "This is a good next step. I guess you didn't hear from your dad?"

"Nah. I didn't expect to." Chris looked completely indifferent. "But God's my perfect father, so I'm good."

Rick grinned. "You can't do better than that." They fist-bumped. "Even if he doesn't come, I bet he did a double take at the email when he saw you were getting baptized."

Chris grinned. The haunted shadow was gone from his eyes. "He probably thought he'd gotten someone else's email by mistake." They laughed.

Over the last three months, Chris had changed in numerous ways. For starters, he looked relaxed and open instead of hardened and wary. He was an eager student of the Bible and active at youth group. Instead of leaving his old friends behind, he recruited a few of them to the group. One had already become a believer while others attended Discovery to learn more. Most of the rest of them drifted out of his life.

Moments later, Pastor Frank took his place behind a podium on the stage. "Welcome, friends and members. We're here today to celebrate the decisions of several people to declare their faith publicly through baptism. I'd like to ask those individuals to come and stand in front of the stage. We'll hear their stories and baptize them one by one. Some of them come from our youth ministry, so I'd like to ask Jesse and Rick to come stand with them."

Four young people and five others rose from the congregation to file to the front of the room. Chris and Rick slid out of the pew and joined the youth there. Rick exchanged a grin with Jesse then looked down the row, spotting the kids from the group who were getting baptized that day.

What a moment. It blew Rick's mind every time he thought of where he'd been a few years ago, compared to now. Turned out, Discovery drew more and more kids from inside *and* outside the church. Several had come to faith already. Among them were kids from the local high school or the neighborhood who had no contact with faith, but had grown curious by the momentum they saw. As a result, the youth ministry grew.

It was a team effort...Jesse, Rhonda, even Pastor Frank and his wife...they all got involved in the wave. They started recruiting and training student leaders as well. Among these was Rod, who'd first invited Chris.

In November, Kelsey began the process of buying The Grateful Fork. As they both guessed, Aggie was only too eager to sell it to her and even dropped the price. Kelsey made a nearly seamless transition going from manager to owner, doing it with as much grace and determination as he'd seen in most areas of her life. She planned to get her own apartment as soon as life calmed down following the completion of the purchase.

One Sunday evening they were together at her parents' house following dinner with them. Turned out Rick enjoyed being around her parents, which surprised him, but didn't surprise Kelsey. During that evening, she suggested launching a monthly buffet dinner for the youth meeting instead of the game. She claimed it would attract more kids, since most kids loved good food, and it would be easy for them to invite their friends. A group meal could also bond the members.

Rick and Jesse thought it was a brilliant idea, so they started in December then had their second gathering the previous week. It was hugely popular with the kids. Kelsey recruited Pastor Frank's wife, Teresa, who helped her create a menu and serve the food. Rick loved having Kelsey alongside him, sharing his passion. He also enjoyed presenting her as his girlfriend and the new owner of The Grateful Fork.

Emotion stirred inside Rick's chest and rose to his throat as he listened to each person's story from where they stood with Pastor Frank waist deep in the tub of warm water. The pastor confirmed the commitment of each person and dunked them backward into the water. When each one emerged, they met with applause from the congregation.

Finally, it was Chris's turn. He climbed down into the tub and stood facing the crowd, his face stamped with bold joy. His voice rang out clear and confident as he shared his journey to faith. He mentioned struggling with drugs and meaning in his life, without too many details. He also talked about Rick, the Discovery group, and the new friends he'd made in the youth ministry.

When Frank plunged him into the water, Rick couldn't stop tears from rolling down his cheeks. He'd never been one for tears before. Never too late to learn. His eyes met Kelsey's, and she too was crying.

When the ceremony finished, Rick's gaze panned the room, where people hugged one another and wiped tears with tissues or fists. He returned to the row where Kelsey stood. "Let's wait here for Chris."

Kelsey wove her fingers through his. "I guess you know now why you came back to Brenner Falls from Arizona *and* why God wanted you to stay here." She gave him a lopsided smile he wanted to kiss, but they were in church. He'd wait on that...

"It's awesome and humbling at the same time." His voice came out husky with emotion. "I don't even have the words." Rick's jaw tightened and he fought tears again then cleared his throat as Chris appeared beside them, having dressed in dry jeans, though his blond hair was dark with moisture. Rick and Kelsey each hugged him.

"You'll never guess, you guys...my dad's here."

"He is?" Rick and Kelsey said in unison.

"Yeah, isn't that wild? I saw him from up front. I haven't talked to him yet, but it looks like he brought Andrew, my half-brother. He didn't tell me he was coming."

"Is your sister here today?" Kelsey asked.

"No, she didn't come but my mom's sitting near the back." His eyes roved to where his mother sat, and he smiled at her across the room.

Rick gave Chris a thump on the shoulder. "Dude, all kinds of good stuff. I'm happy for you."

Chris grinned. "Yeah, it's a big day. My dad was the last person I expected to be here today." He glanced toward the back and nodded with a smile. "I'd better go see him. Thanks for being here, guys."

"We wouldn't have missed it for *anything*," Rick said.

Rick and Kelsey watched him walk confidently down the aisle toward a man and a young boy. They stood talking for a moment then the man drew Chris into a hug.

"Wow, that's something." She blinked away fresh tears. "Whew, lots of emotions. So, what now? Are you free to get some dinner somewhere?" Rick took her hand, and they strolled towards the front door.

"Sure. Someplace cozy on a frosty January night." Rick tightened his scarf around his neck, bracing for the icy gust to hit them. So far, he'd survived his first Pennsylvania winter in many years.

"Pizzarama?"

"Ah, a perfect idea."

Soon they settled across from each other in a booth, surrounded by tangy tomato and cheese aromas. Rick linked his hands to Kelsey's across the table. "Think of the last year, Kelsey. Could you imagine all the stuff that happened?" Less than a year ago, he was still in Flagstaff with no hint of what was to come.

Kelsey simply shook her head, a smile stretching her lips. "Unbelievable."

"I mean, you're the *owner* of The Grateful Fork. That's amazing, for starters."

"And you're a youth minister. Just as amazing."

"When we first met, I'm sure we never imagined these things in our wildest dreams. And I sure never thought I'd be calling you my girlfriend instead of secretly staring at you across the dining room."

She gave him a coy smile. "I'm so grateful God often has different plans for us than we do."

"Ditto. Times a hundred. I guess we were too easily satisfied, and he says, *hold on, just wait, I have more for you.*"

The server arrived to take their order. Turned out they liked the same kind of pizza. "And two waters, please," he told her before she left. "You know, class starts in a week. I've done a few college classes, but not Bible college. I don't know what to expect. I might have to cut some of my hours at work."

"Don't worry. I'll hire someone to take the extra hours. You do whatever you need to."

Rick lifted a brow. "I don't want to earn less, but I guess I won't be able to do it all."

"You might earn less, but you'll still be investing. And you know what *that* does." They exchanged grins. "And with me around, you won't go hungry."

Rick laughed and squeezed her hand.

"I do sometimes wonder how this is all going to work together." Kelsey rubbed his hands with her thumbs.

"By all this, you mean, us?" She wasn't expressing doubt, was she?

"Not *us,* per se. I mean, it's fun to wonder what God's going to do with all of it. The restaurant, the church, the classes."

He drew her hand to his lips and pressed a kiss there. "One thing I've learned, my beauty, is we don't have to program things ourselves. We do the *next* thing. Like when you came up with the buffet idea. We all thought it was a good idea and tried it. And look what happened. It brought kids out in droves. That's what I mean. God'll show us. What I love most about that idea is you're bringing your world into my world, in a way. And for the moment, I'm still bussing tables in your world." He grinned. "So, it might not look like it all fits, but somehow it does." He caught her gaze in his and lowered his voice. "It fits because *we* fit. We'll just do the next thing in front of us, and God'll open the next thing, then the next."

Kelsey looked reflective, as if her thoughts spooled back again to marvel at how the pieces had, in fact, fit together all along. He'd pondered the same thing lately, and it always made him shake his head in wonder and joy.

The server placed two glasses of cold water on the table. Kelsey took a deep sip.

Rick did too, cooling his dry throat. He took on a lazy smile. "So, won't it be fun to see it all unfold?"

"After the last year..." Kelsey's gaze locked into his until he felt heat despite the January chill. "I can't wait."

Then she leaned across the table and kissed him.

I hope you enjoyed reading, **Mistaken Destiny**.

If you did, please consider leaving a review for me (where you purchased it and/or on Goodreads.) It would help other readers discover my books and be encouraged by their inspiring truths.

If you haven't read books 1 through 3, you'll enjoy them too! See the list below.

Read Chapter One of all books (and/or purchase at numerous storefronts or eBooks direct from the author) at www.Kyle-Hunter.com

Get a free novella, *Marissa Rewritten* (Book One in the *Second Chance Series*), when you sign up to receive my newsletter and updates about new books (and other insider goodies) at www.Kyle-Hunter.com.

More books...

Brenner Falls Romance Series

Come to the small town of Brenner Falls, Pennsylvania, where you'll make new friends and watch love blossom.

Good Gifts (Book One) where it all starts...

Nathan Chisholm's high-pressure job in the big city is interrupted by an inheritance he doesn't want, a struggling dinner theater. He returns to his hometown of Brenner Falls, Pennsylvania, so he can sell it fast and return to his normal life.

Leah Albright's plans for her life went up in smoke and she's forgotten how to dream. Instead, she spends her days at a dull job in Brenner Falls and her evenings with musical instruments and her cat. As holidays approach, she fakes cheer to stave off her disappointments.

Nathan and Leah rekindle the friendship they had in high school and attraction brews. But Nathan's leaving town once he sells the theater. And the residents of Brenner Falls, including Leah, don't want their beloved historic theater sold. And certainly not to the developer who's been lurking around.

Nathan finds himself trapped by well-meaning decisions and growing feelings for Leah. He may have gone too far to turn back from the risks to his future and his heart.

Custom Made (Book Two)

Embracing the Broken (Book Three)

Romance in Provence Series

The Provence Series takes you with Bree and Lauren, best friends and business partners, to one of the loveliest regions of France. It's not always idyllic in the land of lavender fields and cliffside villages. Join Bree and Lauren as each woman discovers her unique journey. . . and surprising romance.

Prodigals in Provence (Book 1)
Bree's Story

Bree Sorensen is living her dream as co-owner of a travel company that specializes in tours to Provence, France. But the latest trip isn't fully booked, adding financial strain to her already fragile business. In the land of idyllic lavender fields and cliffside villages, Bree wonders if she'll ever find peace from her troubled childhood, let alone save her career.

Travis Jeffries hides his emotional scars under the glitz of TV travel documentaries. A beloved public figure who often sniffs out travel scams, his smiling persona barely covers the pain of his failed marriage and missionary career years earlier. With his spiritual life a wasteland, Travis fears it's too late for God to welcome him back.

Travis seems like Bree's worst nightmare when she finds he has registered for her latest tour of Provence. One false move and her business could be ruined by his critique. But when attraction blossoms, will these two wounded believers find common ground?

A Promise in Provence *(Book Two)*
Lauren's Story

Lauren Abbott is at a turning point. She's just not sure *where* to turn. Her long-term relationship with Mark is fading fast. Instead, she feels drawn to Jean-Pierre, an attractive Frenchman she'd met the previous summer. When she's laid off from her job as a chef, she plans to go see him in Provence, France.

Mark can't get Lauren out of his heart, even though it's been close to a year since she asked him for space. When she goes to France, he's afraid he'll lose her for good. That is, until he goes there too, as a last-ditch effort to win her back.

At first, Lauren's angry that Mark has followed her to France. But a joint desire to help a young refugee boy leads them to work together. Lauren finds herself torn between Mark and Jean-Pierre. Worse, she's confronted with obstacles in helping the boy and even greater obstacles within herself.

Prodigals in Provence and A Promise in Provence are also available as a Boxset, *Love in Provence*. Both books in one volume.

The Second Chance Series

In *The Second Chance Series*, you'll meet Marissa, Julia, Sydney, and Eden, four college friends who, twenty-five years later, renew their friendships as they find themselves empty nesters and single again. You'll love getting to know these women and following each one in her own book. (Women's Fiction.)

Marissa Rewritten (Book 1: a Novella) An author becomes unblocked.

Julia Redesigned *(Book Two)* Discovery in Florence, Italy.

Sydney Rewound *(Book Three)* Present Clashes with the Past.

Eden Redefined *(Book Four)* Returning to College in Midlife.

Stand Alone Novels

One December (A Romance in Paris)

Circle Back Around (A Return Home to Save the Family Business)

Postcard from Nice (A Novella set in Nice, France)

About the Author

Kyle Hunter is the author of thirteen novels of inspirational romance and women's fiction, weaving Christian truths into the lives of fictional people. Her relatable characters will become like close friends you'll cheer for and learn from as you join them on their journeys. Story settings range from Europe to small town America. As characters face outward and inward challenges, the spiritual and personal insights they gain are encouraging and relevant.

Kyle spent thirteen years living in France, and she's intrigued by faraway places. Currently, she lives in North Carolina where she writes fiction, non-fiction (under the pen name K. B. Oliver), and the travel blog OliversFrance.com. She also teaches French to adults.

www.ingramcontent.com/pod-product-compliance
Lightning Source LLC
LaVergne TN
LVHW010311070526
838199LV00065B/5517